Road to Ruin

The Tales of Drendil (Short Stories)
Fallen Stars
The Collapse of Madira
Dark Magic
Raven's Requiem
The Manticore
Murder
The Basilisk
Minotaur

The Drendil Saga (Novels)
Land of Madness
Downfall
Road to Ruin
Scapegoat

Road to Ruin

B T Litell

RAVENSTEEL
PUBLISHING

Cover art by Cherie Fox @ fiverr.com
Edited by Megan Hundley

First Published in 2021 by Ravensteel Publishing, LLC

Visit my website at: www.btlitellauthor.com

ISBN: 978-1-7379624-0-3 (Paperback)
Kindle ASIN: B094DTN9HR

Write to:
Ravensteel Publishing, LLC.
Attention: Permissions Coordinator
PO Box 274
Canal Winchester, OH 43110

This book is dedicated to my loving wife, Mariana. Without you and your constant support I would not be where I am today. You are my rock, my foundation, my anchor in the storms, and my lighthouse. You are always guiding me back to safety. Without all of your continued support I wouldn't be the person I am today. I love you so much.

Gilded Ocean
Madira
Vihyar
Nahum
Amgan Fields
Shemont
Griffin's Perch
Sorcerer's College
Anselin
Erith
Iron Holm
Shimmering Ocean
Goblin Coast

Table of Contents

Prologue

...Sometime in the year 858...

The sun, currently hidden behind soft, fluffy clouds that floated through the blue sky far overhead, cast ever lengthening shadows as it started its regular descent toward the western horizon. None of the clouds threatened to bring rain, a relief for many students as they crossed the Sorcerer's College grounds with books in hand. Vibrant, healthy, green grass covered every bit of the College grounds where bushes and trees didn't stand. Bushes lined the web of cobblestone pathways that crisscrossed the landscaping and trees stood as accents here and there, seemingly no order to their placement. A throng of students bustled about the College grounds, hurrying here and there as they made their way from one class to another. The classes were held in a series of buildings which surrounded the central, white marble tower that many knew on sight to be the College. One student, among the masses, rushed as quickly as he could without heeding where he walked. Esram had no time to spare as he was already running late for his next class for what he wished was the first time that day. At least he wouldn't have to worry about rain this day. Master Averon would become fussy if the books he borrowed for his classes came back with any amount of damage, especially from water.

Thankfully, Esram learned a spell, ironically from one of the books he borrowed, which would remove water damage even from severely aged vellum. To Esram's knowledge, there was no way to check whether a spell removed water, and its resulting damage, from book pages. Master Averon probably knew either way and simply said nothing about students using spells on the books. Esram assumed all the students knew about the same spell and would use it regularly to repair their borrowed tomes. The wizened librarian probably had rules against students using spells on their books, but nothing yet came from Esram's attempts to keep the other Elf happy.

Esram berated himself in his mind for attempting to learn from three schools simultaneously. According to the College's tradition, he only studied from two schools. They detested his third school and would likely expel him, or worse, if they knew he was studying forms of Magic they not only disapproved, but entirely outlawed. Dark Magic. A thing of great taboo for reasons that Esram never understood. While studying history classes at the College, something required for every student, he learned that, according to the College, the Assembly of Mages conducted experiments. Said experiments resulted in Elves being transformed into goblins, the summoning of greater beings from beyond their world, and several other things which seemed altogether inert compared to some of the things the College taught. Through the War school, one of the most sought-after teachings among the Mages and students, he learned a spell which would take a person's insides and make them their outsides. How, with that caliber of knowledge, was creating an entirely new species wicked? If anything, the College was teaching concepts of immensely more complicated morals.

Esram also learned of two wars, started by the College, which resulted in the complete extermination of the Assembly of Mages. *Well,* he considered, *their extermination only led to the eventual founding of the Children of Chaos.* Again, the College could have kept their collective noses out of business that didn't, in fact, harm anyone else and many lives would have continued. Instead, the College wiped out thousands of Mages like they were snuffing out mass amounts of candles. No additional thought went into the decision to go to war than would be needed to suffocate those candles, either. Morality was a difficult thing to gauge at times, he concluded. Who could really say what was right or wrong in society's eyes? He found himself thankful that his path did not lead toward philosophy as these thoughts generally caused him to develop severe headaches.

Debating this topic with himself did nothing to legitimize his third school of choice, nor did it get him to his next class on time. It did, however, distract him, something he was more than capable of doing on his own with or without a distracting internal debate. When he finally regained his thoughts, Esram realized too late that he was heading right for one of the largest students attending the College: Bryne. Esram bumped right into the larger student, bounced backwards from the impact, and dropped his books. Time seemed to slow as the tomes fell toward the ground, their pages opening up to greet the ground as they fell. Esram felt his heart skip a beat as the books crashed to the cobblestones below. Master Averon would surely notice damage from something like this.

The damage to the books, and Master Averon's inevitable reaction, seemed like a gentle gust of wind compared to the thunderous grimace on Bryne's face. Esram's heart dropped into his stomach as he saw the Elf's face shift from generally displeased to terribly ireful. Bryne seemed to grow larger as his expression worsened. By contrast, Esram felt he was shrinking, his heart beginning to flutter as he imagined what the worst possible outcome would be in this situation.

"You bloody fool! Why can't you watch where you're going, Esram?" Bryne erupted.

"I'm sorry, Bryne. It was an accident. I was just—" Esram started.

"I don't care what you were 'just' doing, Esram. You should know that junior classmen yield to your betters," Bryne stated, his voice low and gravely.

"Listen, it was just an accident. I meant nothing by it."

"Know what else was an accident, Esram?" Bryne taunted. "Your entire existence."

"Knock it off, Bryne. I already apologized. What more do you want from me?" Esram pled, his voice breaking.

Bryne guffawed. "Just hitting puberty, Esram? Let me give you a tip—"

"Knock it off, Bryne. He's already apologized and doesn't need you pestering him," Daethis said, running up and grabbing Esram's fallen books.

Esram felt a warmth inside as he saw Daethis. While she was also further along in the process than Esram—she and Bryne started at the College at the same time—she had taken Esram under her metaphorical wing as his protector. His face burned as he thought about her. He quickly looked away as she bent over to retrieve the books but watched as Bryne stared directly at her. *To think that what I study is somehow more detestable than his behavior,* Esram thought.

"Please leave me alone, Bryne. It was an honest mistake and won't happen again," Esram pled, grabbing the books from Daethis.

"Why don't you do something about it?" Bryne taunted.

Esram snarled at Bryne. "I could do something."

"What? Make a potion? I'm so scared."

"You'll wish I used a potion when I'm done," Esram said under his breath.

"Big words from one so small. Give me your best shot, pipsqueak," Bryne laughed.

"Everyone, get to class," someone shouted from the nearest outlying building.

Esram threw his books back to the ground, not worrying as they fell. What he was about to do would bring a higher punishment than anything that Master Averon could do to him. He prepared a spell he had learned in his illegal school. An orb of pure darkness formed between his hands, growing as he added more seething hatred into his spell. As the orb grew, Bryne, caught off guard by the spell, started casting his own. Before Esram could finish putting his spell together, a bolt of lightning launched from the ends of Bryne's fingers and crashed into Esram's face, sending him reeling backwards and throwing his unfinished orb of loathing and anger into the sky, not harming anyone as it flew until it fizzled.

Burning. An intense heat smothered Esram's face as he fell to the ground, clutching at his face and screaming in agony. His vision went black as he writhed on the cobblestone pathway. Daethis, wanting to prevent the situation from escalating further, cast a wall of air, as hard as steel, into Bryne, pushing him backwards and onto the ground. She immediately cast another spell, this one targeted at Esram, stopping the remnants of the lightning from continuing to burn Esram's skin away. Esram continued screaming as he squirmed on the ground, clutching at his burned face.

Master-level Mages rushed to the situation, having overseen what happened. Esram still could see nothing as he was lifted from the ground and carried away. Daethis stood on the pathway, spells at the ready, watching as Bryne was also escorted into the central tower, a Master nearly dragging him by the ear. Daethis remained on the cobblestone pathway staring at where Esram was, wondering what she just witnessed.

Chapter One

...Sometime in the year 862...

Light. The inevitable, polar opposite of darkness. It crept over the edge of the eastern horizon, the first sign that a new day started. Far to the east, beyond the sight of mortals, the sun peered over the edge of the world. The coming of the sun was accompanied by splashes of color which painted the sky in a unique way. Clouds floating in the sky were now awash with color, spreading the news that the sun was returning from its nightly journey beyond the western horizon. The mortals would see the colors flooding the sky and take it as a herald of good weather for reasons only they understood.

Anselin, the city of Elves, had, for the most part, not yet started to stir. The sunlight only peeked over the distant Ash Mountains far to the east. The city was arranged in disorderly chaos, having expanded since the original city had been built around the site of a star that fell from the heavens. Thanks to the very remnants of that star, the city of Anselin teemed with Magic. Many things happened in the city simply because of its abundance of Magic. However, that also brought those who wished to abuse the power for their dark desires.

The very Magic that flowed through the buildings of Anselin caused the city's equipment to advance decades faster than other cities in the kingdom. The Sorcerers' College was constantly sending representatives to study Anselin in an attempt to understand the workings of the city. They wanted to copy things that the Elven home city possessed. Things like doors which opened on their own when desired or with a simple motion of a hand. Nearly four centuries had passed since the founding of the College, yet in that time they still had not been able to figure out a way to replicate the same phenomena in other locations. It was believed that the proximity to the star is what allowed for such things to work.

King Erkan III, the ruler of the Elven half of the Kingdom of Drendil, concerned himself over neither the workings of Mages nor Magic. He enjoyed the technology that his city boasted. He rarely spent much time thinking of how these things worked. He simply knew things worked and if they didn't, he could complain, and they would be fixed. Some of that may have been due in part to the crown he wore. The silver circlet shaped like the wings of a great eagle came with many privileges but also the responsibility for countless lives.

As he found himself most mornings when the sun was rising over the eastern horizon, Erkan stood alone on his balcony, leaning against the stone banister as he watched his city starting to wake. Every morning that he could, he would spend as much time as he dared on his balcony. Seeing the sunlight reaching over the distant Ash Mountains, where the Dwarves lived, and caressing his city was soothing to him. These days he needed all the soothing he could find.

Erkan looked as far north as he could from the balcony, toward the library which took the shape of a tall tower. Thousands of books and scrolls stood on every inch of shelving that fit within that tower. Centuries of knowledge, carefully preserved, could be perused there. Sunlight, reflected by the clouds in the sky above made the white, marble tower look like it had been painted various shades of red, orange, and purple. This pleased him greatly.

He then gazed as far south as he could see from his vantage point, toward the market in the city. He couldn't see the stalls various merchants rented from their guild, but he knew their haphazard layout well. Everything in the market had a place, and there was a place for everything, despite the apparent lack of order that overwhelmed the area. Textiles, fruits, vegetables, meat, dairy, and other products would be bartered and sold in that very market this day, the same as every day except the one day of rest the city—except the king himself—was granted to honor the Allfather. The Winged Circlet granted Erkan such few days of rest. Even on the days the market was closed, Erkan would read through reports, handle matters, and spend the day preparing for the coming week. Such was his life since he took up the crown from his father who fell so ill he was deemed unfit to rule. On that day, Prince Erkan III took up the mantle of responsibility and, since that day, he rested only when he was allowed.

A temple, the home of Anselin's chapter of the Order of Herons, stood in the center of the town, the steeple rising high above the one or two-story houses that surrounded it. Tomorrow, the priests would hold services for all who wished to attend. Erkan missed the days of being a young Elf and being able to sit in what he always thought to be uncomfortable pews while the priests spoke from the holy texts. He had no time for attending the services now; years had passed since he had even heard the readings. While the pews may have been uncomfortable, the throne he now occupied was tenfold worse. His father had told him no king should be comforted by so much as a cushion while sitting in the throne. Discomfort served as a reminder of the weight of the crown and the power of the throne.

Erkan was not a young Elf, pushing nearly sixty years, something many considered a feat, especially for their king. Few of those sixty years had been gentle; most of the comfort in his life came in his youth. His father passed away just after turning sixty. In the four decades since then, there had been revolts he had personally seen ended, usurpers who attempted to remove him from his family's throne, and many other issues he wished not to think of. He earned each wrinkle and sparkling, silver hair on his head in his tenure as the king. He knew the lines of his face well, from the crow's feet around his eyes to the drooping jowls under his jawline. His eyes, stony and grey, had not changed throughout his years on the throne. Perhaps less joy could be seen in them, but that was expected. Erkan never considered himself a joyful person after the innocence of his youth died a miserable death at the hands of his first year as king.

He lacked an heir, something which gnawed at him lately. He had, after all, never married nor fathered any legitimate offspring. Ruling his kingdom always took priority. Though he made some time for a myriad of women in his lifetime, he possessed no time for a wife. There were likely a dozen children in the city of Anselin that bore his likeness. He wouldn't be surprised if his blood flowed in those children's veins. Yet, he could claim none of them. His citizens grew resentful of him and if he embraced an illegitimate child as his heir there would be chaos. No other king before him had claimed any bastard child as their heir, and he would not be the first to break that tradition. Were he to claim such a child as his heir, the law prevented them from taking the throne until their twenty-fifth birthday. In that time, a regent would be appointed, and he knew no members of his family who would abdicate the throne for a child not raised in the castle under the strenuous life of the nobility.

Erkan pried his thoughts away from his problems, seeing movement in the city below. That was his cue to turn to his duties as king. A stack of papers waited for his review, even now with the sunlight barely touching the city's eastern wall. And he abhorred paperwork. It was a plague upon his life. Yet, as king, it had to be done, and his was the signature most of the forms needed. As Erkan pushed himself off the balcony railing and turned toward his bedchamber, he felt the ground beneath his feet tremble. Simultaneously, a series of explosions sounded throughout the city.

*   *   *

Elias walked the halls of the castle, brushing away minor wrinkles from his uniform with his hands. His belt, which he cinched too tight this morning, caused most of the wrinkles. His grey doublet with black lace frills at the cuffs and around his collar still chafed him, even after nearly a year of wearing it. After the better part of a decade in the regular army, he missed his plate-and-mail armor. He longed for the day when he would get to wear that armor again. This assignment as the king's personal bodyguard was a good thing for his chances at promotion, but did it have to be so *bloody* uncomfortable?

Elias had just finished eating his breakfast and was working his way toward the king's suite on the south side of the castle. There were two hallways he needed to walk down, both littered with guards standing or walking in one direction or another. None of the guards questioned him, not while he wore the grey doublet with the king's black chimera on the chest. His was the only uniform in the castle made in this style. Every other guard wore the same thing every guard wore across the Kingdom of Drendil: a tabard worn over a chainmail cuirass and steel pauldrons. Like his doublet, their tabards were grey with a black chimera. This was Anselin's livery.

Elias rounded the corner from one hallway into the next. As he stepped into the new hallway, he noticed a guard walking toward him. The guard wore no helmet, which was standard for most guards with indoor posts or patrols. Except for formal occasions, they went without helmets. There was little risk to King Erkan or his guards inside the castle. However, something about the guard seemed…off.

His tabard, while grey with a chimera on the front, simply appeared *wrong*. Elias couldn't quite figure out why, but instead of questioning one of the regular soldiers, he decided to arrive at the king's chambers on time. He learned shortly after taking this position that Erkan was a man who appreciated a punctual bodyguard.

Elias passed the guard with the unsettling tabard and made his way toward the king's suite when he felt the ground tremble and heard what sounded like explosions near the castle.

*   *   *

Erkan rushed back out to his balcony, attempting to see where the sounds originated from. He scanned the portion of the city that he could see. Because his balcony faced south, he could see that half of the city, sprawling out before him. Frustrated that his was not a suite with balconies all around it, he briefly cursed the architect who designed the castle. He swore loudly, damning the man and hoping he rotted in a shallow grave. Settled from his tirade, Erkan moved toward the door on the north side of his suite and waved his hand to open the door, which it would do, even from this distance.

The door made a faint whisper sound as it slid open. By the time that Erkan noticed his bodyguard's absence, the guards on either side of the door crumpled to the floor without warning. A quick glance showed that both guards sprouted crossbow bolts from their necks. Stiff, wooden fletching stuck from their exposed necks. Blood poured from the wounds and Erkan knew within an instant that both men had died before they hit the ground. He waved his hand again and the door snapped shut, the lock engaging as it whispered closed.

*   *   *

Elias sprinted down the long hallway toward the king's suite. Chaos surrounded him. Guards ran past him as they held onto sword hilts that hung at their waists. The throng of guards he pushed through reminded Elias of the fish that lived in the northern oceans that swam upstream on their way to spawn and immediately he felt like one of those fish. *What are they called?* He thought to himself, then scolded himself for being distracted. *There are more important things to focus on right now instead of fish.*

While pushing his way through the sea of soldiers running past him, Elias noticed another guard whose tabard seemed off. Once again, he wondered what it was that seemed wrong with the soldier, but quickly returned his focus back to reaching the king. He had to get to the king's suite before anything else happened. His duty, first and foremost, was the king's safety. Nothing else mattered but that. Only when the king was safe and protected could Elias even consider thinking about his own safety or his family's.

Reaching the end of the hall, Elias rounded another corner into the hallway just outside King Erkan's suite. The guards were still there, which was a good sign. At least some soldiers possessed sense enough to remain at their post. He could see the door to the suite opening and the guards turning toward the open door. As they turned, something flashed further down the hallway behind them and both guards dropped to the ground. The door snapped shut the instant the guards' bodies hit the floor.

Further down the hallway, beyond the fallen guards, Elias saw a shadowy figure wearing black leather armor and a cloak of the same color. The figure held a pair of small crossbows and raised one of the weapons toward him. Time slowed as the dark figure lifted the weapon. Elias's hand reached toward his sword through years of instinct. As his fingers wrapped around the hilt, he heard the *thunk* of the string snapping forward and within an instant felt a blinding flash of pain in his lower abdomen as the bolt slammed into him. His mind raced, thoughts of the uselessness of a cloth doublet as his armor overwhelming him. Why could he not at least wear *some* amount of armor under the doublet? The force from the bolt was great enough to stop him in his tracks. Stopped so suddenly, and with a searing agony consuming him, Elias dropped to his knees, only able to watch as his assailant disappeared into the shadows down the hall.

As he knelt on the floor, leaning hard against the wall, he looked to the guards a mere meter away from him. A bolt stuck out of each of their necks, the wooden fletching flush with their skin. A pool of blood formed under each of the guards, and he could hear what would have been their final breaths rushing from the wounds in their necks. They were dead, and there was no one around to whom he could call out for help. No one that could chase after the would-be assassin and track him down. Elias was alone and dying so close, yet so far, from his assigned post. Failure draped over him like a heavy, wet blanket. Someone was targeting King Erkan and he could do nothing to stop them.

The pain in his abdomen was intense, the worst pain he had felt so far in his entire life. He clutched his side and felt for the bolt, finding it easily. The wound immediately tinged the moment his fingers touched the embedded crossbow bolt, and a spike of searing pain jolted through him as he grabbed the exposed end of the bolt. As a soldier he had learned the proper way to remove an arrow from a wound. Yet, at this moment, he found he couldn't care about the proper way to do anything. He had to ensure the king was safe before everything else. His life meant nothing if the king fell this day. Duty beckoned him stronger than the pain in his stomach.

He gripped the exposed end of the crossbow bolt with both hands, trying not to move the bolt as best he could. Even having his hand on the thing made his eyes water with the pain that shot through his body. Summoning all the strength that he could, he pulled on the wooden shaft that stuck from his abdomen and the bolt came free. A sickening, suction sound followed as the bolt came free. He fought against the impending darkness that threatened to envelope him for several moments and felt his stomach lurching as the pain surged. His breakfast splattered against the polished tiled floor entire against his will. What he had thought would be the worst pain of his life multiplied faster than spring-time rabbits, becoming a hurricane of agony within the blink of an eye.

*   *   *

Trapped. Erkan felt helpless and ensnared in his own suite. Someone just killed his guards in the bat of an eye. He could hear something else through the door. Someone had undoubtedly come for him. His end felt nigh. Certain this was his time, he strode to his armor stand and grabbed his polished, never-used sword, drawing it and immediately tossing the scabbard to the floor where it clattered against the polished grey marble floor at his feet. If this were indeed his time, he would not fall without a fight. He certainly would not go unarmed to his inevitable death. Whatever assassin stood on the other side of the door would have to at least work for their goal.

The commotion out in the hallway quieted. Now, rather than the scuffle Erkan had heard, he now heard nothing. Silence. Nothingness heralded his death more than the din that resounded through the halls mere moments ago. Whatever happened out there no longer meant anything. Perhaps another life had been lost. How many times would that happen this day? Surely, the Allfather would pass judgment on Erkan's soul for the lives that were lost this day because of him. A burden weighed upon his soul as, he guessed, blood pooled on the floor outside his suite.

Just that moment, there was an aggressive, offbeat pounding on the door. Belligerent. Determined. Pounding. As Erkan listened to the pounding on the door, it seemed to become synchronized with the throbbing of his own heart until they were the only sounds he could hear. This was a new sensation for him. All sound seemed to cease as his heart's rapid thumping took over reality. *Da-thump, da-thump, da-thump.*

"Highness…open the door! We need to get you…to safety, now," a voice called from the other side.

The voice was a baritone, familiar, and tremendously apprehensive. Yet…could he trust it? This was the only voice he had heard today, and he knew the owner of the voice; maybe the assassins had infiltrated the ranks of guards in the castle. And it was the only sound he had heard since his guards were murdered before his eyes. It would surely be part of the trap. *What sort of people want me dead so badly that they would turn my own bodyguard?* The thought that Elias would fall to an assassination plan was beyond unthinkable. The man had served him more than loyally for the better part of a year, and that was plenty of time for any adverse plots to have been carried out against the king. Still, the thought jabbed at the back of his mind. Who better to turn in an assassination plan than the king's own bodyguard? Surely, there was no one else in the castle who would be as close to him as Elias. Erkan tightened the grip on his sword and called through his locked door.

"Elias how am I to trust that you are here for my safety and not my life?" he called out.

"Highness, you must trust me…I'm wounded. There was an assassin wearing all black…He was armed…with crossbows. The guards out here are…dead. There was nothing…I could do for them…Please, let me in," the bodyguard stuttered through audible gasps.

Erkan had learned fondness for his most recent bodyguard. Elias was human, something the king once thought disgraceful. He spent much of the first month wondering how a human could ever be so loyal to the Elven King of Drendil. Still, the man proved himself time and again. He even married an Elf. It was many years ago, but it was still something Erkan considered as proof enough of loyalty toward the Elven people. Despite the joint kingdoms, there still was a great deal of animosity between the races, so much so that the Dwarves closed their kingdom off from everyone that didn't live underground. The humans, at best, seemed to tolerate the Elves under most social situations. Still, their child was a wonderful young lad who was dangerously curious, but Erkan welcomed that. Most times, at least. The plethora of questions he always asked was not something Erkan always welcomed, yet that was the way of children at times. Undying curiosity and innocence were timeless facets of a child regardless of race or creed. Neither were things that Erkan could discount, having been a curious child at one point in his own life. So long ago was that time of his life.

"You're alone? How badly are you wounded?" Erkan called through the door. He again tightened his grip on the sword in his hands and prepared to kill the man, should he open the door and find the bodyguard had lied. There was a pause before Elias answered.

"The wound is bad, but I should survive. I am alone. I see no further signs of the would-be assassin," Elias gasped, his voice slightly muffled by the door.

Erkan waved his hand before the door and the lock disengaged. The door then hissed and slid into the wall, disappearing entirely.

Apparently, Elias had been leaning against the door for support and nearly fell to the floor when it opened. Erkan instantly dropped his sword, letting the fine steel blade clatter on the stone floor. He reached out his arms, grabbed his bodyguard, and became the only thing that held the man on his feet. He could tell the man was weak by simply holding him. It was like holding a pile of stones that had the shape of a man. He had indeed lied, but not about his being alone. This wound seemed far more severe than he claimed.

"Highness, staying here is not an option. We have to get you out of the city," Elias pled. It was the only sensible thing to do, in his mind. An escape plan had been in place since at least the time that Erkan's grandfather wore the Winged Circlet.

"How am I to leave when the Allfather only knows what is going on in my city? What sort of a king would it make me to leave?" Erkan countered. His voice was firm, unyielding.

"It makes you a living king!" Elias shouted back, though the pain that followed made him immediately regret that choice. The pain in his side raged with every bit of movement. Still, Erkan said nothing, processing the words that had fiercely come from his bodyguard.

"I would rather be a dead king than one who fled while his people were slaughtered," Erkan replied calmly.

"Highness, you still have plenty of years left in your life. We need to get you out of the city before everything goes to complete shit, forgive my language. That is the contingency. We agreed that in the event of a disaster, you would go through the bookcase—"

"You were sworn to *never* utter that location aloud, in the event of prying ears," Erkan scolded.

"I'm sorry Highness. I am trying to get you to agree to leave this place while we still have our lives," Erkan stated.

"I understand," Erkan replied. "Elias, are your wife and child safe?"

"I don't know, Highness. Audra usually has Gordack with her in or around the kitchen. If that is the case, we should cross paths with them on our way out of the castle," Elias replied.

"When we get down there, you get your wife and child, and you bring them with us. I know it's not ideal for getting to safety as quickly as we can, but I want to ensure your family's lineage continues. Today is not a day for more families dying because of my choices."

"Then you are agreeing to leave?" Elias asked.

"Yes," Erkan stated as he turned to the three bookcases in the room.

The three bookcases were taller than both Erkan and Elias combined and filled with books on every inch of shelving available. Some books were leatherbound, others were simply paperbound with a jacket. Each book held some significance to the king, or he wouldn't have placed them in his suite. One of the bookcases contained only large, leatherbound volumes which covered the laws of the dual kingdoms. These laws had been set forth during the early years of the kingdoms' founding and merger centuries before. Another shelf contained various encyclopedia volumes with information about the various topics that would pertain to almost anyone in Drendil. These tomes covered everything from flora and fauna to climate patterns and beyond. Erkan walked to the bookcase on the right and grabbed a plain, paperbound volume roughly the width and height of his hand within a row of similar books and removed it from the shelf. A series of gears groaned from the other side of the shelf.

Within moments, a secret passage opened up behind the central bookcase. Elias learned of the secret passage from his predecessor when he took the position as the king's bodyguard. Unfortunately, the secret of which book opened the doorway was held by the king and queen. Elias was not allowed to learn the book, despite having asked. To his knowledge, this passageway had only been used for test runs, and his role as the king's bodyguard was to keep the king protected long enough for the king to get into the staircase. According to his duties, Elias would have to lay down his life, if necessary, while Erkan escaped down the subsequent staircase.

Elias checked the wound in his side while the revealing doorway opened, and found it was still pumping out blood. He would have to get a towel or something from the kitchen when he got Audra and Gordack. His hand was not enough at this point, and he could feel dizziness setting in. A growing ring of darkness surrounded his vision, and the room was now starting to spin around him. This wound, if left untreated, would most likely prove fatal, he could tell. *Why didn't I leave the bolt in?* he chided himself. He made his choice and would now face the agonizing consequences.

Finally, the doorway finished opening. On the other side, Elias could see a spiraling staircase that he knew ran to the lowest level of the castle other than the dungeons. The staircase was dark, though there were sconces on both sides of the opening with an unlit torch in each. Elias staggered toward the staircase and grabbed a torch, took it to the hearth, and dipped the oil-soaked rags wrapped around the top of the torch into the still-glowing embers of the king's morning fire. The torch flashed to life and Elias once again shuffled toward the staircase. Erkan stopped him before he could start walking down the stairs.

"Let me go first. You are wounded and I don't want you to fall down the stairs," Erkan requested, grabbing the torch.

Erkan started down the spiraling staircase first and Elias followed a few moments later, adjusting his hand on the still-seeping wound in his stomach. His hand felt sticky, warm, and wet with the blood that poured over and between his fingers. Each step brought a new wave of agony as he worked down the staircase, leaning against the outside wall as he staggered downward after the king who he was supposed to be protecting. In any other situation where this exit would be needed, Elias either would have gone first or stayed behind while the king made his escape, rather than following the king down the stairs. Elias knew his predecessors had never intended for him to take this exit.

Elias arrived at the bottom of the stairs a few minutes after Erkan. Sweat raced down his face, soaking his doublet to his waist. In the darkness, he could see a black area where blood stained a large portion of his grey, silk doublet. The world around him was spinning violently now. Struggling to remain on his feet, he leaned all of his weight against the pillar that formed the center of the spiraling staircase. Every ounce of strength he had left was dedicated to remaining on his feet, something which he struggled to do, even with the aid of the pillar.

The entire time Elias had been finishing his way down the staircase, Erkan worked on pulling a series of levers that held the door at the bottom of the staircase in place. There were six levers. At this point, Elias could not remember what any of the levers did specifically. He only knew there was an order in which they had to be pulled to open the door. Getting one lever wrong would restart the entire sequence, and Erkan needed to restart at least half a dozen times. The king swore to himself as he reset the sequence yet again. Elias found it hard to focus on anything other than not falling to the floor and counting the errors took far too much effort.

Finally, the levers were pulled in the correct order—accompanied by Erkan swearing loudly in satisfaction—and the door slowly dropped into the floor, revealing a long, poorly-lit hallway on the other side. Elias forced himself to stand on his own feet and walked into the hall with his sword drawn, though he found he could barely keep a grasp on the hilt. His blade dragged on the floor behind him as he took slow, staggering steps to lead the king to the next hurdle in the escape route. Erkan followed closely behind and rushed around him to the closed door that guarded the tunnel.

"Father!" a young voice cried from somewhere down the hallway. Elias turned and caught Gordack who had been running toward him. The force of the child connecting with his father nearly knocked Elias to the ground, but he, somehow, remained standing.

"Where…is your mother?" Elias panted through the pain in his stomach.

"Father, you're hurt?" the child asked.

"Where is your mother?" Elias asked a bit more firmly this time.

"She's in the kitchen. Some lady in a dark robe came in and told me to wait out here. Should I get mother?"

"No, I will get her…you stay here with the king…Don't get in his way, understand?" Elias asked, trying to give his child a forceful look that he doubted came across the right way.

"I want to come with you, father," Gordack pled.

Elias drew a ragged breath and acquiesced. "Fine. Let's go get your mother."

"What is going on, father?"

"I will tell you later, once everything is safe," Elias promised.

They made their way to the castle's main kitchen, which was only a short walk from where the spiral staircase had dumped the king and Elias into the hallway. Before walking to the kitchen, Elias sheathed his sword, a normally simple task which now caused him a great deal of pain. He removed his left hand from his wound and could feel more blood pouring out after he did so. Once his sword was returned to its scabbard, Elias used his right hand to steady himself against the wall as he walked and held his wound with his left. His steps grew slower as his body continued to weaken.

The door to the kitchen was closed, which surprised Elias, but he figured it may have been necessary. Gordack, given the opportunity, would pester anyone with his nearly incessant questions. It was good that he was curious, but it could be a bit much at times. Hopefully, he would grow out of that someday. Elias did not wish his son to lose all curiosity, only that he would learn the proper time and place to ask his nearly unending questions.

After bracing himself against the wall for a few seconds, finding the strength he needed, Elias reached for the doorknob with his right hand and opened the heavy, oak door to the kitchen and immediately stopped before walking in. Blood. It covered the walls in splatters, pooled on the floor, and reached to the ceiling and the table in the middle of the kitchen. Elias immediately turned around and grabbed his son, a flash of energy coming from adrenaline that surged within him. Not wanting the embrace, Gordack kicked and wriggled, trying to break himself free from his father. Given how weak Elias felt, it wasn't hard for his grip on Gordack to break. As soon as the child was free, Elias grabbed him again and spun so they were both out of the doorway. Elias held Gordack firmly between his blood-covered hands and looked him in the eyes before speaking to him.

"Gordack, please don't come in the kitchen after me," Elias pled.

"But father—"

"Do *not* come in the kitchen with me," Elias begged once again, more sternly this time.

Gordack said nothing but nodded that he understood. Elias finally released his son and went back into the kitchen. Once there, he took a closer look at everything. Given how much blood he could see, there should have been bodies, but he couldn't figure out where they were. Nothing about the scene changed in the time it took to get Gordack out of the kitchen. The entire kitchen was empty except for Elias. He saw a clean towel on the table, with only a small amount of blood soaked into the corner. He took the towel and pressed it against his wound. He could feel the blood had finally stopped seeping from his side, the towel immediately grew wet on his wound. His hand now felt sticky, the blood starting to dry against his skin.

The shuffling of feet came from the back room. Elias looked up and saw Audra moving toward him. *She's alive!* His heart skipped a beat seeing her. But…Something was wrong. Her eyes were not the clear blue of a mid-summer sky. They were now a milky white. Her skin had changed too. No longer did she have a gentle olive complexion. It was now sickly and paler than he had ever seen. There was no loving expression on her face. She somehow looked…dead and still alive. A gnarly wound slashed its way across her chest, from her left shoulder to her right ribs and Elias could see inside his wife's body. He squinted and anger surged inside him at whoever caused this. She continued shuffling toward him, dragging her feet across the bloody floor rather than picking them up. This left trails in the pools of blood on the floor. Still, she was getting closer.

"Audra! Say something. I need you to say something, my dearest," Elias begged. He blinked as tears welled in his eyes, his vision growing into a big blur. He blinked them away and felt their warmth on his cheeks as those same tears now trailed down his face. She said nothing, only shuffling toward him.

Elias knew she was beyond saving. There was only one thing he could do, and that was to put her to rest and end this misery of being left alive after death. With his right hand, he removed his knife from his belt and approached the moving body that, earlier that day, had been his loving wife. As she continued to approach, he felt the weight of what he was about to do growing within him, but he knew that this must be done.

He buried the blade of his knife into his wife's neck and felt more tears streaming down his face as he grabbed her and lowered her once-again lifeless body to the ground. As he placed her body to the ground, he heard a blood-curdling scream coming from the hallway. When he turned, he saw Gordack, a look of terror plastered on his face.

*   *   *

Erkan worked the series of complicated levers that would open the door into the escape tunnel when the ear-piercing scream of a young child distracted him. He intentionally pulled a wrong lever to reset the sequence, stepped away from the door, and looked toward the kitchen where he heard the scream coming from. He saw Elias rushing toward Gordack with a bloodied knife in his hand. The man grabbed his child, dropped the knife, and placed his blood-covered left hand on the child's mouth to muffle the screams. With Gordack now screaming into his father's hand, the hallway once again grew quiet.

"What is going on!" Erkan shouted at his bodyguard.

"Highness, Gordack saw something tragic that neither of us fully understand," the man responded, still fighting to wrangle his son.

"And what is that supposed to mean?" Erkan questioned.

"Audra was killed and brought back to life, somehow. I couldn't leave her in that state, doing whatever bidding someone else wishes. I had to kill her again," Elias said as rivers of tears flowed down his face.

"Say nothing more of this," Erkan begged. "I will never be able to understand this sacrifice you've made. I'm sure your child will understand one day when all of this has settled."

Elias removed his bloody hand from his child's mouth and released the boy, who immediately stepped back away from his father, a look of concern and disgust on his face. He didn't understand now, but Erkan knew he would someday when he was older. Surely, he would understand. Erkan found himself hoping the child could someday forgive his father for what he now didn't understand.

"Elias, I need help with this door, if you have the strength enough for that," Erkan stated.

With both Elias and Erkan working on the levers to open the tunnel door, it only took a few minutes before the section of the wall slid into the ceiling and revealed a dark tunnel that ran so long that they could not see the other end. If the maps that Erkan studied for this portion of the escape route were correct, this tunnel would take them just beyond the southern wall of Anselin, where they could take the nearby road and get to safety at the College in a matter of a few hours. The College would be able to help them, Erkan knew. He hoped they could find whoever was responsible for the tragedies of today. He had no doubt Magic was involved somehow.

As they were getting ready to start the journey into the tunnel, a fizzling sound came from the hallway behind them. Erkan turned and saw a dark, robed figure. It was unclear whether this was a person, some other-worldly being, or something far worse than either of those. As his brain processed the situation, a bolt of lightning shot from the figure's raised hand and crashed into the wall behind Elias. Specks of stone flashed through the air as the lightning destroyed the part of the wall where it landed.

Not wasting any time, Elias grabbed the king and Gordack and shoved them both into the tunnel before walking backwards through the opening himself. *How were we discovered?* Erkan wondered to himself, his thoughts trudging inside his mind. As he stepped into the tunnel, Elias grabbed a conspicuous lever on the wall inside the doorway and slammed it downward, causing the section of the wall that had previously disappeared into the ceiling to come crashing down, locking them in the tunnel. They were trapped in complete darkness with nowhere left to go but forward. They could do nothing other than escape and get to safety. This was their only option now.

"Who was that?" Erkan asked, his voice quavering.

"Father, I'm scared," Gordack whimpered.

"Everything will be alright," Elias reassured both of them. "We just have to reach the end of the tunnel and then we'll be safe."

*   *   *

After a few moments, Elias's eyes adjusted slightly to the total darkness, though he couldn't see anything specific in the tunnel. He knew the door was in front of him, and there were two walls, one on each side. He used his right hand to help guide him as he turned around, found the king and Gordack about a meter into the tunnel, and walked between them both. He kept walking, as quickly as his legs would propel him, though he could tell he was getting slower with each step. The king either didn't notice or thought it was because of the severe darkness where they found themselves. Either way, he was slowing down their escape. *If I even make it to the end of the tunnel,* Elias thought.

With no light in the tunnel, it was difficult to tell the passing of time. Elias guessed that half an hour had passed since they entered the tunnel. He started taking stock of everything that happened today. He recalled the guards with the strange tabards, the assassin in the hallway, and the dark-robed figure. Nothing within those fragmented memories connected together. He felt lost in the darkness, unsure what was happening around him. Confusion swirled his blood-deprived brain into a vortex. What he did know was that their progress through the tunnel was painfully slow. He also knew he had never experienced this amount of pain before. Sharp, stabbing pain that now commandeered his entire abdomen. His wound felt hot even through his doublet. Erkan followed him closely, a hand on Elias's shoulder for guidance, and Gordack followed both of them but kept his distance, likely still processing the events he saw in the kitchen.

Elias could barely walk now. At this point, every moment he remained on his feet was an arduous struggle. During the scuffle getting in the kitchen and having to rush into the tunnel, he had long since lost the towel he grabbed in the kitchen, and he knew that when the fibers of the towel came in contact with his wound, they started to form a clot. With the towel gone, the clot would have been ripped away, making the wound worse than before. He no longer kept his hand pressed against his side to attempt to stem the blood loss. He pushed on, wanting to ensure the king reached safety at the other end of the tunnel.

Something caught his foot as he took another step, his hand against one wall of the tunnel and his other hand reaching for, but not quite touching the other wall. Elias fell, crashing into the floor with a soft *thud*. Something felt wrong and when he put his hand on the floor to get himself up, a new, agonizing pain ran through his right arm, stabbing at his elbow. He rolled onto his left side and tried his best to sit up. His right arm hurt too badly to push himself up. Without help he would be stuck there on the ground. *Surely, this will be my end,* he thought, wanting to embrace the darkness all soldiers knew but feared.

A hand touched him. Erkan. He grabbed Elias under his right arm and brought him to a sitting position, leaning against the right-hand wall of the tunnel.

"We should stop so you can rest. You are pushing yourself too hard with your wound, Elias," Erkan scolded.

"Highness, we cannot afford to stop. Leave me here, and I will catch up later," Elias answered.

"I will *not* leave you here. If you are here alone, you will die. You helped me to see this earlier. Now it's my turn to help you," Erkan said calmly, obviously trying to keep his voice as soothing as he could.

"I promise I will catch up, Highness. Take Gordack with you. Get to the end of the tunnel and get to safety," Elias implored. "I will meet you both at the College. We can get help there."

Erkan took a few moments and processed what he could about the situation. Elias no longer held the wound in his stomach. He had lost a significant amount of blood from that wound, and now he was holding his right arm, supporting a new injury. He couldn't even sit up on his own. If the king left the man now, he would surely die in this tunnel. His child would become an orphan, and out of pity Erkan felt it would be his duty to finish raising the child to manhood. He would be a prince, something much better than he could ever hope for as the son of a soldier and a scullery maid. Besides, this is what the man seemed to want. He insisted on being left to "catch up" later. Erkan could see between the words Elias spoke. They both knew he intended to die here in as much peace as he could muster.

"May the Allfather guide you and your soul," Erkan finally said, cupping Elias's face in his hands. He leaned forward and kissed the man's sweaty forehead, then stood, and started walking toward the end of the tunnel.

"Father! I can't leave you!" Gordack called from his father's side.

Erkan stopped and walked back to grab the child. He had never experienced the duties of fatherhood, and as such had no idea how to handle an emotional child. He lifted the child by the waist and started walking away from Elias. The boy wriggled and writhed in his arms, but despite all of that, Erkan didn't let go. This was what was best for the child, and, just as Erkan hoped earlier, someday Gordack would understand.

They reached the end of the tunnel quickly without Elias as their guide. Erkan felt some guilt about leaving, but knew it was better for the man to go the way he wished than continue and die elsewhere and in more pain. After a few minutes of carrying Gordack, Erkan set the child down. This was a mistake, as he had immediately turned and started running back to his father. Being an elderly Elf, chasing after a child was not something Erkan had anticipated doing in his life, especially not while also escaping Anselin under such duress.

After catching the boy, who was quite fast, he explained the situation the best he could. His father just needed to rest and would join them outside the city when he was well. His conscience scolded him for lying to the child, but the truth would only serve to devastate him. Still, the entire trip to the end of the tunnel, he heard the boy sniffling as he cried.

Leaving the tunnel was much easier than entering it. There was a steel grate that had to be opened, but Erkan alone possessed the key for it. He unlocked the door and he and the child made their way through without any issues. When Gordack was not looking, Erkan reinserted the key and locked the door behind them. He knew Elias would not recover from his wounds, and there was no sense in leaving the grate open for anyone to potentially follow them. There had been that mysterious Mage in the hallway, after all. And while he knew the door was secure to others, he doubted the Mage would be held back from getting into, or through, the tunnel. As he locked the grate, Erkan breathed a prayer to the Allfather, asking that Elias's soul be guided to whatever afterlife awaited him this day. That small thought soothed his conscience. Somewhat. Erkan had grown fond of his bodyguard and would sorely miss the man.

As the maps had shown, the tunnel opened up to the wilderness just south of Anselin. While it was the wilderness, there were few trees to provide cover for their escape. Half a kilometer east, a road ran south and curved out of sight beyond a thick spinney. Erkan knew that road would lead them to the Sorcerers' College if they followed it long enough. He also knew that whoever was assaulting his city likely knew he would escape this way and that staying off the road would be in their best interest. They started walking south toward the College. It was the only thing they could do right now. Even outside in the open air, surrounded by trees, Erkan felt as trapped as he had after Elias closed the door to the tunnel. His pursuers would likely know his every move and could anticipate his path better than he could. Nowhere they could go felt safe. Now, to add complications to the situation, he had a child under his care.

Gordack walked just ahead of Erkan, trudging his feet through the grass that came up to his waist. Erkan knew the child had to be confused, but as long as they reached the College, they should both be fine. They continued until Erkan reached an oak tree with a strange symbol carved through the bark into the flesh underneath. It was a circle which contained a hexagon. Lines went from the center of the circle to the points where the hexagon touched the outer edge. Small triangles set halfway along the sides of the inner shape also touched the edge of the circle. He had seen this symbol before but could not recall where. He continued studying the symbol, keeping Gordack in his peripheral.

"Your Highness! There has been a situation," a voice called behind him.

Surprised to hear anyone calling for him, Erkan turned and saw the same dark-robed Mage he saw in the hallway. A boulder of despair dropped into his stomach as he regarded the shadowy figure standing before him. Whoever the Mage was, they were an Elf or an exceptionally tall human.

"Who are you, and what do you want from me?" Erkan asked.

"Oh, what happened to your little protector? Is he still alive in that tunnel that where you trapped him, I wonder?" the mysterious figure asked.

"Who are you and how do you know so much?" Erkan asked, curious about his assailant.

"You don't know who I am, do you? You're about to know me well." The other lowered his hood and revealed the face of an Elf, severely scarred on the left cheek from just below the eye to beyond the jawline.

"I still don't know you," Erkan confessed.

"Prepare to know me!" the Elf yelled as he stretched out his hand.

"Gordack, run! Get help from the—" Erkan started when he felt something engulf him. It was like a fire, but different. It somehow was both blazing hot and ice cold at the same time. He didn't understand how such a thing could happen.

*   *   *

Gordack turned in the direction the king pointed and ran. He ran so fast he thought his legs would fall off. He didn't stop for a long time, and when he finally did, he looked around with no idea where he was. He looked all around, trying to figure out where he was but still nothing seemed familiar. He looked in the direction he had been running and thought he saw something really tall and very far away.

He turned around and saw his home city of Anselin, the spires on the castle, temple, and the tower of the library rising high above the walls.

It was at that moment a bright flash of white and yellow engulfed the whole city. The light was so bright he had to cover his eyes. He hadn't been alive for long, shy of ten years, but seeing that light scared him more than anything he had seen up to that point. And earlier that day, he had seen his father stab his mother with a knife in the servants' kitchen at the bottom of the castle in Anselin. He kept his face covered for what felt like forever, and when he finally removed his hands from his face, he couldn't see anything left of Anselin. The horizon in that direction was clear. His home was gone. Lost forever to something he didn't even understand. It wasn't anything good, that much he knew. He turned around and ran toward the tall thing in the distance opposite where Anselin once stood. He ran as long and fast as his small legs would carry him.

Chapter Two

...A Few Weeks Later...

The light from the sun no longer touched Shemont as it slinked lower than the walls that surrounded the human capital city. Dusk approached rapidly, and soon the whole city would be bathed in the glow of torch and moon light. Guards walked the nearly empty streets, their eyes on constant swivel as they looked for threats or those who were not supposed to be out this time of day. As with most nights in the city, merchants left the market with their horses or donkeys pulling small carts with unsold goods. Various items went through the market ranging from salted meat, vegetables, and fruits to weaponry that anyone in the city might need. Despite the presence of the guards, thieves still reigned nearly uncontested. People were living in fear of the rise in crime. Meanwhile, the king did nothing but send out more guards.

Much of the chaos came in the wake of the Fall of Anselin a few weeks prior. The news struck Shemont hard; people started to panic as thoughts and fears led them to think they would be the next target for such an attack. King Orson II did what he could to soothe the nerves of those living in the city, but words only carried so much weight. These days, especially. An entire city of the kingdom had been wiped from the face off the continent and with nothing done to stop the attack. Nothing could have been done to prevent it either. Rumors, spread by those who knew nothing of the matter, stated the attack was from a group of Dark Mages; others said it was a coordinated effort by a single person. Regardless of what the rumors said, everything came back to one thing: King Erkan was presumed dead. Unfortunately, after the attack on Anselin, a body was never recovered. Only one person, a half-Elf child, had survived the whole ordeal and based on his account, King Orson concluded that his counterpart was dead. Criers had been announcing the king's funeral for the whole week since he was declared dead. Even now, criers stood on most street corners as they shouted the details of the funeral for any last-minute updates.

Reaching the end of the market, a pair of guards turned east and walked toward The Dwarven Cave. One guard, new to the rank-and-file, stood tall and rigid as if his spine were made with a steel rod. The other was older and slouched, his head bobbing with each step he took. They stopped briefly outside the tavern, talking about whether they had time to stop in for a quick drink and whether they would be able to drink and not get caught by the captain. One of the guards argued against stopping in, though he lost his argument quickly. The guards turned and stepped through the door into the nearly empty tavern. Two other guards occupied the tavern. One, a middle-aged man, slumped onto the counter just to the right of the door. He sat on a heavily-worn stool that seemed to have seen better days. The man wore the livery of the guard, a crimson tabard with the king's golden griffin embroidered on the chest, metal pauldrons, leather bracers, and heavy leather trousers. He carried a sword on his left hip and a shield on his back.

"Should we wake him and send him home?" one of the two newcomer guards asked, pointing at the passed-out guard.

"Don't bother him. He's doing nothing wrong," the other said. "Let's just find somewhere to sit and get *one* quick drink. That's it, then we have to get back onto patrol."

"Would you relax already?" the older guard complained. "The captain'll never know we even stopped in here. What's the harm in having just one beer?"

"Let's just sit down before someone gets suspicious of us."

The guards sat at the counter near the passed-out guard. The older guard sat at the corner near the sleeping guard, while the younger one sat to the left of the older guard, constantly looking over his shoulder while trying, and failing, to not look guilty. The older guard saw this, smacked his companion in the side and muttered something. They called over the stout man behind the counter who took one look at the younger guard and pointed toward the door.

"I won't be caught dead serving guards on duty. Get out before I call the captain!" Frank hollered, rousing the attention of two off-duty guards in the tavern who left their table and followed the others out the door. Frank grabbed the cudgel under the counter and paced back and forth until he heard the argument outside calm down. The two off-duty guards returned to their table and nodded at Frank who breathed a sigh of relief before returning his club to its place.

As a tavern owner, Frank could be held responsible for what happened inside the Cave. Overserving anyone, serving guards who were on-duty, and serving those the law deemed too young to be consuming liquor would all result in the Cave being shut down swiftly and mercilessly. King Orson granted no mercy in this matter. Thinking of this, Frank walked over to the end of the counter, replaced the cudgel, and checked on Sir Michael the Valiant. The man snored softly, a hand still on his mug of ale. Frank knew Michael was fine. The knight was simply stressed and needed some rest. Lately, he visited the Cave more and more, something Frank considered a concern but ignored. He tapped Michael on the shoulder, making sure he tapped hard enough to get through the armor but not so hard that he hurt the knight.

Michael stirred and sat up lazily. "Frank, what have we talked about?"

"That I should wake you before last call and not sooner. I'm just checking on you," Frank stated, holding up a pitcher with some watered-down ale.

"You can refill my mug, Frank, if that's what you're asking. I've had a pretty shit day and can use some encouragement," Michael resigned. "Actually, it's just been a shit few years if I can say as much."

"Anything you want to talk about, lad?" Frank asked, almost afraid of the answer.

"It's not really anything, Frank. My life has been filled with so much death and misery. How is a man to adjust to people being in his life if they just die?"

"That's quite a loaded question you a—"

"It's a rhetorical question, Frank. I'm not really looking for an answer at this point. Thanks for the top-off though. That'll come in handy," Michael said, raising his tankard to his mouth and taking a gulp.

"After that, why don't you head home. I'm sure George is worried about you," Frank suggested.

"That's the thing, Frank. George always worries about me. Told me himself while we were going after a minotaur up in Shaulis Woods."

"You don't think anything of that?"

Michael shrugged and drank from the tankard, emptying it. "He worries about me because of what happened to his previous knight. Since he told me that I've mostly stopped taking hunting assignments from the king. I think that relieves some of the worry, but I've got nothing else to do but manage the guards and other knights. What am I supposed to do?"

Frank refilled Michael's tankard again. "Find a balance, lad. There's got to be some assignments you can take on that won't worry the piss out of George. What kind of missions are you handing out to the other knights?"

"Mostly simple stuff. Find Jack's missing chicken, retrieve Vivian's cat from a tree, and the like. Nothing worth really taking on myself. I get a stipend for managing the knights, as a commander. That's enough for me, I guess," Michael said, looking a bit defeated.

"Perhaps the king will have something for you after the funeral," Frank suggested.

"Maybe," Michael said, starting to take another sip from his tankard. "Wait, what day is it again?"

"It's the sixth, I think. Let me check," Frank said, setting down the pitcher of watery ale and waddling over to the other end of the bar where he kept his calendar. "Yeah, today is the sixth. Why?"

"The funeral is tonight!" Michael shouted, stumbling off his stool and nearly toppling it. He caught the stool, righted it, grabbed his coin purse, slammed five gold coins on the counter, then rushed through the door.

Frank, confused by the whole ordeal, looked to the two guards sitting in the tavern still. "The funeral's next week, though, right?"

"So far as I've heard," the sergeant confirmed. "I'm not going to argue with him though."

"Yeah, why argue with a drunk?" the other guard said.

"Watch your mouth," the sergeant said. "That's a knight commander, and you'll show him respect even if he's not here."

Frank looked to the door and chuckled to himself, wondering when Michael would realize his mistake and if he would come back afterwards or just go home and rest. *I hope he decides to get some rest,* Frank thought to himself.

*   *   *

Sir Michael the Valiant, and the currently inebriated, ran down the road from the Cave to the cemetery as best he could. He had already tripped twice, both times catching his balance before he could tumble all the way to the ground. He surely was a sight for anyone who might be watching. He didn't care if anyone watched. He needed to get to the cemetery after a brief detour at his house to change. He didn't want to show up to the funeral late, drunk, and wearing the wrong colors. By tradition, those at a funeral wore black. Wearing a crimson tabard would make him standout like…well, a red thumb, and he simply couldn't afford to bring that level of attention on himself while not sober.

Michael rounded the corner to the alley in front of his manor and slowed down to avoid tripping, yet again, on a large, loose stone which George had complained about quite a few times. From outside, Michael could tell that the squire was cooking as he saw smoke rising from the chimney and could smell the searing meat that would end up in a pie or stew. *That's odd that he's cooking if the funeral is so soon.* Surely George was waiting for Michael to get home before heading there. Michael shook his head and continued walking up the lane toward his front door.

He struggled with his keys trying to find the correct one for the front door. After an embarrassing amount of time, he finally found the right one then fought with the door to get the key to enter the lock. He chuckled to himself and knew that if George, or anyone else, could see him, it would be an entertaining sight for sure. Within a few moments the key went into the lock, turned, and Michael heard the bolt snap inside the door. He turned the key to the left half a time, removed the key, the rushed through the door where he encountered George in the kitchen wearing his regular clothes, cooking a meat pie.

"Welcome home, sir! I wasn't expecting you for at least another hour," George said, placing a piece of dough on top of the dish containing the rest of the meat pie filling. He started sealing the dough pieces together using the second knuckle of his first and second fingers on both hands.

"I'm here to get ready for the funeral. We're going to be late, George!" Michael shouted as he dashed toward his room to change his tabard.

"The funeral isn't tonight, though, sir."

"It's on the night of the sixth, George. *Today* is the sixth," Michael argued.

"The funeral is next week," George called from the kitchen.

Michael stopped, black tabard in hand, and thought as hard as his sluggish brain would let him. His thoughts felt fuzzy and delayed. Finally, George stepped into the doorway of Michael's room and looked, quite puzzled, at the knight before chuckling slightly.

"Are you alright?" the squire asked.

"Yeah, I just…you're sure it's next week?"

"Quite certain, sir. Come sit in the front room. I have an ale ready for you in case you need to unwind after your long day at work."

Michael closed his eyes as he thought then opened them and returned the black tabard to his wardrobe. "Thanks. I was just at the Cave, though. Dinner smells great, George."

"Minced beef pie, one of your favorites. Come. You need to sit and relax. Dinner will be ready soon."

"Thank you, George," Michael said, walking to the front room and finding a ceramic mug filled nearly to the brim with a cold ale that George made himself.

Michael sat in the high-backed, leather chair, took off his boots, and put his feet on the ottoman. He grabbed the mug and sipped at the foam. While George had only started making his own beer a few months ago, he was quite a brewer. This ale tasted better than what Frank served, something he hated admitting, even to himself. Michael sank further into the chair and closed his eyes as he continued to relax. He stayed this way, sipping at the beer every so often, until George came to tell him dinner was ready.

*   *   *

The sound of pages turning and the occasional popping from the wick in the candle were the only sounds Sir Joshua the Ravenous could hear. The College, especially in the upper levels where the bedrooms were located, was generally always quiet, but at night even the general quietude turned into utter serenity. Joshua preferred reading in his bedroom at this hour of the night for the simple reason that he was undisturbed by even the simple annoyances of his day-to-day life. As a Councilor, especially of a school with no actual students, Joshua experienced significantly fewer interruptions throughout the day, but those he did encounter were usually grave matters he needed to attend to right away. Dark Magic. Its use had increased since he took the position of Councilor. Perhaps the use of Dark Magic was the same, but he was detecting more of it than before. Either way, the Children of Chaos were still incredibly active.

Despite the interesting subject matter of the book, the myriad of rituals practiced by the Children, Joshua found it hard to focus on the book. He read the same sentence repeatedly but found he had not comprehended any of it. His mind strayed to the attack on Anselin. *How did it happen without anyone knowing about it beforehand? Who was behind the attack? Did anyone other than Gordack survive?* So many questions prattled around in his head, yet Joshua had none of the answers. Of everyone in the kingdom, he was expected to have the answers as the Councilor of Dark Magic. Yet, when these questions came up, he could provide no answers for whomever asked. The entire purpose for his position on the Council was to answer to important people, and he didn't have the answers they were looking for. *What a great Councilor I'm turning out to be.*

Joshua closed the book, wished he could focus his mind enough to read, and placed the tome on his nearly immaculate desk. He had a stack of papers, neatly organized, the single candle on a simple candlestick, and the book on his desk. It held nothing more than that unless he was actively working. He hated a cluttered desk.

Joshua had meditated before reading but that focus he made broke almost immediately as he started reading and going through the process again wouldn't have done anything beneficial. Instead, he decided to investigate what he felt was calling to him. Joshua stood, walked to the door, grabbed the polished brass doorknob, and opened the door. He stepped into the hallway, then closed and locked his door before turning left and working his way further up into the tower, as he headed for the balcony at the very top of the College's central tower. He liked going there, at night especially, so he could gaze up at the stars and contemplate this mortal existence. He could also just barely see where Anselin used to be on a clear enough night. Tonight, he thought, would be too cloudy to see much, but he could at least get some fresh air.

As he walked down the hallways and made his way to the top of the tower, he was accompanied by only the sound of his shoes' faint whispers on the carpet and the marble floor between the rugs. He enjoyed the solitude and the time it brought for clearing and organizing his thoughts. Moving, rather than sitting in one spot, always let him do that more effectively. He reached the top of the tower faster than he expected and opened the door to the balcony, stepping out into pitch darkness. He guessed the time to be around midnight, if not later, and closed the door behind him before finding a good spot on the balcony to lean against the railing. He propped himself up with his elbows against the stone banister and let his eyes adjust to the totality of the darkness. Not even the moon brought any light to disperse the blackness that surrounded him.

Once his eyes adjusted, Joshua gazed around the tower, able to see for leagues beyond the marble tower he now called home. To the northwest, a forest stretched all the way to where Anselin used to stand. The trees, massive and ancient, tried their best to be the tallest thing around but failed miserably thanks to the might of the College's central tower. Far to the north, where the Elven homeland used to sprout from the ground like a small sapling, from this distance, Joshua could see a faint hazy glow. It was too dim to ruin his night-adjusted eyes, but something about the glow called to him. Anselin. *The* former *Anselin,* he reminded himself. The city fell less than a month ago and he knew it would take time to adjust to it no longer existing. The entire kingdom needed to adjust.

There was something familiar about the glow, despite Joshua not having seen it before. It tickled at the back of his mind like a downy feather. He could have sworn there was something in a book that explained what the glow came from, but he would have to check with Master Averon. If he didn't wait until morning the elderly librarian would grow extremely grumpy in a matter of moments and that was not something anyone wanted to deal with, least of all Joshua. He was known as the outsider in the College. The former priest who had wooed the headmaster with his brilliance and landed a spot on the Council when others were required to earn that position. His taking the position on the Council had been hugely beneficial for everyone, however there were still those who despised him for it.

Looking at the faint glow on the horizon for a few moments longer, Joshua decided he could risk waking Master Averon. He could save some of the frustrations the librarian would display with some well-developed questions and an interesting research topic. Averon loved helping those with guided, direct questions. He loved helping those with questions in general, but he grew fussy toward those who didn't even know the questions they needed help researching. This, the glow coming from the former Anselin, would bring about a great deal of questions for the librarian to answer, something in which he would be hugely interested. Joshua pushed himself off the banister and returned into the tower on his way to find the librarian. *Allfather let him at least be receptive to my presence this late at night,* he thought, closing the balcony door behind him.

*   *   *

A sea of grass, already covered in beads of dew squeaked as the wind whispered across the wet blades. The lightest of fogs seeped over the gently rolling hills that spread out before the lone oak tree in the field. Thanks to moonlight, the fog shone a gentle bright white. Esram, waiting for the others, watched the fog as it swirled with the breeze. He leaned against the singular oak tree that had sprouted probably a century before after a squirrel buried an acorn for later and simply forgot about it. No other signs of other trees existed in this field so this wasn't a result of deforestation. Esram felt the nodules of the bark pressing into his back as he knelt in front of the tree.

He closed his eyes, shutting away the serene scene before him. With his eyes closed he slowed his breathing and focused on the sounds around him. The branches of the tree above him whispered their secrets as the wind danced through them. Insects chirped in the tree and the field around him, and he heard the flapping wings of a bird as it landed in the tree. He heard it croak and knew it was a raven or some other corvid. He then heard the gentlest of sounds as grass was matted underfoot. Someone else was here. Daethis was the only other member of his order that announced her presence with a corvid.

"You're late," he said, not opening his eyes.

"*You're* early. I'm right on time," she replied, her voice dripping with a honey sweetness as it always had since that day long ago.

Daethis sat beside him, giving him just enough space. His left hand tapped a rhythm on his knee, the only motion he made besides breathing. He ignored the burning sensation in his face, the constant reminder of the mistake he made going toe-to-toe against Bryne all those years ago. *That bastard will pay for this*, Esram promised himself. It was just a matter of time before they would have their revenge.

"Where are the others?" Esram finally asked, opening his eyes.

"They'll be here," Daethis promised. "Give them some time."

"What's the point of calling meetings if others—"

A portal opened and Oleg stepped through followed by Boris. Maja was still missing. *Perhaps she's gotten cold feet given her position in the College,* Esram thought. It wouldn't be the first time someone from the College left the Children. Those who left were dealt with swiftly to avoid detection and compromise. Oleg, a tree of a man, made no effort to be quiet while he walked. He stood over two meters tall and was almost entirely muscle even at over twenty stone. When he spoke, as rare as that was, he surprised many people with his sharp wit. Boris, nearly the complete opposite of Oleg in every way, spoke often and rarely said anything of value, walked almost silently and could only be described as avian in his appearance. A twiggy, hunch-backed Elf with a beak of a nose and thin, wispy, black hair, he could have easily been mistaken for the ravens Daethis preferred.

"Why do we have to meet out here, Esram? It's too cold for some of us," Boris griped, only adding to Esram's dislike toward him.

"Seclusion," Oleg answered. "Harder to find out here."

"We were all supposed to arrive separately," Daethis reminded with her lilting voice that many mistakenly trusted as friendly.

"Enough. We have to wait for Maja before we can even begin the ritual. Does anyone know where she is?" Esram asked.

He got no response, but the newcomers sat on the ground near him. Oleg tried his best to cross his legs like Daethis but gave up and ended up sitting with his legs straight out in front of him. Boris squatted on the ground, which only added to the image of him being a bird-person. Esram took a deep breath and looked up at the portion of the sky he could see around the branches of the oak tree overhead. Some clouds blotted the sky here and there, but he could still see enough of the constellations. He always loved the stories behind the shapes people saw in the stars. Deja, the phoenix, who guided travelers on their journeys, was found to the north. It was the brightest of the star patterns and the only one that didn't move in the night sky. Esram looked west and saw Tusur, the great dragon that would one day devour the world. *How wrong that myth is,* he thought to himself, chuckling softly.

"What are you laughing about this time, Esram?" Boris asked, his voice barely more than a squawk.

"The stories of Tusur being the one to devour the world. It's our master who will bring the mortal world to its knees, not the great dragon, if we can have anything to do with it," Esram said, getting nothing from the others.

Esram returned his attention to the stars, looking south of Tusur for the great huntress centaur, Isothie, who was tasked with keeping the great dragon at bay until the end of times came. As he locked eyes on the formation of the stars, a portal opened and Maja stepped through, making a beeline for the oak tree and the others before the portal even closed. She made no effort to look like she *wasn't* meeting anyone here in the event of prying eyes being around. Esram subtly shook his head, deciding against yet another lecture on the importance of discretion. Maja especially needed to be discrete considering she was part of the Dark Magic school. *Infiltrated right into the belly of the enemy,* Esram noted, confident in her ability to steer the College away from the Children.

"Why do we always meet here instead of at the actual site?" Maja asked, walking up.

"Discretion," Esram said simply. Why waste words on those who refused to listen. *I wish I could be as ruthless as Kalathan,* he sighed.

Maybe someday after the world descends into Madness. Maybe then he would finally rule with an iron fist.

"Stop worrying. No one saw me leave," Maja said, half reassuringly.

"There's got to be another reason for *this* tree, Esram," Boris chimed in.

"It brings me peace," he lied, knowing he could care less about tranquility and calm. He wanted to be able to watch everything around him easily.

Boris snorted and spat at that. "I will never understand you dendrophiles."

"There's much you will never understand, Boris," Esram mocked. "Regardless, we are all here now. Let's go to the site."

Daethis nodded and deftly opened a portal to their far-away ritual site. The sharp smell of saltwater spray came through the portal. Maja, Boris, Oleg, and Esram walked through the rounded doorway in the air, followed finally by Daethis. On the other side of the portal, they found themselves on a large island far to the west of the lone oak tree. The Iron Holm was the Children's sanctuary, partially for its seclusion, partly because few knew of the island's existence. How an island could go unknown when it sat within sight of the mainland's western-most coastline, Esram couldn't begin to understand. He bothered himself not with *why* people didn't know about the Holm and instead accepted that they had never been disturbed or discovered there. This place felt more at home than the wooden structure he lived in and called his home on the mainland.

The center of the island was formed like a bowl, supplying a perfect location for their forbidden rituals. Esram found it preposterous that communicating beyond their own realm was a practice the College forbade, simply because the Assembly of Mages had gone somewhat overboard during their initial experimenting. Entire species would simply not exist without the Assembly and their efforts. The creatures others called *monsters* were all a result of those experimental rituals. Minotaur, manticore, goblins, and others had all been created or summoned into this world by the Assembly. Esram also found it utterly ridiculous that the College forbade talking with other realms, yet when they needed help, especially their Superintendent of the Dark Magic School, they summoned or sought aid from the Vor. That same Councilor even removed one of the Vor from their portal and brought it into this realm! *How can the College sit there and tell us what is* dangerous *and then do things that are astronomically worse?*

Esram snapped his focus back to the matter at hand, rather than focusing on the hypocrisy of the College. The Children of Chaos had much more important business to attend to right now. With Anselin destroyed, they needed to speak with Kalathan and get the next step for his process of bringing the world into disarray and destruction. Chaos *would* descend upon the world, and with his own hands would he fulfill that destiny. Esram would rule under Kalathan with an iron fist and all those who mocked him or had shown cruelty to him would be his slaves.

Having performed the same ritual for speaking with Kalathan many times, the steps now came easily to the Children. The spell they cast created an orb slightly bigger than a melon which floated above the altar. Through that dark, shimmering orb suspended in the air above the stone slab they would speak with Kalathan and hear his terrible voice in reply. If their master chose, he would bring darkness over the bowl in the island. Doing so prevented them from seeing his face, something none of them wanted until he took physical form in their realm. Soon. They knew not what would happen if they looked upon his true face, but legend spoke of agonizing death.

The orb flickered briefly then stabilized. Its surface shimmered and rippled like water, though it was an entirely different substance. They had set up their side of the communication bubble correctly and now they would have to wait for Kalathan to speak to them. His voice would cause their hearts to tremble, their bones to rattle. Such a terrible, deep voice he possessed, yet they all craved his attention. The very core of their beings would shake at the sound of his voice. Esram looked around at the other Children of Chaos whose eyes turned wholly black once the ritual started. His own changed as well but he couldn't see them. Darkness leeched from their eyes into their skin. This effect only happened when they were in communion with Kalathan, though extended time in his presence could make it permanent. They had to keep their sessions short for the time being. Soon, they could show their true forms to the world.

"You have carried out my Will, Children," the deep, growling voice called from somewhere hidden within the orb.

"Anselin is no more. I saw to the king's death personally. His end, much like his life, was that of a coward. The kingdom is shaken and will crumble easily at your touch, Dark One," Esram replied.

"I don't understand why we had to destroy the star," Boris interjected.

"That is what I ordered," Kalathan barked

"I just don't get why we couldn't—" Boris started when the terrible voice grew more intense, cutting him off.

"Do you question my Will?"

"No, I just don't understand why we couldn't keep the star intact and use its power to—"

Darkness enveloped the group, cutting off the imbecile as he spoke. Boris always doubted their calling. He didn't belong with the Children. They never should have allowed him into the fold, but Esram obeyed Kalathan's orders. The darkness grew so great that Esram couldn't see his own hands before his face as he continued the spell to maintain the orb. So lightless was this sensation that the darkest night seemed like daytime.

"You have doubted me for too long," Kalathan rumbled.

An ear-shattering scream rang out, piercing the veil of utter darkness. Boris. Even without seeing it, Esram knew what had happened. Kalathan removed the soul from the bird-like Elf's body and devoured it on the spot. Another thing he found himself envying his master. The ability to completely remove someone's soul while they still lived made him want to giggle with glee, but he refrained. Only just.

As the scream subsided, the darkness dissipated like a fog ran from mid-morning sunlight. Soon, they could once again see their surroundings. The orb rippled and wavered as it floated above the altar. Small stones surrounded them at the bottom of the bowl. Stone slabs surrounded the altar on one side. The slabs used to be benches for whatever purpose the Iron Holm had served long before the Children discovered it. A body lay on the ground, motionless and still. Lifeless. Boris had indeed died during the eclipsing darkness. That was the price of doubting Kalathan, and the Children all knew that going into this. The voice continued from within the floating orb.

"Go. Find Vor'Kath's broken sword where he fell outside his tower. Take the shards to the witches in the tundra; they will know what to do with the pieces you bring them. Continue carrying out my Will, Children."

"When will we get to summon you into this world, Great One?" Esram asked.

"Soon. Retrieve the shards first. The witches are expecting you."

The orb closed, leaving no room for argument. They had their orders, and it was their duty to fulfill them. Vor'Kath had fallen in the south of Drendil in the fields outside his assumed tower. The shards would be there, hidden by some form of Magic. They certainly would have their work cut out for them. The College had since taken control of the tower and there would be Mages crawling all over the grounds. Thankfully, they had someone inside the College who could ease the burden of this assignment. Esram looked to the others, who kept their gazes locked on Boris's lifeless body lying on the ground. The darkness faded from their eyes now that the ritual was over. They had work to do.

Chapter Three

ir Joshua the Ravenous, a knight of the order and a Councilor for the Sorcerer's College, strolled through Shemont on his way to the castle. He normally would have used a portal to enter the castle directly but, with the fall of Anselin, Magic use was restricted within the city's limits, even for one of his status. Instead, he used a portal to take him from the College to just outside Shemont and walked the rest of the way toward the castle. He crossed the market and noted, looking up at the dozen spires of the castle, that the crimson and gold standards bearing the king's livery had been replaced with solid black pennants. The kingdom was mourning the fall of King Erkan III as well as the city of Anselin. For centuries, two kings ruled over the kingdom of Drendil. Now, with this tragedy, everything fell on King Orson II who had not taken the burden of being the sole king well. 'Stressed' would have been putting it lightly.

After waking Master Averon from a deep slumber, Joshua spent the entire night pouring over manuscripts looking for the answers he sought about the glow coming from the former city of Anselin. Master Averon, surprisingly, seemed less than frustrated about the disturbance, especially given the interesting subject matter Joshua brought him. They returned to the balcony together and, after witnessing the glow for himself, Averon almost immediately knew which books might hold the key to the mystery. Together, they poured through the annals of Drendillian history looking for what caused the glow. Joshua was a step closer to solving the mystery.

"Sir Joshua, I was hoping to find you here," a familiar, stuffy voice called as Joshua approached the castle's courtyard where years before he, Michael, and Týr had temporarily captured Vor'Kath in a spell that turned him to stone.

"Headmaster Sanev, it's good to see you. I wasn't expecting you to be here as well," Joshua said in reply, slightly lowering his head toward Sanev.

"I'm here on College business. I have to speak with the king about Anselin."

"I do too. I have a theory about what happened, thanks to some digging that Master Averon and I did late last night. I, sadly, haven't slept yet."

"I guessed as much. I heard someone had woken our grumpy librarian, but I hadn't heard who. Did you find everything you seek?"

"I have a theory. I think…Actually, I think I'll wait until we're with his Highness. I would rather not explain twice," Joshua said.

"I'm hoping he can see us shortly. Jacob said the king has been quite frazzled of late as he pours over the laws and the incident reports we have generated. Have you spoken with Gordack yet?" Sanev asked.

"I haven't, but that's on my list of things to do. I want to see what he has to say about everything. Hopefully, he can shed some light on the matter."

"He has surprisingly little to say about the subject. I think he's still in shock. The poor soul," Sanev bemoaned.

Joshua hadn't heard the full story of how the half-Elf child arrived at the College, but he knew there was some trauma involved. Gordack was, as far as anyone knew, the only person to have survived the attack on Anselin. His memories could be the only direct account of what happened, and Joshua feared the Mages were already chomping at the bits to get their hands on any kind of information they could pry from him. Joshua shook the thought from his mind as the Master General came out of the castle far enough to motion for the Mages to follow him. Tall and lanky, Jacob looked like he was wearing his father's uniform, which Joshua still found amusing. Master General Jacob assumed the position as the head of the military after Alwin, the previous occupant, retired the year prior.

"His Highness is ready for you, Headmaster, though I do ask that you reach your point as soon as you can. He's been a bit…testy lately. Also, I cannot promise you will have anywhere near his full attention," Jacob said, motioning for Sanev to follow him into the castle. Joshua started walking too and Jacob cocked his eyebrow. "I'm sorry, Sir Joshua, but there's only enough time for—"

"Oh, we're here for the same matter. Joshua will come with us if that's perfectly alright," Sanev said leaving no room for questions from the Master General.

"As you wish, Headmaster. Please be quick about your business with the king, though."

Joshua and Sanev followed the general into the castle, down the main hall with its statues, marble pillars, stained-glass windows, and red carpet going from one end of the room to the other. They entered a spiraling staircase that led to both the upper and lower levels of the castle and exited a few floors up. They stepped into a long, narrow hallway with guards posted at both ends. Jacob led them to the far end and into another spiral staircase that only led up. They took the stairs, Jacob two at a time, and eventually came out into another hallway with intersecting passages. This hall had more guards posted than the previous one and some even patrolled, walking rigidly from one area to another. They stopped, one on either side of the hallway, and saluted, clenched fist to heart, as Jacob passed. Rather than returning the gesture, he instead acknowledged them, told the guards to carry on, and then walked between them.

They passed offices with various markings carved into their wooden doors. Guards stood posted outside some of the offices but not others. One, marked with the six stars that made up the constellation Deja, the phoenix, Joshua knew to be the Master General's office. One guard was posted outside that office, his armor and weapons pristinely polished. The guard, armed with a halberd and a sword, stood at the ready and grew somehow stiffer as Jacob guided the visitors through the hallway. The guard raised the halberd to a fully upright position until just after the Master General passed him then returned it to an angled position. A red and gold tassel dangled from just beneath the swooping blade.

Finally, after traversing a few other passageways, they arrived at a dark, wooden door with two burly guards standing to each side of the doorway. They carried a sword on their left hips as well as a halberd in their hands, the end of the haft planted on the floor. Rather than the simple, metal helmet that most guards wore, their helmets were adorned with plates that portrayed terrifying, snarling faces. These masks, covered in gold and red lacquer and a varnish that made them gleam, seemed intimidating enough to deter nearly anyone wishing to reach the king without an invitation. Joshua looked the guards up and down without being too obvious and noted that, in addition to their swords and halberds, they also carried a set of knives, and their gauntlets were spiked. Their armor reminded him a lot of Bruce, the king's guard in Prikea, and the armor he wore.

Master General Jacob knocked twice on the door and waited for the king to call from inside before motioning for Joshua and Sanev to enter. Sanev opened the door and took no time waiting for the king to motion toward a chair before taking a seat in one of the two chairs in front of King Orson II's desk. Joshua waited momentarily and sat in the other chair on Sanev's right. The king, a middle-aged man of above average height with white hair at his temples, and scattered elsewhere throughout his auburn hair, stood hunched over his desk, several large tomes open before him. His fists were clenched tight as he leaned into the top of his elegantly carved desk with the leather ink pad protecting the wooden surface.

King Orson's office, while not as big as it could have been, would be intimidating to anyone who saw it. Various hunting trophies adorned the wall to the king's left, while bookshelves, lined from ceiling to floor with books and scrolls, on the wall behind and to the king's right. Joshua looked at the wall of trophies and noted a minotaur and manticore head, both of which he knew Michael had given to the king during two of his assignments. Other heads, such as a deer, bear, and an elk, were more common and were likely the king's own kills. Regardless, it was an impressive collection. The manticore head, especially, added to the daunting aura the office held. Joshua took his eyes from the snarling beasts and once again looked at the king, waiting for one of his guests to speak.

"Thank you both for coming," King Orson said, taking his eyes away from his books for only a moment. "Shall I assume both of you coming at the same time means you have a related topic for my attention?"

"Highness," Joshua started, "I'm here about the attack on Anselin."

"I, as well, wish to speak about that, Orson," Sanev said. Joshua cringed at the headmaster's informal manner of speaking to the king.

"Joshua, how many times have I told you that you don't have to be as formal around me. You're a Councilor now. To an extent we are nearly at the same level of importance. Given your particular role on the Council, I would say you're far more important to the kingdom than I am."

"Highness, my formality with you is a hold-over from my days as a priest. That habit will die when I do," Joshua explained.

"I won't force you to be uncomfortable then. Do whatever you wish, Councilor," the king said. "I don't have much time. There's still much to be done for Erkan's funeral and so little time for that. What news have you for me?"

Joshua looked at the headmaster, trying to determine who would go first. Sanev nodded toward the former priest who cleared his throat before speaking. "Well, Highness, I think I may have an idea about what happened in Anselin."

"Don't titillate me like this, Joshua. Please, just tell me what you know."

"Sorry, Highness. Anyway. I believe that whoever attacked the city targeted the star at the heart of Anselin and somehow caused it to rupture. I noticed a glow coming off the horizon last night and, after some preliminary research, this is my initial conclusion. The only other time something like this has been documented was after the Dwarves lost Madira in what was determined to be a similar incident. From what was gathered, a Dwarf was mining and struck a star which then exploded into a mass of molten light."

"Quite a discovery, Joshua," Sanev said, his voice barely more than a hoarse whisper. "Why would they destroy the star, though? It contained untapped amounts of Magic that could have been harnessed by anyone with whatever ill intentions they had."

"You mean to tell me that whoever killed my counterpart *and* hundreds of thousands of innocent Elves did this by breaking the star

Anselin was built around?" the king asked looking up from his books. "How could they have gotten to the star undetected?"

"I can't really say about either of your questions just yet. I have no idea why they would destroy the star, but I think by doing so they didn't need as powerful a spell to do what they did. I would have to actually venture to Anselin to find out what happened there, but given what I think happened, I doubt it would be safe for anyone to go there for long. There are untold amounts of Magic freely emitting from the site and prolonged exposure could—"

"How long would you need to tell what happened there?" the king asked.

"Not more than a few hours."

"What risks would there be for exposure to the Magic in that time?"

"Highness, it's hard to say. I'm sorry, but I don't have an answer for that. I'm guessing that the closer someone gets to the star the more Magic they will encounter. In order to find out what happened, I would have to go to the star itself. Something like that could be dangerous in minutes if not sooner. Something like this hasn't been tried in nearly four hundred years."

King Orson sat in his chair and folded his hands on the desk in front of him. "History lessons aside, would you be able to handle this?"

"I believe so, Highness."

"Headmaster, what are your thoughts on this?"

Sanev inhaled sharply before speaking. "We need to find out what happened in Anselin. I dislike the idea of putting someone in danger with this, but we have to find out the truth of this matter. There is no doubt that this was intentionally malicious, but perhaps we can glean some insight into who is behind this attack and why. We must do what we can to discover our adversaries and prevent them from moving further with whatever plans they undoubtedly have."

Orson looked at his visitors for a long moment before speaking again. "Do you think they'll come for Shemont?"

"Honestly, Orson, I have no way—" Sanev started when Joshua cut him off.

"Sorry, Headmaster, but without knowing who is behind this we can't even begin to say where they may go next. It would be unwise to consider yourself and your family safe from their plans, but then you would be living in paranoia and that's not good for anyone, Highness. You are already under enough stress with now being the sole ruler of the kingdom, even if that is a temporary measure. We don't need to add to that by making you look over your shoulder for the foreseeable future."

"Dammit! What else am I supposed to do?" Orson roared. "Since getting the news that Anselin and Erkan fell, I jump at even the slightest noises. I already look over my shoulder, fearing what may be there or around a corner. I am already living in fear. Never before has there been an assassination like this. Kings and queens have fallen in the past but never like this. Someone at least was known to be behind the massacre. Now, we have a king fall, and no one even has an inkling at who did it or how. *How* do we fight this?"

"Highness, I didn't realize—" Sanev started

"Save your sympathy, Headmaster. Give me something worthwhile that will ease my distress. I cannot lead a kingdom like *this*."

"Your Highness, there's nothing that we can do for the immediate future. There are other matters, such as the funeral, which should be seen to first. I know finding out what happened in Anselin is important, but it can honestly wait a week. Maybe by then the Magic there will be safer for whoever is going to investigate," Joshua said.

"I want you and Michael to investigate what happened there, Councilor. I think this assignment would be good for him. He's been cooped up lately and something happened while he was hunting the minotaur," the king said, pointing at the stuffed head on his wall, "that prevents him from wanting to do more hunting. He's clammed up about the subject entirely."

"Michael would be a good addition for the investigation," Joshua agreed. "I know you want some answers soon, Highness, but perhaps we should continue preparing and researching between now and the funeral. Afterwards, I will take Michael up to Anselin. Whatever we find will be reported immediately."

"Yes. The first priority should be the funeral. This is going to be a particularly tough one and not simply because we never recovered the body if there is one to recover."

"Then I think that settles everything," Sanev said, standing up. "We wish not to take up more of your time. Please let us know if you have further need for us, Orson."

*   *   *

College battlemages, Masters from the War School, patrolled the grounds of the neatly kept tower. Maja had never seen so many of them in one place before. *I hardly knew the War School was so large*, she admitted to herself. They had good reason to guard this tower. Vor'Kath once claimed this as his own and before then it belonged to an Assembly Mage. The Masters patrolled the grounds, keeping as vigilant a watch as they could. Maja could easily have subdued them, but she wanted to avoid causing an incident. Anything like that would get back to the College directly, and her position within the Dark Magic school would be compromised. She needed to act normal. She was on a mission but not one she could discuss. The Dark Magic school continued coming to this tower to investigate the site of Vor'Kath's demise. It was a subject that should fascinate anyone in the school. Maja, instead, hated coming here. The Vor harbored such potential and he wasted it. He lost a battle to mortals because of carelessness.

Maja herself came to the tower repeatedly during her earlier days with the school as she actually was interested in learning how the mortals had defeated someone as supposedly strong as Vor'Kath. He should have been too difficult to bring down. The mortals had help from the other Vor, though. *The College certainly has double standards,* she thought to herself as she approached a cluster of Masters on patrol. She recognized each of them but only enough to know their names and that she needed to avoid confrontation with them. She could feel their strength even from a few paces away. One of them would be able to overpower her. Three? That would have been a nightmare. One broke away from the pack and approached. Douglas was the weakest of the three Mages, but she still felt wary as he approached. She was sure he could sense the darkness in her. The betrayal.

"Back again, Maja?" Douglas said as she approached the tower.

"Only wanting to do some more poking around if that's fine with you. There's always rumors of more Dark Magic here that we haven't found yet. I can feel it, actually."

"This place gives me the creeps. The aura here is too strong if you ask me."

"Every site like this is the same. You get used to it in my line of work," Maja said.

"Whatever makes you happy. Do you need access to the tower tonight or just the grounds?" Douglas asked. "If you need to go into the tower you'll have to talk with Garrick. He's in charge tonight."

"I shouldn't need access to the tower. Pretty sure Garrick hates me for some reason."

"I can talk to him if you end up needing to go into the tower. Feel free to do what you need. None of us will bother you."

"Thanks," Maja said, walking away from the other Mage.

After Douglas returned to the group of Mages and they started walking away, Maja sighed in relief, then started casting spells as she looked for the site of the battle between Michael, Joshua, and Vor'Kath from roughly a year before. She knew the battle happened outside the tower but was not quite sure where. Traces of Magic stained the ground all around the tower. Finding the exact spot would be tricky at best.

She started walking around the tower until she started getting traces of Dark Magic that had to come from Vor'Kath. Something about the Magic of the Vor was different since they were beings of pure Magic. She followed the trail and soon found what she sought amid a patch of overgrown grass: the shards of Vor'Kath's sword. Eight pieces of a broken Magic sword. She released the spell she was using to follow the traces of Magic and cast another to retrieve the sword pieces. She didn't want to touch something this powerfully dark with her own hands. That would cause potential issues she didn't want to deal with right now surrounded by dozens of War School Mages. *Better not to have a fight with them anyway,* she decided.

With the shards safely retrieved and contained within a Magic-imbued satchel that would mask their presence from others, she created a portal and left the tower behind. As a member of the Dark Magic school, she had an obligation to return the shards of this sword to the College for examination; however, Kalathan said to bring them to the witches in the tundra. She hated dealing with witches but knew that Esram wouldn't mind at all. Maja used a series of portals to leave the tower. The first portal took her to her rooms in the College, then to the Dark Magic school's underground building that only members of the school knew about, then she used a third portal to take her to the lone oak tree where the Children always met Esram before heading to the Iron Holm. She hated going through portals so rapidly. She took a step through one, closed it then opened the new portal. She traveled hundreds of kilometers in the matter of a few steps which always made her feel dizzy. Thankfully, Esram already waited under the tree for her. He knelt on the ground with his back against the trunk of the tree and the fingers on his left hand tapped a four-beat pattern on his knee while he waited.

"What took you so long?" Esram asked, stopping the tapping on his knee as he stood.

"Sorry, some of the College's Mages were checking on me and I couldn't get away from them any sooner than I had. I was afraid they would start asking questions soon," Maja replied.

"The witches are waiting. You have the fragments?"

"All eight of them. Do you know what we're doing with these?"

"We need the shards for the summoning ritual. That's all you need to know for now," Esram said.

"Good. I will give you these," Maja said, handing over the protected shards of Vor'Kath's sword, "and you can go to the witches. I would rather not deal with them at all."

"Very well. You're aware of what comes next, correct?"

"Of course. Meddle and mislead for the sake of chaos."

"Very good. Go. You're needed elsewhere," Esram said, taking the shards and opening a portal to the tundra.

Chapter Four

...Later that week...

The sun started setting as people still gathered at the cemetery just outside of Shemont. A mass of people congregated outside because there was no more room for anyone inside the cemetery. An iron fence surrounded the area and people leaned against the fence as far as they could. The road that led to the graveyard was packed with people still trying to get in for the ceremony. Never before had such a turnout happened for a single funeral, but this was not a typical funeral. Elves and humans alike traveled from across the kingdom to pay their respects to a fallen king, something which had not happened for quite some time within the kingdom of Drendil. Inside the fence, those with social status gathered before the pyre which would be lit after sundown. Those gathered still were limited to standing room as even their numbers were greater than the chairs lined up within the area that was free of tombstones. Generals, knights, those of noble houses, Councilors from the College, and the royal family all gathered within the fence. Everyone within the fence, and many of those without it, wore black, following the kingdom's mourning traditions. As the colors in the sky faded to the grey of twilight and finally into the blackness of night, the most important of those within the kingdom took their seats in preparation for the ceremony.

Sir Joshua the Ravenous and Sir Michael the Valiant stood behind the small group of chairs. They would, together with the king and his brother, light the pyre at the end of the ceremony and remain here until it fully burned away. Earlier that week, Joshua had gone with the other Councilors to where Gordack, who sat in a chair not far from the queen, said the assassination happened. While this gave the Council the first, albeit distanced view of the ruins of what remained of Anselin, they found nothing else. No sign of a body or even a fight beyond the still glowing remains of the city. Joshua had found a symbol carved into a tree which Headmaster Sanev identified as belonging to the Children of Chaos. That only served to further confirm their theory that Anselin was attacked. Nothing that happened was accidental. King Orson took that news gravely, imposing further restrictions on Magic use around the city of Shemont, if that were at all possible. Rather than a fine, Magic users now faced a minimum of three days in the dungeon if they were caught casting spells within the city. He also increased the presence of his guards who were now being more thoroughly vetted before taking up posts within the floors surrounding the king's office.

"This is a grim setting," Michael whispered. "I hate how much death there is in our lives, Joshua. Why does it feel like we're surrounded by it?"

Joshua placed a hand on his friend's shoulder. "Death is a natural part of life, Michael. However, I agree with you. So many around us have died since we came to Drendil."

"Is it all related to the Children of Chaos in some way or another?"

"Yes, in some way or another everything has been caused by the Children."

"There's got to be something we can do about them," Michael said, finally breaking his eyes from the pyre.

"We will talk with the king about that after the ceremony. Be patient, Michael."

"Patience is a virtue, but not one I'm fond of," Michael replied.

"It is one of the hardest virtues to cultivate," Joshua agreed.

"Thank you all for coming. I apologize for there not being enough room in here for everyone," King Orson said, addressing the crowd as the light in the sky finally dwindled. "King Erkan was a great man, regardless of what people may say about him. He dealt with many problems throughout his reign. Famine, revolutions, coups. He took everything in stride and never faltered. He stood, loyal to his duties, to the end of his days. Some called my counterpart a coward, but I have never met anyone with more of a warrior's resolve than Erkan. He fought countless foes throughout his life. Usurpers who fought for his throne, violent protesters who sought only to discredit him as the rightful king, those with unfounded accusations, and other enemies, unseen or otherwise. This loss is not the end, though, for through us Erkan lives on. So long as the kingdom prospers and continues to grow, we shall remember him and the sacrifice he made not long ago. This pyre behind me may be visibly empty, but it carries a weight no number of Drendillians ever could. With a heavy heart we, as a kingdom united by grief and distress, bid farewell to King Erkan III, Elven king of Drendil. May the Allfather guide his soul to the afterlife and protect him to the end of days."

With that, Joshua, Michael, and Reifous I, the queen's brother, started their walk down the aisle toward the pyre. They walked slowly and deliberately as they made their way to the king. Once there, Orson grabbed a lit torch and lit Joshua's torch, which then lit Michaels and finally Reifous's. Together, the torch-bearers moved toward the pyre and as one set their torches against the four corners of the oil-soaked pyre built on a stone outcropping that stood over an inlet of water. The fire immediately took to the pile of wood and within a few moments the torch-bearers were already stepping away from the flames. They filed to one side to ensure everyone gathered could see the wood burning. Without a body on the pyre, Joshua thought it a hollow display, but he knew the symbolism the king wanted from this. This wasn't a pyre for King Erkan alone, it was for the whole of those lost in Anselin.

The pyre burned in complete silence, save the sounds of the wood popping as the fire consumed it. At least an hour passed before the fire began dying down and those who had come for the ceremony started leaving. Those gathered within the cemetery fence stayed, waiting for those on the other side of the fence to filter down the single-lane road that led back to Shemont. With the ceremony officially over, Joshua looked to Michael and King Orson to speak with them.

"Sire, I haven't mentioned the investigation to Michael yet. Would you like for us to speak now?" he asked.

"What investigation?" Michael asked.

"I want both of you to look into Anselin and find out what you can about what happened there. We already know who did this, but I want to know how and see if we can figure out the why of it all. Something still isn't sitting well with me about this whole affair," the king said, his face still cast in dancing lights and shadows from the funeral pyre.

"What all will be involved with the investigation?" Michael asked.

"We will have to go to the very heart of Anselin and see what happened to the star, if we can learn that at all. It may be dangerous because of the amount of Magic still pouring from the collapsed star. If you don't want to be part of this I understand," Joshua explained.

"No, I will go. I've been wanting to have something to do other than manage the guards. George may not be happy about the nature of the assignment, but he'll accept that I need to go. When do we head out?"

"Why don't I stop by tomorrow morning, and we can head to Anselin after breakfast?"

"George will enjoy that. He has asked about you ever since you took the spot on the Council. I don't think he's seen you since the tournament," Michael said.

"Sorry, I've been quite busy with my duties lately. I don't mean to be so secluded."

"No need to apologize, Joshua. Sometimes life just gets in the way of things."

"How is your arm? Has it fully recovered from the wound you got from the basilisk?"

"It still gets sore right before a storm comes through. I think I have full range of motion though. Thank you, again, for saving me from that," Michael said.

"I never heard the full story about the basilisk," the king said. "Maybe you two can stop by the office tonight and tell me about that?"

"That sounds like a great idea, sire," Joshua said. "I have a fresh bag of tobacco if that furthers your interest."

"It certainly does, but if the queen asks, I never said that," the king said then held up a finger to his mouth and winked.

Michael tapped the side of his head and nodded. "Your secret is safe with us, Highness."

"Why the need for secrecy?" Joshua asked.

"He's supposed to be quitting his pipe, Sir Joshua," the queen said, her voice firm yet somehow forgiving as well.

"Your Grace, we mean no harm with this. If you wish him not to smoke then I won't bring my tobacco. I wasn't aware that his Highness was quitting," Joshua said, a touch of shame in his voice.

"It's not my choice. He's the one who said he should quit. He's an adult and can make his own choices. Who am I to judge?"

"One night won't ruin my ability to quit, my love," the king said.

Queen Lydia scrunched her face at this. "You have to be happy with your choices, Orson. That's all I'm going to say of the matter. Don't stay up too late?"

"I won't," the king said.

"Sire, can I make a portal from here to my chambers in the College?" Joshua asked, fearing the punishment the king had placed for Magic use around Shemont.

"If you're asking if I would lock *you* in a dungeon cell for taking us to the College, the answer is no, Joshua. Yes, there are the restrictions inside the city, but that really only applies to spells that could threaten the city."

"I understand, Highness. I simply wanted to make sure," Joshua said as he cast a portal and motioned for King Orson and Michael to go through first.

Joshua hadn't brought many visitors to his personal chambers within the College. While not modest in size, the lack of decorations certainly made the room feel emptier than it really was. He had a desk, some chairs in the event that people did come to his office, and a single bookcase with a few books standing on the shelves. His collection of books didn't begin to compare to Orson's either in number or variety of subject matter. The king's books mostly dealt with laws, traditions, customs, treaties, and the like which any ruler would need. Joshua's books, on the other hand, covered subjects such as the known rituals of the Dark Mages, bestiary found throughout Drendil, and various other arcane subjects. Joshua walked to his desk and opened a drawer, retrieving both his pipe and the fresh bag of tobacco he purchased from a merchant who used to visit Anselin but now stopped at the College.

King Orson took a seat in one of the chairs across the desk from Joshua before the Mage could ask about opening a new portal. Joshua looked confused, but when Michael also took a seat, it was clear they meant to catch up here. Joshua sat down, opened the bag of tobacco, and started filling his pipe. Michael did the same. The king simply sat and watched as both of his knights carefully placed their dried tobacco flakes into the bowls of their pipes and proceeded to light them. Joshua took a long puff on the mouthpiece before exhaling an average-sized cloud of tobacco into the air above his desk. Technically, tobacco use was not allowed on College grounds, but that rule was bent by many of the staff.

"I have an extra pipe if you would like to smoke, sire," Michael offered.

"Thank you, but I'm fine simply sitting here," the king replied. "While we are here, let's talk some business first before we start catching up on what's been going on."

"What do you have in mind?"

"First let's talk about Anselin. I know you are both heading up there tomorrow to investigate what happened. As you can imagine, I would like to be the first to know what news you gather about the incident. I know the headmaster has probably already asked the same, but I would like to think I get at least some amount of precedence in this matter," King Orson said, looking longingly at the clouds of smoke above Michael and Joshua.

"Of course, sire. We can bring the headmaster with us if you would like," Joshua suggested, blowing another small cloud of blue-grey smoke into the air above him.

"Whether he comes or not isn't a concern of mine right now. I just need to know," the king said, adjusting in his chair. "Actually,

Michael, if I could have that spare pipe you have, I would appreciate that. This has been the wrong month to try and stop smoking, I will say that much right now."

Michael removed a plain, short-stemmed pipe from a pouch on his belt and handed it to the king. Joshua handed over the bag of tobacco that sat on his desk and the king started filling the bowl hastily. Once that was accomplished, he grabbed a match from Joshua's desk, struck it, and puffed at the pipe vigorously. Within a few moments he was blowing tendrils of smoke from both sides of his mouth with the stem between his teeth. A few minutes of silence later, he sighed in relief and leaned back in his chair before propping his left ankle on his right leg.

"Can I ask why you are trying to stop smoking, Highness?" Michael asked.

"Lydia is concerned about my health and after a talk we decided it would be best if I quit. I have been without a pipe for a week now and while I feel better, the cravings are severe. Thank you, Michael, for your spare pipe. Why do you carry two? If you don't mind my intrusion."

"In case I'm somewhere with George and he doesn't have his. He smokes so infrequently that he often forgets to bring it with him," Michael answered.

"Do you still have your pipe, Highness?"

"I do, but Lydia keeps it with her, so I don't use it regularly. She thought about having Jacob watch it, but she doesn't trust his resolve in the matter."

"Is the Master General easy to sway?" Michael asked. "He doesn't seem like a pushover to me, but I don't know him all that well."

"Only when it comes to things he considers an order," Orson said after blowing a ring of smoke into the air and sending a smaller one through the first.

"What time are you stopping by Freenel tomorrow, Joshua?" Michael asked, changing the subject.

"I will probably stop by just after the seventh bell if that works."

"Come by at the eighth bell and we can eat together. George makes a good breakfast."

"Sounds like a plan then," Joshua agreed.

Michael emptied out his pipe into a small ceramic ashtray that Joshua removed from his desk. Michael then gently tapped the bottom of the bowl and scraped the ash from inside before returning the empty pipe to his pouch. The king also emptied his borrowed pipe and returned it to Michael. Joshua tapped the ashes out of his but filled it another time before grabbing a book from a separate drawer from his desk. He opened the book and set it on his desk facing his visitors. Both Michael and Orson leaned in to read the paragraph Joshua pointed to.

"This is what I fear we will find in Anselin tomorrow," Joshua clarified as the other two leaned back into their chairs.

"So, you think—" Michael started when Orson cut him off.

"Why would they have done that?"

"One reason alone: intimidation," Joshua answered.

"Who would need this level of intimidation?" Michael asked.

"There's only one being that craves domination over everything within our mortal realm," Joshua said. "Kalathan."

* * *

Three crows flew into the tree where Maja stood waiting. Together they cackled and cawed in the branches above. *Daethis.* She was the only member of the Children that announced her presence. Maja didn't know why she used corvids. While beautiful birds, she detested how noisy they were. *Must they make so much noise?* The birds, not far overhead, continued making noise until their master approached. Daethis walked with such grace that Maja could hardly hear her footsteps. *Elves.* Maja didn't hate the Elves but was jealous of their grace and long-lasting beauty, something the humans didn't have for themselves. Daethis walked under the tree and cast a spell which silenced the crows without harming them. With the birds quiet now, Maja felt that she could finally tell Daethis about what she had learned. The spell hadn't been complex and went unnoticed by the Councilor while he smoked with the king in his office, something which Maja knew was against College policies.

"The Councilor is taking the drunk one to Anselin in the morning," Maja said.

"This is all part of the plan, remember?" Daethis reminded.

"I still don't like that we are giving him so much information about what happened."

"Yours is not a place to dictate what must be done and why," Daethis chided. "We must simply allow the plan to unfold as our great master has told us."

"I'm not trying to question the logic of the plan," Maja said. "I simply don't like that we are giving the College so much information. We went through so much to keep our plans for Anselin secret. Why give them up now?"

"The College must think they are getting close to us for the plan to work. Trust is essential, little one," Daethis said, the insult stinging less with the way her voice lilted.

"You know I hate when you call me that," Maja grumbled. "What happens after they discover what we did there? You know they will figure it out. The Councilor is a cunning one."

"Once the witches have the dagger prepared, we will lead him there so he can see the shards from Vor'Kath's broken sword. The temptation of the darkness is too strong for him to resist. He will have to touch them, but you have to seem distracted by the writing on the walls of the cavern. Are you able to do that?"

"I *am* fascinated by the language of the Vor. I'm sure I can be distracted for long enough that he touches something he's not supposed to. But again, why is this part of the plan?"

"We need him for the ritual. His strength alone could summon Kalathan into this world. With his help, we will destroy the very world he loves so much," Daethis said, malice dripping on her voice. "This whole ordeal will be delicious."

"How are we so certain that he will be called by the shards?"

Daethis smiled, just the faintest flash of movement in the corner of her lips. "The witches are crafting a spell special for him."

"Excellent."

"His time is coming, Maja," Daethis promised. "Good work on that spell. I knew you would be the right one for this."

"I'm happy and eager to serve our master. What else do you need from me?"

"Nothing until after he learns the truth of what happened at the star. Go get some rest."

"The night is still young. We should do something," Maja suggested.

"We cannot. It would bring too much risk of getting caught. Leave here and wait for the next step. Go back to the tower if you need to do something to stay occupied. I'm sure you can keep up the masquerade by going there."

"Certainly."

Daethis nodded her approval and removed the spell she placed on the tittering crows still in the branches overhead. The birds flapped their wings impatiently until the Elf whispered something and they took to the sky, flying above the tree and circling before taking off south. Daethis took a few steps out from under the tree, her feet not even whispering against the grass. She stopped, turned, and looked Maja dead in the eyes, her face expressionless.

"You have a big part to play in this. You will have to make sure the Councilor comes to the Iron Holm unscathed. We will deal with him once you're there with him."

"I look forward to it," Maja breathed as Daethis disappeared into thin air.

Chapter Five

ir Joshua the Ravenous stepped out of a portal outside the capital city of Shemont and walked through the few yards of grass that stood between him and the packed-dirt road that cut east and west across the land. From this vantage point he had a great view of the lake that surrounded Shemont. The air had a tinge of algae and moss, something he loved. He stopped at the side of the road as a merchant wagon barreled down the road and looked to the east where, far away, the Ash Mountains rose above the horizon, hiding the first sliver of the sun as it peeked into the sky after its nightly journey across the other side of the world.

The morning, while crisp, promised that the day would be muggy and warm, verging on miserable. With its proximity to the lake,

Shemont felt swampy during every portion of the summer, something that made him thankful for living at the College almost full-time now. He no longer dealt with the overwhelming humidity. Unfortunately, his position on the Council meant he still visited Shemont quite a bit more than he wished. Days like this one, where his forehead gathered beads of sweat even standing still, made him miss Prikea where a cool breeze swept across the city at all times. The ocean there was cool and didn't provide as much humidity. Many things about Drendil made Joshua miss his homeland, and the weather was certainly not a small factor.

With the merchant wagons passed, Joshua started walking down the road toward the city. He enjoyed the time walking to the city, despite the convenience of portals. Even with the king saying the night before that non-threatening Magic was fine, Joshua still didn't wish to take his chances on three days in the dungeon. He had avoided being thrown into a dungeon his entire life and this wasn't the time to try something new, he figured. He also didn't mind the walking. It was good exercise. Any doctor would be pleased to hear about this change of pace. Plus, the walk wasn't that far from where his portal brought him to Michael's knightly home, Freenel Manor. Joshua frequented the home shortly after attaining his knighthood and knew it to be a quaint home, perfectly fit for a knight of the order.

He quickly reached the city gates after crossing a stone bridge. He walked through the gate without any problems as the guards knew him and walked the city streets toward Freenel Manor. As he approached the knightly home, he could smell meat roasting as smoke floated from the top of the chimney. George was already cooking. Joshua rounded a corner onto the small alley in front of Michael's home and then down the small lane lined with blossomed trees that lined the walkway. Joshua was thankful for even the minimal amount of shade the trees provided.

Joshua used the polished brass knocker on the door and rang thrice on the metal plate. He heard the pitter-patter of feet inside as someone approached the door and finally, after the sound of two locks disengaging, the door opened and Michael's squire, George, appeared in the doorway. Given the surprised look on the man's face, Joshua knew he wasn't expected, which surprised him greatly.

"Sir Joshua! What a pleasant surprise. Are you here to visit Sir Michael?"

"Did Michael forget to mention that I was coming by?"

"I haven't seen him since the funeral. I was starting to grow worried, actually," George said, his voice more than concerned.

"You don't know where he is at all?"

"No, but if I had to guess, I would say he might be at the Cave as he calls it. I can run there and check if you don't mind watching breakfast," George suggested.

Joshua walked back down the few stairs to the stone pathway back to the road. "No, George, that's quite alright. I will go find him."

"Thank you so much, Sir Joshua! Please make sure he gets home safely."

"Before I leave, do you tend to the grounds yourself?"

"Please don't mention this to Michael, but I actually have someone come by once a week to keep things spruced up. If you would like I can have them stop by Valenton and talk with Harold for you."

"I would really appreciate that, George. Harold writes me often about the state of the grounds. He gets so distraught about them, and I would rather he not worry about something so simple if he doesn't have to," Joshua said. "Take care, George. I should be returning momentarily with Michael."

Once the door closed, after more unnecessary thanks from George, Joshua once again admired the well-kept grounds before returning to the street that ran between Michael's manor and the one next door. Each sported split-rail fences that lined the properties, something Joshua appreciated. They did nothing to stop anyone from getting onto the properties, but they looked nice and that was generally all that mattered. Once on the road, Joshua made a beeline for The Dwarven Cave, a tavern not far from Michael's home. He met back up with the main road, turned left and walked two blocks down until he could see the sign bearing a dwarf carrying a pickaxe on his shoulder. The dwarf, carved in a simple, artistic manner, was coming out of a dark cave. Above and below the Dwarf were the words that made the name of the tavern.

Joshua knew the Cave, as the regulars called it, well. It was a humble tavern that didn't stand out from the other buildings in the city. Stucco and wood on the top half of the building and stones with mortar at the bottom was the style of most buildings in Shemont. The sign was the only way to tell anything was different about this establishment compared to the house next to it. Joshua walked up to the door and hesitated until he heard what sounded like cavorting inside then opened the door. The gentle *ding* from a bell above the door announced his arrival.

"Sir Joshua, it's good to see you again!" Frank called from behind the counter.

"It's good to see you, too, Frank. I'm here to find Michael. George hasn't seen him since the funeral, and I know I sent him home late last night."

Frank pointed toward the end of the bar. Joshua closed the door and found Michael sitting on a worn-down stool with his pipe in one hand, tendrils of smoke fluttering from the fluted bowl and a mug of beer in his other hand. Michael took a deep drink from his mug, set it down, and looked to the door. A big smile crept over his face as he realized who he was looking at and he started waving his pipe and the mug of beer around as he grew excited.

"Joshua! Have you finally come to have a beer with me?"

"No, Michael. I'm here so we can go to Anselin like we discussed last night. Don't you remember that?"

"We can't go to An...selin," Michael hiccupped. "It's been destroyed,"

"That's why we're going, Michael. We have to investigate what happened there."

"We can talk about that after we have a beer together, friend. It's been so long and mourning alone is terrible," Michael said, looking to Frank. "Bring us two beers, good sir."

"Ignore that request, Frank," Joshua said, not taking his eyes off Michael.

The other knight wilted. "You don't want to drink with me?"

"Michael, we have work to do."

"I don't want to work right now. I'm happy where I am."

"We are *going* to Anselin. First, we're taking you home so you can get some of the food George has made for you, and then we're going to find out what happened to an entire city of innocent Elves. Come along, Michael."

"No! I won't go with you. *You* can't make me go, Joshua."

Joshua took a deep breath, reached into a small pouch on his belt, removed some papers, unfolded them gently, and slammed then on the bar in front of Michael. "I wish you had a choice in the matter, but his Highness says otherwise, Michael."

The expression on Michael's face shifted from sad to serious as he picked up the papers and struggled to read them. He shook his head and blinked, trying his best to fix his vision after what Joshua assumed was a night of heavy drinking. Joshua watched Michael read the notice, his lips moving silently as he read through the king's orders. Ale and stale tobacco wafting off Michael. Michael once again shook his head, read through the notice from King Orson once more, then tapped the still-burning ember from his pipe. He cleaned the bowl and removed the stem from the pipe before tucking it into the pouch on his belt. Dismounting the stool, Michael smoothed the wrinkles from his tabard and looked at Joshua.

"We should be on our way. Would hate to disappoint the king."

"Thank you, Michael. I can't do this on my own."

Joshua grabbed the handle on the door and pulled it open, holding it for Michael. The other knight staggered through the door and shuffling down the street toward his manor, almost like someone else were controlling him. Joshua grabbed a few coins from his purse and placed them on the counter, nodding at Frank as he did so. Frank waved and returned to wiping down the counter. With Michael's bill paid, Joshua joined him in the short trek to Freenel Manor. Joshua stayed a pace behind Michael and watched carefully as his friend walked, somehow gracefully avoiding the loosened cobblestones in the road. Together they reached the knightly estate within a few minutes. Michael stood at the door and fumbled with his keys, trying to find the right one but Joshua lifted the knocker and let it drop a few times. A crow cawed nearby and fluttered off, flapping its wings vigorously as it took to flight from one of the trees lining Michael's walkway. George came to the door promptly and opened it, greeting the knights when he did so.

"Welcome home, Sir Michael! I was worried about you all night. I hardly think I slept."

"No need to worry, George. I'm safe. Joshua has reminded me that we have an assignment up in Anselin today. I will be out of the house the rest of the day, but rest assured, Joshua will be keeping an eye on me," Michael said, stumbling across the threshold and toward his bedroom.

Once in his room, Michael opened his wardrobe, removed a crimson and gold tabard from inside and placed it on his pristinely made bed. He hurriedly removed the solid black tabard he wore for the funeral, returned that to his wardrobe and threw on the other. He emerged from his bedroom still fastening his belt and tucking the loose end around itself. Michael looked at Joshua and nodded. He was ready to leave. Michael made his way toward the door but stopped when George called to him from the kitchen.

"Sir, before you head out, I would recommend you eat some of the food I've prepared."

"What do you say, Joshua? Care for some breakfast?"

"Sounds lovely, Michael."

The knights walked into the kitchen and retrieved filled plates from George. Joshua's plate held three round, fried cakes, two sausage links, and three eggs. Scents of pepper, garlic, and onion floated from the plate. Joshua's stomach let out a quiet rumble as he took in the sight of the food. George grabbed a ceramic carafe and walked to the table in the adjoining room. Joshua and Michael followed, sitting across from each other. George poured two cups of coffee and left the dining room so they would have some peace while they ate. Neither Joshua nor Michael spoke while they ate their breakfast. There was simply nothing for either of them to say.

*   *   *

The road leaving Shemont rose slightly as it led to the bridge that crossed the water surrounding the city. The morning grew warmer as the sun rose higher into the sky. Small, fluffy clouds floated through the sky, pushed by an even softer wind that swept across the land. Trees on the other side of the water swayed in the gentle breeze, their branches waving at travelers on the road. Joshua and Michael walked in silence as they crossed the bridge. Once they reached the other side of the bridge, Joshua walked away from the road, returning to where his portal brought him earlier. He cast a spell that opened another portal taking them to the College. From there it would be a short ride on horseback to the ruins of Anselin. Joshua feared how Michael would fare on the horse but figured he would be fine after a few minutes. Michael was strong and would adapt quickly, no matter how drunk he might still be.

"Joshua," Michael said, breaking the silence that had hung between them since leaving the Cave.

"Yes, Michael?"

"Do you think I spend too much time at the Cave?"

"That's a loaded question, Michael. No one can really say whether the time you spend there is too much time or not. Only you can decide that."

"I know. I wanted to see what you thought about it though. You're a good friend, Joshua. I value your opinion."

Joshua closed the portal and looked at his friend before answering. "It's clear to me that you're trying to forget something that's happened to you. Are you well, Michael?"

"I don't know how to answer that question, honestly. Some days I feel fine but others the thoughts are too heavy to bear. I don't know what to do."

"Talking is a good start. What kind of thoughts do you have?"

"Sometimes they're thoughts of home. Others they are about the death that has followed me since we came here and all the people we have lost. I don't like those thoughts."

"I'm so sorry, Michael," Joshua said. "I'm always here if you need someone to talk to about this. As a priest I learned to listen to others' problems and help them work through them. Would you like to give that a try some time?"

"I'm not sure, Joshua. I think I've been dealing with this on my own for so long that I don't even know where to start. So often lately I just feel lost and broken. Is that a normal feeling? I don't want to burden you with my problems."

"You're never a burden, Michael. No matter how you feel, no matter what you're going through. You are *not* a burden. I will always be here for you."

"Thanks, Joshua. We should head to Anselin."

Good idea," Joshua said, opening another portal.

Like every other portal that Joshua opened, this one shimmered and rippled like the air over a fire. The doorway in the air took up space yet seemed not to even be there at all. Joshua hardly noticed the fascinating nature of portals after the first few months of casting the spell that created them. The beauty of what happened when crafting these marvelous creations just faded over time. He figured it was no different, really, than anything else in life. The more of something you saw, the more immune you grew to it. Even the most breathtaking thing in the world could become mundane quickly.

Joshua waved Michael toward the portal and waited for him to walk through before following him. As happened every time he traveled through a portal, Joshua's skin tightened and tingled as a wave of cold splashed over him. The chill followed from his hand that went through first creeping up his arm and over his hairless head. Every bit of exposed skin immediately prickled in tiny bumps. Breath escaped his lungs and his chest felt tight, as if he had jumped head-first into a pool of water on a brisk fall morning. This sensation followed him a few moments after stepping through. He looked back at the surface of the doorway and watched it shake and waver like a pond where a child had just thrown a handful of stones into the water. With both of them through the portal, Joshua released the spell and the doorway dissipated like a morning fog after the sun came rose over the horizon.

The portal took them to the northern edge of the College's grounds where the stables stood. Horses whinnied inside and Joshua heard the stamping of shoed hooves against dirt. Manure and hay hung in the air, both smells that made Joshua's eyes start to water. Michael already started walking toward the stables and was about to speak with one of the hands inside when Joshua approached. He had arranged for two horses to be prepared before heading to Shemont earlier that morning and was told to only say when he was ready. The College didn't rent out their horses but offered their use to select few as they were needed. Councilors, the Headmaster, and other heads of schools or departments were given free reign over using the horses when they were available.

"Welcome back, Sir Joshua. We have your geldings saddled and ready to go," the lead hand said as the knights approached.

"Thank you. We will have them back tonight, hopefully before the sun has fully set," Joshua said, grabbed the reins of his black gelding.

Michael mounted the piebald gelding beside Joshua and together they started off, heading down the path that connected the stables to the north-south road that would be less traveled now that Anselin was no more. They rode north and soon had the horses in a cycle of trotting and galloping. Trees on their left, the Shaulis Woods, passed by in a blur. Joshua knew Michael hunted down a minotaur here but didn't know the full story behind that expedition. *Someday I will ask him,* Joshua thought to himself. Perhaps after all of this was through he would want to sit down and talk about the things that bothered him. Joshua yearned to help relieve Michael of his burdens.

The knights rode in silence for some time, continuing the cycle of galloping the horses then bringing them back to a trot to rest. Joshua bounced in his saddle and looked over at Michael who kept his eyes forward toward the horizon as he did the same. These were good horses, young and full of energy. It made Joshua miss his own horse, but Coal retired around this time the year prior. He simply didn't enjoy being ridden any longer and that was problematic. Plus, Joshua traveled by horseback less often than by portal now that he knew he could use a portal even without visiting a place first. The proximity of the spell was still tricky to master, but it remained an effective means of travel.

"I miss Watson," Michael said as they reached the end of the Shaulis Woods and started riding through an open plains area.

"Did something happen to him?"

"He caught an ailment of some kind. Had to put him down a few months ago," Michael replied, his voice breaking.

"I'm sorry to hear about that, Michael. He seemed like a good horse for you."

"These things happen sometimes. It's nothing to be bothered about."

"We're getting close to Anselin. Let's keep our eyes open for anything out of the ordinary, Michael," Joshua suggested.

Chapter Six

S ir Joshua the Ravenous and Sir Michael the Valiant approached the ruins of Anselin from the south. They dismounted their horses and walked the packed dirt road with scattered rocks toward the former city. Michael gently kicked a rock as they walked down the road with the toe of his boots. The rock skipped and tumbled across the dirt, kicking up small, almost imperceptible puffs of dust as it bounced down the road. It finally settled just in time for another soft kick which sent it tumbling down the road again. Michael continued kicking the rock down the road until Joshua stopped and looked at his travel companion.

When Michael stopped walking down the road, Joshua cocked his head to the side. "You have an odd look on your face. What are you thinking about?"

"How many times are we going to almost die on this continent, Joshua?" Michael asked in response. "Honestly, there are times I wish we hadn't taken this journey together. I miss Feldring something fierce. Life was simpler there and things didn't try to kill me."

"I understand that Michael, I really do. Have you thought about the good that we've done since coming here, though?" Joshua asked. "For starters, Vor'Kath is dead, all thanks to you for that. If we had kept him alive, or had he killed us, Shemont *and* Anselin likely would have both fallen by now. The other continents would be no safer either. The whole world would be teetering on the brink of chaos."

"I know, Joshua. I'm tired of the number of times I've been on death's door though. Vor'Kath, the manticore, the hellhounds, the basilisk. Each of those fights almost ended with me dead. I have never been closer to death's door than after fighting the basilisk. I thank the Allfather almost every day that you were able to find me in that desert in time. You never did mention how you found out the name of that lizard," Michael mentioned.

"Oh, did I forget to mention that? Well, I was looking for the name of that forsaken desert and was hoping that the fauna book I had in front of me would tell me something helpful. As soon as I saw the drawing on the page about the basilisk, I knew you were in trouble. Rushed to the nearest librarian who wanted to have a debate with me about the ability for the thing to turn someone to stone with its gaze,"

Joshua sighed before continuing. "All I remember is that *I* had trouble fighting that thing. I can only imagine how your fight with it went."

"From what I remember, my side of the fight was over pretty quickly," Michael said. "We never did find anything special out in that desert, did we?"

"No, we never did. It's a shame," Joshua sighed. "What happened with the manticore? I never got to hear that whole story."

"That's actually where I got my signet ring," Michael explained, showing Joshua the silver ring with the running rabbit engraved into the flat face. "I ran into another knight, Lady Sela the Gentle, when I was in Haran. She saved my life and scared off the manticore. We got into a brief altercation and the village elder kicked Sela out. We ran into each other in the mountains the next day while hunting the beast. I still don't think those mountains are natural, by the way, but that's neither here nor there. Anyway, we were discussing my plans to go after the beast when it ambushed us. After another quick fight with it, she got impaled by the tail. I tried to save her, but she yelled for me to go after it. By the time I killed it and got back to her, she had already died. There was nothing I could have done."

"I'm so sorry, Michael. I can't imagine how that must feel. You said her name was Sela the Gentle, right? That seems like an odd name for a knight in the order," Joshua noted.

"I thought the same thing when I learned her name. Thought it was odd. I guess I forgot how much that bothered me until now. There's something else that has bothered me, but I buried *that* until talking about all of my shortcomings as a knight," Michael said, leaving much unsaid.

"These aren't anything less than life lessons, Michael. How can we fully appreciate the light without first knowing the deepest darkness of night? What are you concerned about though?" Joshua asked, almost afraid of what his friend would say.

Michael inhaled deeply before finally answering. "Have I really earned my knighthood?"

"Why do you wonder that?"

"I'm not sure. I just don't hear many other knights in the order talking about how *they* have almost died half a dozen times. I'm sure they would scoff at me if they heard this conversation. How can I feel even adequate compared to the other knights? You saw how they acted at the tournament: like I didn't belong there competing with them."

"Consider this really quick, Michael," Joshua countered. "We have only been knights for, what, eight years?"

"Somewhere around there, yeah."

"These other pedigreed knights have been members of the order in one way or another since they could hold a training sword. Very few of the knights aren't from some kind of noble house or knightly lineages. Many of them see us as outsiders still. We have come in, from nowhere, and entered their prestigious little club. If they scoff at us it's only because *they* feel threatened by our presence in their lives. You are proving them wrong by simply doing what you continue to do, Michael. Don't stop now or you'll prove them right," Joshua replied. "Also, there is a big difference between fighting another soldier and fighting a whole manticore."

"I see your point. Sometimes I just think that Orson made a mistake, you know?"

"Do you think he would have given you a title you hadn't earned?"

"His humanity allows him a few mistakes even as the king."

"That is correct. However, I will argue that making you a knight was not a mistake on his part."

"What's that?" Michael asked, pointing up the road.

"I believe those are the city ruins. Let's pick up our pace a little if that's ok with you."

"Fine by me."

They started jogging and Michael stopped kicking the rock down the road with them. Without realizing it, they had finally come within sight of the ruins of the former Anselin. What had once been a marvelous city now looked like nothing more than a box of burned matches dropped onto the ground. What were once houses and shops now were little more than burnt out piles of rubble, the charred remains of the city. There was no sign that a wall ever surrounded the city. The soft glow of white light had dimmed, partially because the sun was above the horizon, and partially because whatever light remained from the star had faded. A cloud of dark dust covered the city. The same breeze that had danced through the tops of the trees now picked up the ashen remains of the city and threw the dark powder like a child threw a handful of stones.

*   *   *

Insects chirped and birds sang as the sun beat down on a lake. A cabin stood on a raised bank on the southeastern shore. Four windows broke up the walls of the cottage; one window overlooked the lake, two looked over the field that spread south and west of the unkempt shack. The last looked toward the Shaulis Woods. The window overlooking the lake was open allowing in a small breeze that smelled of algae and fish. Still, that breeze smelled better than the stale, dusty air, and the crafting of potions within the cottage. Despite being an alchemist first and foremost, Esram still found the brewing process quite foul-smelling. Still, he needed the potions for later stages of their plan. *The Councilor* will *be part of the ritual willingly or otherwise.*

A jackdaw flew through the air and landed on the one open windowsill in Esram's lakeside cottage right as he poured the contents of a carafe into a series of bottles. The corvid ruffled its feathers upon landing and shook itself smooth. Esram watched but didn't need to pay any further attention than that. Daethis had arrived. She would be stepping through a portal in the room any moment. *At least she is consistent*, he thought. It would be one thing if she announced her presence only sometimes with a corvid, but she always sent one as a forerunner for her arrival. *Strange, though, she rarely uses a jackdaw,* he thought, looking at the black and silver bird again. It looked at him momentarily, its head tilting back and forth as it watched his movements intently. Something about the bird was off-putting, but Esram didn't know what. It seemed to know too much. The bird looked too intently at him with its beady eyes the color of moss-stained grey marble. The bird chittered and flew away with a heavy fluttering of its wings. Finally, as Esram could barely see from his table with the alchemy equipment, the jackdaw perched in a low hanging branch of the nearby tree. The bird's master had arrived.

"You so rarely call me here, Esram, that I feared something was wrong," she said.

"Nothing is wrong, Daethis. I just wished to discuss our dearest friend, the Councilor. Has he arrived in Anselin yet?"

"He should be getting there now. Would you like me to continue watching him while he's there?" Daethis offered.

"No, don't get yourself caught. I'm sure they'll notice if there is a corvid in the ruins."

"What if there are hundreds? There are bound to be bodies there for the carrion birds to feast on. We could blend in and still watch them even from here."

"That's not a bad idea, Daethis. How do we go about getting the other carrion birds into Anselin to disguise our agents?"

"Oh, dearest Esram, they're already there feasting on the mass open grave we left behind after our attack on the city. Slipping a few more into the city will be no challenge," Daethis said with a smirk that lit up her eyes.

Daethis cast a spell and within moments hundreds of corvids cawed and cackled from the nearby trees before they flapped their wings and took to flight. They circled over the cottage until they all were flying in a single group. Daethis cast another spell and whispered something in ancient Elven. Esram felt ashamed of how little of the language he knew, but he picked up something he thought was "pester" or "follow." Maybe it was "gesticulate," he couldn't tell. All he knew is Daethis whispered something and the flock of birds that circled his cabin overhead suddenly dispersed as quickly as they appeared. All the birds flew north toward the former Anselin. Once they passed out of sight of the cabin, Daethis smiled and curtsied like a College apprentice who had just shown a simple spell to a full-fledged Mage. Esram chuckled, shook his head, then returned his attention to the alembic and other tools on the table before him. He had much work to do.

"You're not going to praise me, Esram? That's very unlike you."

"Apologies, dearest. I have these potions to focus on. How else are we supposed to get the Councilor to participate in the ritual?"

"We could always use spells. They last longer than the potions would anyway. There's the added benefit that we don't have to have someone continuing their application for the effects to stay. We could simply set the spells, anchor them, and he will be clay in our hands," Daethis said, walking up to Esram and putting her slender hands on his tense shoulders.

"Not right now, Daethis. I have too much to do. Maybe later?"

"Whatever you say," she replied, squeezing his shoulders slightly before letting go.

Free from his distractions, Esram returned his full attention to the mortar and pestle on his table with the partially-ground, dried herbs. He continued crushing them until everything was a fine powder. This he placed in part of his alembic which he then set over a small fire. Inside the alembic, the powdered herbs and plants mixed with distilled water and would create the liquid that would later be refined into a finished potion. Esram had learned this process during his many years at the College and perfected the study since his expulsion. He still remembered that day. Every glance in a mirror, every reflection in a clean window reminded him of the mistakes he made exposing himself too soon. He could have, instead, done what Daethis did and complete the training cycles required for Mage status at the College then simply fade from their attention. Few remembered her at the College though she would be welcome to come and go as she pleased. Esram, however, would wear the scars that marked him as a Dark Mage for the rest of his days. The headmaster at the time thought that a more than suitable punishment. Ordinarily, the College would brand Dark Mages. *Why don't they just hang us?*

The thought bothered Esram, not for anything but the confusion he felt with asking himself. The College claimed to detest Dark Mages, yet never did anything to prevent them from continuing to study, grow stronger, or recruit others unless they were a threat to the College. Esram had never harmed another student, so he was deemed as not dangerous to others and allowed to live. *Oh, what a mistake that decision turned out to be,* he chuckled to himself.

"What's funny, dearest?" Daethis asked.

"Just thinking about how the College should have put me down if they wanted to make a change. Instead, they neither branded me nor stopped me from continuing my practices of Magic outside of their control."

"You never hurt anyone. You only started a spell that apparently threatened or intimidated Bryne."

"Considering that alone, they should have expelled him instead of me."

Daethis traced the tips of her fingers along the deep, jagged edges of the scar on the side of Esram's face, something she did from time to time. Esram didn't mind her curiosity over the scar. In fact, her fingers tickled more than anything else. Everyone focused on the scar, something he wished would happen less. The scars went from the left side of his mouth, starting between his lips and his jawline. One of the scar's tendrils journeyed up to his eye and beyond his hairline. Another three went across his cheek toward his temple. A fifth went to his earlobe, and yet another zig-zagged down beyond his jawline toward his collar. He had long since given up trying to hide the scar. Everything, save a hooded cloak, simply failed to cover everything.

"You should come with me. Your potions will still be here when we get done," Daethis teased. "We'll be quick."

"Later, Daethis. My mind isn't in the right place for you."

"I'll focus on what the birds are seeing, then. Come find me when you're ready for me."

"Of course. Thanks for understanding."

Chapter Seven

Anselin, the former Elven capital of Drendil, is a city Michael always wanted to visit. Now, being there, he wished he could have seen the city before its destruction. He and Joshua walked through the broken pieces of the ramparts that surrounded the outer edge of the city. It took a bit more work to get into the city than expected, but once through the gate, moving through the now-empty streets was much simpler. Michael tried not to focus too much on what went on around him. Piles of ash and dust crumpled beneath his boots as they walked down the main boulevard that came into the city. Despite it being nearly noon, the entire city seemed to have been plunged into the gloom of night. Michael could hardly see more than a few yards ahead. Joshua provided a solution to this: a floating orb of light suspended in the air over his right shoulder. The orb followed them as they walked and provided enough light to see their surroundings. Michael wished he couldn't see even that much.

Bones. Skeletons littered the ground, scattered amid the dust and ash that covered everything in the city. Of those that Michael could see, none bore any remnants of clothing, skin, or other soft tissue. Marks in the dust showed animal tracks. *They've been picked clean by the carrion eaters,* Michael shuddered. He knew this was a part of life, but within the block of the city he and Joshua had walked, they passed nearly fifty skeletons picked completely clean of anything remotely edible to the scavengers. His stomach lurched thinking of it. He looked up, trying to keep the bone-littered ground out of sight. His was a life filled with death and destruction, but never anything to this scale before. *How could anyone do this?*

A slight breeze danced through the city, picking up and carrying the same dust and ash that covered the ground into Michael's eyes. He stopped, groaned, and started blinking repeatedly trying to remove the dust. Within a few moments, after vigorous rubbing and blinking, he cleared his eye, but now it burned. Things didn't belong in his eyes, let alone flakes of ash from the ground. He started walking with his head down until Joshua looked over and cast a spell that put a white bubble around them, the same as when they camped together on their way to Griffin's Perch a year ago. The wind stopped and Michael sighed with relief and lifted his gaze right as he heard and felt a crunch beneath his boot. A chill ran up his back and he shivered again. *I will not look at what I stepped on,* he said to himself adamantly. Doing so would only lead to heartache and despair.

Every step brought agony to Michael's head. Dehydrated and still a little drunk from his night of drinking at the Cave, he now had a pounding headache and a parched mouth. *This is supposed to be a quick trip*, Michael thought, regretting his choice at not grabbing a waterskin before leaving. Despite how much Joshua touted this as being a short trip, he should have grabbed some water. *This is what I get for not being in the right mind before leaving the house for an adventure*, Michael berated himself.

"Joshua, what are we looking for out here? If it's bones and ash, I think we've found what we were looking for," Michael said.

"How cruel of you, Michael," Joshua replied, shaking his head. "We are looking for anything that stands out. Honestly, anything unusual could help. The goal is to get to the center of the city where the star was and see if we can find anything there."

Joshua waved his hands, and Michael felt the hairs on his neck stand up as the Mage cast a new spell. This one placed a translucent, blue rectangle in Joshua's hands. He grabbed the edges once the spell solidified and held the box out at arm's length in front of him. He moved the blue box around, examining everything around them before frowning and continuing down the boulevard toward the center of the former city.

"What's wrong, Joshua?" Michael asked.

"I don't know if you remember, but this is a similar spell to the one I used when we were looking for those hellhounds that killed the lady outside the Cave," Joshua replied.

"I vaguely remember that. What's wrong with the spell though?"

"Oh, there's nothing wrong with the spell. The problem is I'm seeing far too many Magic traces all over everything. Maybe it's residue from what happened, but it shouldn't be *this* overwhelming," Joshua explained, continuing to hold the rectangle in front of various things he found to examine them further.

Michael sighed quietly, knowing he would likely regret the answer that would follow his question. "What's a trace?"

"Oh, I guess I should explain that. Look here," Joshua said, motioning with a nod of his head at the box he held in front of a skeleton. "See how there is an aura coming off the bones? Well, that's a trace, or a residual piece of Magic leftover from a spell. Not all Magic leaves them, and different types of Magic leave different types of traces. Everything that I'm seeing, though, is coming from the same spell. Nothing is standing out as different."

"Do you know what's causing that?"

"Well, this is my first time visiting Anselin, but from what I've read and heard about the city, they used the Magic from the star to power everything in the city. They had doors that would open on command, lights that didn't rely on oil, candles, or spells, various things like that. If I were to guess, these traces are from that Magic system they used throughout the city, or..." his voice suddenly trailed off and his face wrinkled in concentration.

"What? Did you find something different?"

"I found something *very* different," Joshua said. "See here, how everything has that green hue to it? Well, if we look over here..."

Joshua moved the box he held, passing over some piles of bones into the empty street. Everything he could see was green. As they reached the middle of the street a red streak showed in the sea of green. Everything around the new trace was calm and simply floated there. The red streak, though, wavered aggressively, moving like flames as they consumed logs. Joshua knelt to examine it further and moved the blue box he carried so he could see where the streak went.

"Why is that one red?"

"That's a great question, Michael. I wish I could answer that question without having to investigate further."

"Should we follow it and see where else that trace goes?"

"Excellent idea," Joshua beamed. "It's almost like you read my mind."

"I'm sure that's why you brought me along," Michael guessed.

"Certainly. Let's find out where this trace goes. Maybe we can figure something out by seeing where it goes."

Joshua stood and started walking, carrying his blue rectangle, still held at arm's length. He walked down the boulevard, stopped in an intersection, turned north, and started going down a different street. For what felt like a couple hours, this pattern of walking down one street only to stop and take another continued. Michael felt his legs growing heavier as they walked, and his mouth felt more parched now than it ever had before. Together, he and Joshua walked down six streets and covered more than a dozen blocks within the city. Nearly every intersection they crossed looked the same as each of the others. Throughout the city, no matter where they went, skeletons littered the ground. Here and there, carrion birds still picked at the remains of these innocent Elves. Buildings, once houses and shops, now stood as reminders of what they once were. Crumbled ruins were all that remained of the city now. Michael felt his heart growing heavy with all the destruction around them.

The gloom surrounding the city grew stronger the deeper they went into the ruins. As they pushed on, Michael felt his skin crawling and his stomach fluttered. Beads of sweat started collecting on his forehead and his mouth watered fiercely. His knees trembled. Hands shaking, Michael bent over and closed his eyes as everything came rushing out of his stomach onto what was once the corner of an intersection. Now, the street and thoroughfare simply crossed paths through ashy remains of the city. Not a month before merchant wagons would have barreled up the wide streets to and from the market on their way to sell goods. Now, the only sound was the soft splatter of Michael's stomach emptying itself onto the piles of ash and dust beneath him. For the first time in so long, Michael didn't feel he could blame this on any amount of consumed alcohol, though he wished he could blame the drinking as he started dry heaving.

"We must be getting closer to the star. The Magic is getting stronger," Joshua said, stopping in the middle of the intersection while Michael continued retching.

Michael looked up and spoke between the intense spasms in his stomach. "Then why…aren't you getting sick?"

"I didn't spend the whole night drinking, Michael," Joshua replied curtly.

"That's uncalled for, Joshua. You know that."

"I was just trying to lighten the mood. This whole scene is heavy."

Michael wiped his mouth on his tabard and stood up, finally feeling better. He nodded at Joshua, showing that he was ready to continue. Joshua continued looking around the intersection, seeing where the trace went and clearly following something else. Michael knew something was wrong despite not standing over Joshua's shoulder. The face Joshua made said enough. He normally was better about hiding his emotions, something Michael understood. Joshua lowered the box he used to follow the traces and slumped his shoulders before turning to Michael.

"This intersection has so many traces running through it. I can hardly tell where the one we followed goes. It looks like it stops near where you're standing, actually."

"Where does that leave us?"

"Undeniably stuck unless we can find where it picks up. *If* it picks up, that is."

A thought struck Michael while Joshua explained their predicament. "Didn't Kerron show you a spell when we hunted those hellhounds? Are you using—"

Joshua slammed the palm of his hand roughly into his forehead. "Of course! How did I forget that spell? It would help if we were following a Dark Magic trace, after all."

"Glad I could help," Michael said.

"Thank you. This is why I brought you along."

"You're welcome. Any chance we will be backtracking toward the way we entered the city?" Michael asked.

"It's possible, but unlikely. We have to get to the star near the center of the city," Joshua explained. "The traces are simply helping us to understand what happened."

"That makes sense. Do you have that spell ready?"

"I just need a few moments to remember it. This is probably the most useful thing my predecessor did during his tenure."

As Joshua said, it only took him a few moments to have the new spell cast and a different translucent rectangle in his hands. He closed the spell that created the first and started looking around the intersection with the new spell. As he looked, his face contorted again, and he once again lowered the box in defeat. He looked to Michael but stopped and held up the spell. He started beaming, excited about something.

"What did you find?" Michael asked.

"I thought we would have to double back a bit, but just over your shoulder there's an incredibly strong trace that I think we should follow. It's different than the other ones I've seen today and not just because it's Dark Magic. This one is…complicated."

"Let's see where it goes then," Michael suggested.

Joshua walked past Michael and down a side street with what looked like a bakery and another indiscriminate shop on either side. The facades of the stores were now broken and scattered through the intersection, mere remnants of what they had once been. Michael reached out his hand and touched the former bakery, running his hand along the bricks as he walked behind Joshua. The moment he touched the stone wall, a wave of something…wrong…flashed up his arm leaving a tingling in its wake. He had never experienced something like that before and immediately removed his arm to avoid it happening again. With his arm free, but the tingling sensation still there, he started shaking his hand to bring back the feeling in his fingers. His hand was numb like he just struck his elbow on a cabinet or the corner of his desk.

Michael followed Joshua through the side street as they made their way toward the center of the city and the star that waited for them. Michael had only heard about the star and was curious to see it. *If any of it is even left,* he reminded himself, recalling the description of what happened to the city. Being here and seeing the pure destruction, Michael doubted even a fragment of the star remained in whatever had once contained it. Still, it would be curious to see where one of them had been. Michael continued following Joshua until they reached a giant crater at what seemed like the middle of the city.

Chapter Eight

Joshua and Michael climbed a small hill as the former priest followed the Dark Magic trace they picked up further back in the city. After reaching the top of the hill, Joshua could see all the way into the crater where the star used to exist. This hole in the ground, near the castle ruins, came from what he suspected was the detonation of the star that resulted in nearly a million innocent lives being lost in an instant. Now, standing at the brim of the crater, Joshua knew that's what exactly happened. Whoever was behind this attack wanted to make this process as quick and noticed as possible. They couldn't destroy the whole city quickly without detonating the star. Not without hundreds of Mages working together. *I doubt there are even that many Children of Chaos anymore,* Joshua scoffed to himself. Long ago, during the Mages Wars, the Children numbered in the thousands. Their numbers dwindled during the second war as the College and the Children met on the battlefield. Both sides lost indeterminate amounts of Mages. Joshua felt no sympathy for the Dark Mages lost during the wars. They chose their fate by siding with the Children.

Joshua knelt at the edge of the huge, cylindrical crater, letting go of the spell Kerron taught him. He no longer needed to follow a trace to the star. He would cast the spell again soon to investigate what exactly happened here, but for now he could only stare at the center of such massive destruction. This was merely the crescendo of the attack. He needed to learn where it started and how it happened. This was the part of his job as the Superintendent of the Dark Magic School that he disliked. The Headmaster and King Orson always expected him to have answers to questions he never anticipated. He greatly disliked disappointing anyone by not having the answers to simple, albeit unanticipated, questions. He desperately needed to find the answers to what happened here in Anselin before heading back to safety at the College. *We need to move deliberately and quickly,* Joshua thought, trying to ignore the tingling feeling in his skin that had only grown stronger the closer to the star's crater they came. *I can only imagine what this must be like for Michael.* The Magic was reaching dangerous levels. They wouldn't be able to move any closer to the crater without potentially fatal levels of Magic flooding their bodies, even with the protective bubble. That was, right now, the only thing that let them get this close to the crater without severe consequences.

Joshua stood and cast the spell that allowed him to see the traces again. He looked around and saw a group of three traces near a low point in the edge of the crater. He tapped Michael on the shoulder and together they made their way to that cluster of traces. Clearly, that area was where something happened to the star. He waved the rectangle around looking at where the traces went. They came from the north, disappearing around a corner. Beyond that, Joshua could see nothing that told him what happened here. He took a few steps to follow the traces to see if he could glean anything more about them to no avail. He walked back to the edge of the crater and noticed something strange about where the star used to sit.

"There's a barrier. I won't be able to go in there," Joshua said.

Michael spun around on his heels so fast he wavered a little. "You *want* to go in there? Joshua, you've lost it. It's too dangerous. The walls are nearly vertical. Getting down there will be easy but getting out will be nearly impossible. What if you get in there and can't use your Magic? We don't have any rope for you to get out. What could you possible want to do in the crater?"

"Michael, that's where the star was. If any of it remains, we could advance the kingdom by decades overnight. *Everything* in the kingdom would advance. Our architecture, armor, weapons, even our lifespans could improve. Do you not want something like that?"

"Joshua, think about what you're saying. Think about everything that's happened today. I touched a building earlier and my arm hasn't *stopped* tingling yet. I vomited earlier and it wasn't because I spent the night drinking. The entire time we've been in this forsaken place, something has been happening to us. I won't stop you if you really want to go in the crater, but think about what you're suggesting first," Michael argued.

"Do you not want people to be able to get treated for ailments we don't know how to cure? Think of the possibilities here."

"I absolutely would love that, Joshua, but—"

"Then we have to get through this barrier and see if even a piece of the star remains."

"You think we can advance the entire kingdom with just a piece of the star?"

"Maybe not everything, but we could pick *something* and make advancements where we can. What do you think?"

"Have you considered that the advancements Anselin made are part of why the city was destroyed?" Michael asked.

Joshua paused. "I hadn't considered that possibility."

"Doing the same thing, even to a part of Shemont, could only be putting that same target on our own backs."

"You really don't want me to go down there, do you?"

"It just doesn't sit well with me, Joshua."

"Alright," Joshua conceded, "I won't go into the crater then. We have to figure out what happened here, though. Here. You hold the viewer, and I will work on something."

Michael grabbed the viewer with both hands and held it like Joshua thought he would hold an infant: nervously and unsure. Joshua chuckled then removed a small, leatherbound book from inside his robes and started flipping through the pages. He knew there was a spell in the book for reassembling a spell from the trace it left. He simply had to find it first. After a few minutes, Joshua found the spell, read through the guide a few times, then cast it. This spell book was one that Sanev recommended, but Joshua had never cast the spells in it before. He had no idea what to expect from this particular spell. Still, the Headmaster said this could show them what they needed to know.

Joshua cast the spell and a cloud immediately started forming before him. He connected the cloud to the traces he found just outside the crater and light started sparking to life. He saw images of three people standing in hooded robes in an empty street in Anselin. Together, almost instantly, the three raised their hands and started casting spells together. The two on the outside opened portals, one each. The outside Mages turned, and Joshua thought something about the woman on the left seemed familiar. He couldn't place why, but something about the shape of her nose triggered something in his mind. *That's something to dig into later,* he thought. He returned his focus to the spell that showed him the past. The third Mage, from the center of the group, made a spell, one Joshua had never seen before, and anchored it in front of the portal to her right. She stepped up to the left-hand portal and cast another spell, a wall of air, into the orb of immensely powerful, dark lightning she made previously. The orb hurtled through the right-hand portal and she immediate stepped through. Both portals closed at the same instant. Finally, a flash of light brighter than the sun came over the cloud. Nothing further was shown in the spell. Unsure of what he saw, Joshua closed the spell and cast it again. And again. He continued recreating the cloud until he knew the spell they used to destroy the star. Until he understood what happened here. Until Michael finally tapped him on the shoulder and broke his focus. Joshua took a deep breath, shook his head, and blinked until Michael came into focus.

"I'm sorry. What's happening?" Joshua said, his voice shaky.

"You were locked in a trance or something. You cast your spell over and over again. I couldn't see what it showed but I saw your face freeze. Are you alright, Joshua?"

Joshua looked past Michael's shoulder and saw a flock of dark birds flying away from the castle. "Yeah, I'm fine. We should start heading back though."

"I agree. I don't like being here. This place makes my stomach hurt," Michael noted.

"We should get out of here and get back to the horses. I hope they're fine on their own."

"They're horses. They should be content with just grazing."

Joshua closed the spell for the viewer that Michael still held unsurely. As the spell closed, lightning shot through the clouds overhead toward the castle ruins. The lone spire, still standing amid the rubble of what had once been a magnificent castle made of layered walls, many spires, and long halls, crumbled after the bolt of lightning crashed into its weak-looking base. The sound of stones crashing against each other sounded louder inside the nothingness that Anselin was. Joshua felt something…strange.

Michael's hand went to the back of his neck. "Did you cast a spell, Joshua?"

"No. We should get out of here now," Joshua suggested. "I don't think we're alone here."

"Great," Michael replied, his voice thick with obvious sarcasm.

"If you don't mind, I'm going to portal us out of here. Hopefully, whoever else is here doesn't decide to follow us. I would hate to have a confrontation with whoever is capable of destroying a star."

"That's fine by me. Let's get away from these wretched ruins."

Another bolt of lightning rushed through the sky, this one only jumping between the thick, dark clouds overhead as Joshua opened a portal back to their horses. A clap of thunder boomed, and the wind picked up. Michael stepped through the portal and Joshua looked around, trying to find whoever was there with them. Stepping backwards toward the portal, he thought he saw the outline of a robed figure walking toward him down a side street. The figure, large and bulky, moved quietly and with great grace. *An Elf, perhaps?* Joshua didn't recognize this robed figure. Something behind him, unseen, grabbed him under the arm and yanked him backwards.

*   *   *

Oleg chuckled to himself as the Councilor was pulled through his own portal by his drunkard friend. Esram told him to interfere as best he could, so he did. The lightning was an easy enough spell to cast. Staying out of sight, with his size, was the only challenge in the ruins of Anselin. Now he just had to speak with Esram about what he saw the Councilor learn. He knew the Councilor would be devastated when they learned what happened to their horses. Oleg felt bad about that, but he was just following orders. He looked around, ensuring he was the only person around and created a portal. He stepped through, knowing he would make two more before he finished his journey at the lakeside cabin. Esram spent much of his time there but seldom asked for the other Children to meet there.

Oleg stepped through the last of his series of portals, took three steps, and knocked forcefully on the cabin door. He stood tall enough that he would have to duck to get through the doorway, but that was normal for him. He stood just over two meters tall and most other people he ran into were much shorter. He had spent much of his life larger than everyone else around him. Joining the Children made no difference to him as he was seen as a freak everywhere he went. Unfortunately, because of his size, Oleg was easy to spot and often depended on spells to blend into crowds. Still, that much was fun. He enjoyed taking another form at times, even if it meant he would be uncomfortable. Oleg relied on spells that altered his person rather than illusions as they often didn't work in the intended way with his height.

The door opened slightly at first then the rest of the way. Oleg stooped down and stepped into Esram's humble cottage. Acrid smoke which carried the scents of many herbs filled the cabin despite the open windows. An alembic and other alchemical tools sat on the table, their contents working away into what would later become potions. Oleg had much respect for Esram, who showed lots of patience with this process. Oleg knew he didn't have enough patience to wait for herbs to boil and distill themselves into a potent concoction of plants. He would rather take matters into his own hands, literally if needed. Despite his former status as a Master Mage, he still preferred physically besting his opponents when the need arose. The College revoked his title as Master years ago after he squeezed someone to death to protect a fledgling Mage. They didn't care about accidents or anything else. They only saw that he killed another and removed him from the College. *Fools.*

"Have they left Anselin yet?" Esram asked, not looking at Oleg longer than needed; his attention was instead on the tableful of alchemy tools and his future potion.

Oleg nodded and answered as simply as he could. "Yes."

"One of these days," Esram said, slumping his shoulders slightly, "you will talk to us in complex sentences, Oleg."

"So you think."

"Are we to assume the Councilor now knows how we destroyed the star?" Daethis asked from the other room, her hood down on her shoulders.

"He knows."

"That's all we needed. Good work, Oleg," Esram said as he ground more herbs to powder with his mortar and pestle.

"I can go now?"

"Feel free to. You have done your part," Esram replied. "Or stay here if you would like."

Daethis shot Esram a quick glare when he said that. "Don't feel obligated to stay though, Oleg. I'm sure you have your own matters to attend."

"I will leave."

"Very well. Meet us at the tree for the next ritual," Esram reminded.

Oleg turned toward the door, stopped with the knob in his hand, and looked at Daethis. She seemed taken aback by his attention. Oleg said nothing but winked at her, then opened the cottage door and left. Outside he cast another portal spell and left. He stepped through to a plateau that overlooked a small village. In the town below him were many people creating a stack of firewood for the night's celebration. None of them knew that Oleg had kidnapped their elder weeks ago and was playing the part. Quite well, he thought. Tonight, they were celebrating him and his ability to bring rain to the village after a drought they didn't realize he caused. Oleg smiled knowing all of this. He quickly cast a spell that transformed him into the little village elder who walked with a cane and had a hunch in his back. He used another portal to jump to the small hut the elder lived in. He closed the portal and opened the door to oversee the celebration preparations. He smiled and limped his way around the village.

Chapter Nine

Joshua turned around, ready to hit whoever grabbed him until he saw Michael pulling him through the portal. Once he was through the portal, Joshua released the spell immediately to keep that robed giant from following them. The last thing they needed right now was to fight a potential Dark Mage on their own effectively in the middle of nowhere. While Joshua may have been able to handle it—he and Michael *had* defeated Vor'Kath after all—it wasn't high on the list of things he wanted to do today. Once the portal closed, Joshua broke free from Michael's grasp and turned to face the city. Lightning continued flashing through the sky for a few moments and thunder boomed after each bolt. After a few seconds, the lightning stopped, and the wind died back down to the gentle breeze that it was earlier.

He turned his back on the ruins of Anselin and started walking down the road toward the small copse of trees where they left the horses. Michael joined him shortly and they walked in silence until they reached the trees. Joshua looked up from the road, where he had been watching his feet as he walked the dusty road and felt a pang of fear and dread wash through him. The horses were strung up by the branches of the trees, their entrails scattered on the ground beneath them. Blood pooled beneath the horses and the saddles and other accoutrements were nowhere to be found. Joshua sighed and looked to Michael who paled seeing the horses.

Michael swallowed the lump Joshua knew was in the knight's throat. "What monster would do this? These horses didn't deserve this."

"The same monsters that did that," Joshua said, pointing back toward Anselin. "*They* didn't deserve that fate either. The Children of Chaos are living up to their name."

"What happens now?" Michael asked.

"I suppose the only thing we *can* do is portal back to the College and let them know what we discovered. The stablemaster will be quite cross about this, but I will give him some money to buy some new horses. That should smooth things a bit."

"Let's get to the College then."

Joshua opened a portal and motioned for Michael to step through. Before stepping through, the Mage took a final look at the slain horses, closed his eyes, and shook his head. *They'll be stopped soon*, he promised himself. He only needed to speak with Sanev and Orson to outline what they found in Anselin, then they could formulate a plan to eradicate the Children. He was ignoring the fact that he must find the Children as well, but that would come in time. The members of his school were working tirelessly to find the Children and he had full faith that they would do just that. He stepped through the portal and onto the College grounds. Michael stood not far from the portal, hands on his hips as he looked about. This wasn't his first time visiting the College, but he hadn't been there in some time.

Nothing had changed since the last time Michael visited the College. The grounds, still just as green as ever, spread out in the area between the road from Shemont to Anselin and the Shaulis Woods. Shrubs and trees littered the grounds in near chaos. Several walkways split the grounds, forming a spiderweb of stone paths between the outlying buildings. The main pathway to the central tower was lined with seven paired stone fire pits stood on both sides of the walkway. Each pair of fires burned a different color, each representing the different schools of Magic present at the school. Red, orange, yellow, green, blue, purple, white, and black flames lined the walkway. Joshua knew the schools well. His formal Councilor's robes contained a stripe with each color. The black stripe he wore was larger than the others. Only Headmaster Sanev, as the head of the College and the Council, wore stripes of equal sizes. Each school emphasized different areas where the Mages could focus their training: fighting, teaching, studying, healing, diplomacy, traditions, and Dark Magic. Many students felt called into the fighting, diplomacy, and healing schools, which were the most populated schools within the College. Others picked less popular schools for their own reasons. Joshua never judged a student's choice of schools.

Joshua and Michael walked up the pathway toward the central tower. As they climbed the stairs, the doors opened. Joshua learned, after joining the Council, that an anchored spell sensed when people approached the doors and would open them automatically. Similar spells had worked doors and sources of light in Anselin before the attack. Anselin was able to forego the actual spells thanks to the city's proximity to the star which provided Magic to many mundane tasks. Joshua found himself hoping for spells like these to be found throughout the kingdom. Someday that would happen, he was sure.

The first floor of the tower was a large lobby and a few small offices in the back. Just inside the doors sat a desk that, at all times, was occupied by an Apprentice who checked in visitors using the large ledger on the desk. They also directed visitors to their destination and kept tabs on the schedules for the Councilors, Headmaster, and a few other important people within the College. Most Apprentices saw their time sitting at the desk as a punishment. The Elf sitting there today was using her shift to better herself and further her studies. Based on the cover of the book, the large rune emblazoned in the leather, and the intensity with which she read, Joshua assumed it to be a spell tome for one of her classes. Joshua approached the desk and stood there for nearly a minute before she realized anyone was standing in front of her. She started when she saw him, nearly threw the book down, and stood to greet the Councilor. Joshua wanted to get upset with her for being distracted, but he could hardly begin to think of what to say. Telling a student not to study for the six hours they had to sit at a desk seemed backwards to him. *She's being productive. Best to leave that be,* he thought.

"Good afternoon, Councilor. I hope you've had a great day so far," she blurted out, the lilt in her voice absorbing the worry he knew was still there.

"Not at all. It's been a terrible day to say the least. I need to speak with the headmaster at once. Is he in his office?" Joshua asked.

The Apprentice checked the book and nodded. "Yes, he should be in a meeting with—"

"That's fine. What I have to tell him is a bit more important. Thank you very much, Apprentice," Joshua said, making a portal and waving Michael through.

"You're very welcome, Councilor."

Joshua stepped through the portal, something that was technically not allowed within the College, and found himself standing outside of Sanev's office. The shimmering surface of the portal rippled after Joshua stepped through. He closed his portal and reached for the polished brass doorknob on the black lacquered door. Before he could grab the knob, though, the door opened and Farryn, the Superintendent of the Healing School, stepped out with a grim look on her face. Joshua could only assume her meeting went poorly. He chalked that up to either Sanev being in one of his moods or the subject matter not pleasing him. *I wonder which it was,* Joshua thought.

"Good luck in there, Joshua," Farryn said under her breath.

Joshua nodded deeply to her. "Thank you."

"Ah, Councilor, I was hoping you would stop by at some point today. Have you been up to Anselin yet?" Sanev asked, looking up from some papers on his desk.

Joshua stepped into the headmaster's office with Michael following closely behind. "We actually just got back from Anselin."

"What have you discovered?" Sanev asked.

"Let's go to Shemont so we can speak with the king about this. He asked to be the first to know. I dislike being caught in the middle of two powerhouses in the kingdom, so I hope you understand my trepidation here," Joshua said.

"Of course. I was actually wondering if we would have the king be a part of this conversation. Your concerns are fair, Councilor," Sanev said, standing behind his desk. "Do you wish to change into your Council robes first? This seems like official business."

Joshua sighed before answering. "If you don't mind, Headmaster, I won't change first. Once again, I dislike being caught between you and the king on these matters. I investigated Anselin as the head of the Dark Magic school *and* as a knight of the kingdom."

"I was simply asking, Sir Joshua. There's no need for consternation here. Shall we head to Shemont, then?"

"Whenever you're ready, Headmaster," Joshua said.

Michael, Joshua, and Sanev walked out of the headmaster's office and down through the tower on their way out the door. Students they passed looked gravely concerned and did their best to move out of their way as they walked. Joshua enjoyed the reverence students showed to the Councilors but felt the extremes they went to showing that reverence was unnecessary. The Councilors were still people, after all. Without having to fight their way through the throng of students returning from their classes, they made easy progress out of the tower and onto the grounds. Portals, while not allowed within the tower itself, were allowed on College grounds. Joshua thought the rule pointless but understood they wanted students to practice safety at all times. *But why make that rule only to allow portals immediately outside the tower?* Still, rules were rules. Joshua stepped onto the grass to the side of the main walkway mostly to get out of the way of the students trying to get back into the tower. After getting onto the grass, Joshua made a portal that would take the trio to just outside Shemont to avoid the Magic use penalties the king still had in place.

*   *   *

Master General Jacob exited the castle, his armor just as pristine as always. He kept one hand on the hilt of his sword to keep it from swaying as he walked. The other hand swung easily at his side with each step he took. He made his way down the stairs and into the courtyard and approached the trio of visitors. He bowed slightly toward them before informing them the king did, in fact, have some time for their visit. They promised a speedy visit which seemed to visually soothe the Master General.

After following Jacob through the maze of staircases and hallways, they finally arrived at the king's office. The door, with a guard on each side, had a golden crown carved into the wood. Master

General Jacob knocked on the door, waited for the king to call from inside, and opened the door for the visitors. Sanev, Joshua and Michael walked into the office; the two Mages took a seat in front of the desk and Michael went to the corner where he leaned against both walls. To his right, just above his head was the stuffed manticore head he had given the king as a trophy after that hunt. King Orson leaned back in his chair and looked at his visitors, now ignoring the mess of papers spread across his desk.

"Should I assume, seeing the three of you together, that this visit is about Anselin?"

"Yes, Highness," Joshua said before filling Orson and Sanev in on the details of what he and Michael found in Anselin. He left out no details, from Michael getting sick to the tingling feeling they both still had in their arms.

"What an absolute crock of shit," Orson said. "Can anyone tell me what motivated the Children to attack such a large target? Haven't they been harder to find than a tick on a dog since after the end of the second war?"

"They have indeed gone into hiding. We have found a few among their numbers here and there but that's been it. Most of the time they are entrenched in society in ways we would never know," Sanev said.

"Highness, I have some theories but nothing that's concrete about their motivations," Joshua said, leaning forward in the chair.

"Let's hear these theories then."

"All the theories are roughly the same. They all point back to Kalathan—"

"Councilor, please refrain from uttering that name aloud," Sanev stammered.

"Must you name him here?" King Orson gasped at the same time.

"I'm sorry, but to be honest it's just a name," Joshua reminded. "Yes, it's the name of the Light Eater, but it's just a name regardless. Our fear is what gives it any amount of power."

"Sorry. You were saying, Joshua?" Orson said.

"All of my theories point back to him. I fully believe the Children of Chaos have filled the vacuum that was created when Michael and I took down Vor'Kath. Who else, beyond Kalathan, would benefit from the kingdom being this close to the brink of…" Joshua started before his voice faded away. He clearly didn't want to finish that thought; Michael perked up.

"On the brink of what, Sir Joshua? Please finish your thought," the king requested, his voice barely louder than a whisper.

"Collapse. The kingdom is in complete turmoil with Anselin gone, Highness. People are frightened and a loud noise away from sheer panic," Michael interjected.

"Highness, what Michael means is—" Joshua started.

"I said what I meant, Joshua. The kingdom is on the brink of collapse either by someone else's hands or our own. Since Anselin fell, supply chains have shattered either because goods are no longer coming from the Elven capital or because merchants are afraid to travel out of the fear that they might get overrun by hordes of terrified people in the streets."

"Michael, I…didn't realize you were so informed about current events. I just—"

"You just thought I spend all of my time in the Cave drinking? I may be there often, Joshua, but I listen to Frank's concerns and those of his other patrons. Don't be upset, Joshua. I'm not," Michael said.

"Getting back on topic," Orson said, his eyes lingering on Michael before returning to the Mage in front of him. "Joshua, you think that Kalathan is involved with this in some way or another?"

"Yes, Highness. I believe he is behind the attack on Anselin and the assassination of King Erkan. I can see no other reasonable explanations."

"Have you talked with the kid about what he saw? I think he may know more than he's let on already."

"I have not personally spoken to him yet, Highness. There are spells we can use to get more information from him if he's being withholding," Joshua suggested.

"Joshua, we cannot simply *delve* a child because they are trying to block out a traumatic memory. What kind of thinking is this?" Sanev asked, his voice beyond incredulous.

"I've delved other people many times before. Michael is one of them. It can help us get information that we seek, especially if Gordack is keeping anything from us or simply refusing to speak," Joshua suggested. "If you would feel better about it, we can have Farryn there to monitor him for any signs that we should stop."

Sanev sighed. "I guess that's all we really can do. We should head back to the College and probe the mind of an impressionable child then. Sire, have you anything else for us?"

"Not for the three of you. Come back with your findings, whenever you may have them. I have a meeting with the head of the

Merchants' Guild and while he will understand if I'm tardy, I would rather not keep him waiting. Anything further for me?" Orson asked, standing.

"I have nothing further," Sanev said.

"Nor I, Highness," Joshua replied.

"Nothing on my end," Michael said.

"Good. You have your tasks. Please see to them."

Orson walked around his desk, opened the door, and the four of them filed out. The king locked his office door with a large, ornamental skeleton key before walking away, the guards following closely behind him. One guard followed on his left, the other on his right close enough they were almost stepping on the backs of the king's polished, brown, leather boots. Michael, Joshua, and the Headmaster left the castle and the city before they took a portal back up to the College. Michael hated the cold sensation that portals gave him, but he was appreciative of the quick form of travel. A trip from Shemont to the College would take at least two days otherwise.

Chapter Ten

Six gulls flew in the air overhead, their cries killing off every scrap of silence there could have been. Waves crashed on the shore not far away, only adding to the cacophony of sounds. Esram hated the sounds of gulls, but the waves were perfectly fine for him. *What have I become?* he thought to himself. He normally despised nature. Thinking about it, he assumed the chaos in the waves is what he enjoyed hearing. Water battered the rocks and over time wore them down to nothing more than sand. He imagined small crabs scuttling along the beach getting carried out to sea by the waves as they crashed onto land. Everything around him felt chaotic, thinking of it that way. The gulls, circling the Iron Holm overhead, only flew so they could find food. Scavengers, the lot of them. They didn't care for the ecosystem or the environment. They merely ate because they needed to. By the same token, something would eat them for basically the same reason. Chaos. It surrounded him even without Kalathan speaking to him directly. He pondered a bit longer and decided he did, in fact, like nature, but realized it was really only the chaotic temperament of it that drew him in.

"Esram," Daethis said, breaking his focus from the waves and gulls, "are you waiting for something? We're all here."

Esram shook his head, bringing him back to the task at hand. He glanced around the ritual site and saw Maja, Oleg, and Daethis all gathered around the altar. He couldn't remember why he started to focus on the nature around him, but clearly there had been a reason. He wondered how he kept the others waiting while his thoughts wondered to crabs and gulls. He cleared his mind and started casting the spell that would create a dark orb for them to speak with their master. Kalathan. The Eater of Light. The Chaotic One. He had many names, most of which did him no justice or were simply cruel. Still, he had likely earned most of the names.

"Let's get started," Esram said as the orb formed above the altar.

Just as every other ritual, this one happened the same way. They joined their Magic powers together, each casting a portion of the orb and connecting the pieces together with Esram's. Together, the pieces formed a singular orb that would bring them at least the sound of their terrible master. Kalathan wasted no time once the orb had formed. He started speaking immediately, his voice booming and deeper than normal.

"You're late, mortal. You know I don't tolerate tardiness."

"Many apologies, master. My thoughts were elsewhere. It won't happen again," Esram replied, trying his best to calm Kalathan.

"See that it doesn't. Have you taken the gathered shards to the witches yet?"

"My lord, I gathered eight shards from outside the tower," Maja said.

Esram spoke up. "Those were taken to the witches in the tundra as you told us."

"The witches will take some time to work the hilt as they need to. The rest are worthless for our plans. Will the College fall into our trap?"

"They will run for the cave like a fly to a dung heap. I will make sure of that," Maja said.

"Do what you must. I *will* walk your realm in a short time. Make this happen," Kalathan urged them, his voice somehow deeper than earlier.

With that the orb dissipated and Esram turned his attention to Maja. "You're sure the Councilor will fall for this trap?"

"After Anselin he's been itching to catch us doing *any*thing. We will have the witches cast a spell that the Dark Magic school won't be able to miss," she replied.

"The spell won't need to be grand to get their attention," Daethis reminded with the ever-present, sweet lilt in her voice.

"It will be just grand enough to attract the College's attention, I can assure you of that," Maja said. "What did they learn in Anselin?"

"They learned enough," Oleg chimed in, a sly smirk on his face.

Daethis shook her head and chuckled a little. "We can glean a world of insight from you, Oleg. It's truly astounding."

"Let's not start infighting," Esram said. "That will quickly put us in a position where the College wins. None of us should want that."

"Have we finished the plans for the ritual?" Daethis asked.

Oleg cleared his throat and shifted his weight. "We are still using them for it right?"

"That is still the plan," Esram answered.

"Do we have anything left to plan?" Maja asked.

"I don't believe so. We just have to get the Councilor to the cave and then here," Daethis said. "Everything else should be easy."

"Now that we've done what we came here to do, we should all go back to what we were doing. I shouldn't have to say this, but let's stay discrete about this plan. There's no need to tip our hands just yet," Esram reminded.

*   *   *

Sanev detested having so many people in his office and not only because it wasn't a grand office like King Orson's. Five people, including himself, made it feel cramped. He looked around the room and wondered why they hadn't used the Council chambers for something like this. Obviously, they needed Gordack, Joshua, Farryn, and Bryne for the delving, but something should have been done about the location they used. Still, that was a small price to pay for the information they could glean from the child's mind right now. They had yet to ask about the day of the attack; upon his arrival, Gordack was shaken and traumatized. It was clearly not the right time to ask him about what happened, other than to get preliminary details from him. *What if we come out of this with more questions instead of answers?* While this was possible, Sanev argued with himself that it was less likely. Besides, preventing the kingdom from falling into what seemed like an inevitable collapse felt worth the risk of more questions.

Sanev looked at the child sitting in the chair, a look of fright on his face. Joshua stood behind the child. This was Joshua's first interaction with Gordack. From what the College previously learned, Gordack's father served in the army, as many Elves in Anselin did. What set him apart from others, however, was that Gordack's father was the king's Aegis, the official title for the king's personal bodyguard. Unlike the army structure within the human side of the kingdom, the Elven Aegis was a sacred position passed down to a hand-selected guard. This tradition survived five generations of kings and an untold number of Aegises until the fateful day when Anselin fell to Dark Mages. The only reason the College knew this much about Gordack's lineage was from the terrified sputtering that happened after his arrival.

"Am I in trouble? I didn't do anything."

"You're not in trouble. Far from it, in fact," Joshua said, placing a comforting hand on the half-Elf child's shoulder. "We only want to learn more about what you saw on the day of the attack if you'll allow us. We intend to find whoever did this terrible thing to Anselin and bring them to justice."

"Please, tell us what you saw that day," Sanev asked.

"I was in the kitchen with mother but then everything went dark, and the ground shook a lot. All the light came back, but no one was in the kitchen with me. I got scared and went into the hallway to find mother, but she wasn't there. I kept walking hoping I would find her. That's when I found Father and the king. They appeared out of nowhere. Father was holding his stomach and his clothes were wet and dark. Father took me to the kitchen to find mother. He went in by himself, but I heard something and went in and that's…that's when I saw him *killing* Mother. I screamed and ran, but he chased me. The king got upset because I was too loud."

"What do you remember happening next?" Joshua asked.

"We went into a tunnel behind a weird door. Someone was casting spells and father closed the door to keep us safe. There weren't any lights there either. It was really dark and scary. Father said he knew the way though and the king trusted him. Then while we were walking he fell over. The king said for us to leave Father behind so he could get better and join us outside again. The king walked a lot faster than Father did, and I almost had to run to keep up with him," Gordack said.

"You poor thing, leaving your father behind during an attack on the city," Farryn said, her voice dripping with concern. Sanev assumed that was from her background as a healer.

"Did anything happen after the tunnel?" Sanev asked, getting them back on track.

"We were walking through the grass. I was in front of the king, and someone showed up. I didn't know the other person. The other man wore black robes like yours and his face was hidden. The king was supposed to know who this was. That's what he said."

"Did you hear or see anything else when you saw the new man?" Joshua asked.

"The king screamed and told me to run. That's what I did."

"What else happened?" Sanev asked.

"I was already running but I stopped and saw the king covered in black stuff. Then there was the bright light. That's all I remember."

"Joshua does any of this help you with your research into what happened?" Sanev asked.

"I think it helps. Everything is still pointing back to Kalathan. It's possible this spell is the same one that Vor'Kath used that almost swallowed me in darkness. I think the delving is more necessary now than it was before," Joshua answered.

Bryne shifted his weight then spoke for the first time. "Is there any chance this person who killed the king *is* Vor'Kath?"

Joshua shook his head. "No, there's no chance that Kalathan would have taken Vor'Kath back, if he *has* resurrected since that day at the tower. I have no doubt that he died that day."

"I have to ask that we begin the delve soon," Sanev suggested. "We are likely to cause added trauma to this poor child if we prolong the process too long. Farryn or Joshua, which of you would like to lead this effort? I don't know, between the two of you, who would be the better choice for this affair."

"I'll lead the spell," Farryn said.

"Look specifically for anything around the king's death. We want to avoid dredging up more memories than are needed," Joshua suggested.

"It's imperative we can find out whatever we can about this person," Sanev said. "I agree with Joshua on this matter. Let's avoid adding to the child's trauma while trying to find what we can about the attack."

Farryn started the delving spell; Joshua and Bryne joined her spell to increase the power behind it. They didn't need an intensely powerful spell for a child such as Gordack, but it would be easier to retrieve traumatic memories with more people casting the spell. Sanev stood by his desk supervising the effort. Farryn slowly lowered the spell over Gordack's head and then slipped a few of the tendrils into his mind. Over the chair where he sat, a cloud formed as part of the spell. Light flashed from inside and pictures showed on the surface of the cloud. These pictures, flashing for mere seconds, represented minutes to hours of memories held within Gordack's subconscious. The casters moved their spell through his mind until they found the correct timeframe for the memories they sought. Images flashed across the surface of the cloud, all grim and terrifying. Blood. A knife. Darkness. Everything flashed for moments at a time until… They found the memory they hunted and slowed the spell to only focus on one moment.

King Erkan III. The Elven king of Drendil. Darkness washed over him in a wave and consumed his very being. Agony filled the room as Gordack's mind recalled the sound Erkan made as the darkness consumed him. Sanev watched as Joshua staggered, dropping out of the spell, and falling to his knees. Anguish washed over his face. Sanev knew not what Joshua thought, but if this was the same spell that Vor'Kath cast about a year ago, it may have brought up memories that Joshua had suppressed. Those kinds of memories didn't begin to fade in that time. Sanev took his eyes from Joshua and returned his attention to the cloud floating in his office over Gordack. So much could be learned from this.

"Find a previous memory. This one is too late," Sanev suggested.

Farryn sent the spell backwards and stopped a few minutes prior. The dark-robed figure stood before Erkan, cowl covering his face completely. *This is it,* Sanev thought. *Let's see who led this attack.* The image shifted and stuttered. Within a few moments the Dark Mage lowered his hood and reached out his hand toward Erkan, the spell ready to cast. Sanev focused intently on the face. Dark, deep-set eyes, a hooked nose, a weak jawline, and a chin that a team of rescue personnel could likely not have found. All of this seemed familiar, but Sanev couldn't place who it was. Then the caster turned ever so slightly. Scars. A huge, jagged scar that reached from the jawline to the hairline and from the mouth to the ear. The entire left side of the caster's face was a scar. *There is but one Mage I know with a scar like that.*

Bryne looked up. "Esram!"

"By the Allfather is that really him?" Farryn asked, the spell collapsing as she looked up in surprise. Gordack fell limp in the chair.

"Joshua, are you alright? You dropped out of the spell when you saw the darkness," Sanev asked, his voice concerned. "Farryn, please check on the child."

"I'll be fine, Headmaster. I just need a minute," Joshua replied. "Seeing that spell brought back some unresolved memories I didn't expect to encounter for a long time."

"Bryne, are you sure that's Esram?" Farryn asked, the back of her hand on Gordack's forehead as she cast a spell to check his vital signs.

"I won't ever forget that face in all the days that I live. Not after that day," Bryne replied.

"Who is Esram?" Joshua asked, finally standing.

"He was a student here who fell to the lies and temptations of the Children of Chaos. He was the last student any of us would have expected that from. He focused his time in the classroom, was on track to graduate early, and rarely got into trouble. Then, one day, he snapped and attacked Bryne in the open," Sanev explained.

"I defended myself before he could get a spell off. He took some lightning to the face. That's where he earned his scars," Bryne chimed in.

"What happened after that?" Joshua asked.

"I expelled him from the College. At the time he was in such pain and agony that I didn't think he would be a threat to anyone. It was uncertain he would live even a week. I made the mistake of underestimating him. I should have put him down when I had the chance. Instead, I showed ill-advised mercy to someone who had not earned even a fraction of what I showered upon him. If ever there was a time when life slaps you with your mistakes, this is one of them."

"We are allowed to make mistakes, Headmaster," Joshua said. "It's how we recover from them that shows our true colors."

"This isn't a concept that's lost on me, Joshua," Sanev claimed. "What have you learned from the delving?"

"The darkness confirms a few things for me. First, we are dealing with someone who has curried favor with Kalathan. Second, this won't be easy. Third, Anselin was by no means an accident. It was a deliberate, calculated strike. Lastly, Esram orchestrated the attack and is likely the mastermind behind all of this."

"Is there anything else that you can tell us with any certainty?"

"Only that I desperately need something as quickly as we can get it."

"Tell me what you need, and we will get it to you posthaste," Sanev promised.

"I need every book the library has about Kalathan."

Chapter Eleven

The College library, neither hectic nor empty, felt the same way it always did: serene. Students sat at a few tables as they studied various books. Joshua walked by one table and slowed down to see the types of books the students were reading. He saw a stack of mystic spell tomes which covered subjects such as telekinesis, invisibility, and transmutation. *That's interesting subject matter,* Joshua thought to himself. He often heard tales of Mages trying to buy goods with iron tokens they changed to gold. Unfortunately, those stories all ended the same way: the Mage would go to leave with their newly "purchased" goods and the spell would break, revealing their cheap nature. When the merchants figured this out, the Mages often ended up in the pillories with vegetables thrown at their heads. As strong as their morals should have been, Mages continued to attempt to change the very basis of materials into something entirely different. These spells worked, though temporarily. Joshua thought that was the true lesson behind the stories. Something may work for a time, but that doesn't mean it actually worked the way it was intended.

Joshua found himself walking toward the central desk where Master Averon currently stood, scrutinizing the condition of several recently returned books. His long, well-kept beard, white and grey in color, hung nearly to the middle of his sternum. Master Averon, known to all the students as a hard-ass for the condition of the books, had served the College for decades as a librarian. When he started, so the tales said, his beard had only been a few inches long and showed far browner than it currently did. As Joshua approached the desk, he noticed that the Elf didn't use a spell to investigate the condition of the books but instead relied on a series of increasingly smaller looking glasses. He scanned the books a page at a time looking for anything that seemed out of place. With his focus on the books, he didn't notice Joshua's approach. Councilor Joshua waited a polite amount of time for Master Averon to notice him, but still ended up having to knock on the tabletop to get the librarian's attention.

Master Averon jumped and nearly dropped his monocles. "I'm sorry for not seeing you. What obscure subject can a member of my staff can help you with today?"

"I'm afraid I can only trust you with this matter, Master Averon," Joshua answered.

"Councilor, you can drop the 'Master' accolades. If anything, you are the superior in this conversation. Respect should travel from me to you," Averon said, not entirely looking up from the book he examined.

"Personally, I prefer to maintain working relationships built on mutual respect," Joshua replied.

"Whatever makes you happy, Councilor," Averon said, setting down his glasses with a warm smile. "What obscure subject may *I* help you research today?"

"I'm currently looking for books about Kalathan," Joshua said, keeping his voice as low as he could.

"Ah, the Light Eater. I'm afraid that, if we have any books on that subject, they are locked in glass cases to protect not only the books, but those who may read them. Those kinds of works are not only *extremely* rare but also quite tempting to the younger, more relaxed students. Come with me. I will show you what I mean."

Master Averon took Joshua to a room in the back which contained several locked bookcases, their glass doors covered by complex spells. The old librarian took several minutes looking through the darkened glass before he settled on a particular bookcase. More minutes passed as he disarmed the spells before he finally opened the bookcase. The smell of dusty, unread books flooded the room, a smell Joshua loved deeply. Really, he loved the smell of all books but especially enjoyed old, dusty books. Master Averon grabbed two black tomes from inside the cabinet and brought them to a small desk in the room. He set them down gently and motioned for Joshua to come take a look.

Joshua walked across the small room to the table and looked at the two books. Leatherbound and rather on the small side, there wasn't anything overly impressive about them. A rune, embossed into the leather of each book showed what looked like a letter from the Vor language, but Joshua wasn't well-versed enough to know which letter it was or what the rune represented. Given the subject matter he was here to study, and Master Averon's unwillingness to have these books out in the general library, he assumed the rune represented Kalathan or something along those lines. Joshua reached for the book on the right. He felt a strange throbbing in the air as his hand approached the book. Something was certainly wrong with this book. The air grew icy cold as Joshua's hand grew even closer to the book. The throbbing grew faster until it became a pulsing sensation. *Come to me,* a deep, booming voice called inside of Joshua's head. He had heard that voice before. He wanted so badly to touch the book, but not knowing what to expect made him wary. He retracted his hand, the pulsing instantly grew slower, and the air returned to its normal temperature.

"You feel it, don't you?" Master Averon asked.

Joshua nodded, not breaking his eyes from the book. "What exactly is that sensation?"

"Despite having this book in the library's collection for nearly three *decades*, I still don't know what causes that sensation. It's not something everyone experiences."

Joshua's heart started pounding. "Not everyone feels that? Do you know anything about the others who have felt it?"

Master Averon shook his head slowly. "Unfortunately, no. This isn't a book that people commonly request, so I still don't have enough information on their demographics. Perhaps it's caused by previous exposure to Dark Magic?"

Joshua's heart continued pounding, the sound growing intense in his ears. "That seems like a likely explanation."

Come to me, the same voice whispered. Joshua closed his eyes and shook his head, trying to rid himself of the voice. He entered the abyss in his mind, the place where everything faded away. The Order of Ravens had taught him to access the abyss from an early age. From here he could touch the Magic. Except. Something shimmered in front of the Magic in his mind. A shadowy, shimmering…something. He had seen this before, a long time before. He had reached to it back then, unsure of what blocked the Allfather's glorious light in his mind. The last time he saw this was the night before he became a full-fledged member of the Order of Ravens. The night before he became a priest. He had reached out and touched the shimmering darkness in his mind. Now, decades later, it had come back and now called to him. *Join me.*

"Councilor?" Master Averon asked. "Is everything alright?"

"Yes," Joshua lied, "I just have a headache forming is all. Maybe it's from the pulsing sensation from the book?"

"That's likely. Come, sit down and rest. We can try again with the books later. I know a spell that can block the sensations so you can read through the books."

Joshua followed the librarian and sat in the single chair in the room. "Thank you, Master Averon. You're not nearly as terrifying as the students claim."

Averon chuckled. "That's because you're neither a student nor irresponsible with borrowed books, Councilor."

"Master Averon, do you have any information about former students? Specifically, I'm looking for information about students who have been expelled."

"Ah, the ledger should have that. We have surprisingly few students get expelled so when one of those instances come up, it gets heavily documented. Let me grab that book for you." Master Averon disappeared for a few minutes and returned with a set of five books. "Do you have a particular student in mind or are you just curious?"

"There's one student I wanted to look up: Esram."

Master Averon froze mid-step. "You're sure you have the name right?"

"That's what the headmaster said the name was. Bryne and Farryn confirmed it."

"May the Allfather save us," Averon breathed.

"What's wrong?"

"Esram is a…cunning Mage. Did the Headmaster tell you why Esram was expelled?"

"He covered something about a fight between Esram and Bryne that resulted in the scars," Joshua waved his hand over the left side of his face, "that identified him."

"You *saw* Esram, and he wasn't stopped?" Master Averon stammered.

Joshua quickly filled the librarian in on the details of the delving spell. "So, I asked about expulsion records to see if anything was listed about his home or anything like that. Maybe we could find a clue about where he might be hiding."

"No, there's nothing like that in the student records. That wasn't a bad idea, though."

"Esram was a member of the Children of Chaos, correct?"

"Now, that is where some of the uncertainty comes in. We don't really know if he was a member of the Children or the Assembly—"

"The Assembly of Mages survived the first Mages' War?"

"Unfortunately, they did. Also, they weren't the only sect of Dark Mages to exist at that time. They are where the Children ultimately originated."

"Are there any books here in the library on that subject? I'm curious about all the different offshoots specifically." Joshua asked.

"If we have anything, those books would be in your section of the library, Councilor," Master Averon answered.

"Wait, I have my own section in the library? How have I not known this?"

"Have I not mentioned it to you already?" Averon asked, dragging his fingers through his beard. "It's not a surprise that you didn't know about it, really. It's not a very popular section of the library by any stretch of that word's definition. Many of our students would rather learn to throw apples or cheese at one another for whatever reason they have for such childishness. Well, your school, like all the other schools, has a dedicated section here with books to read more about your subject matter. The Dark Magic section is in the back along the western wall."

"Thank you, Master Averon. I will let you know if I need anything further to further my studies," Joshua said, bowing his head slightly.

"May the Allfather guide you on your journey, Councilor."

Joshua left Master Averon who returned his attention to the book he inspected earlier. On his way there, Joshua passed a few groups of students intently looking through books about the dangers of portals while others giggled while looking at hand-drawn depictions of anatomy meant to aid the healers in their studies and understandings. The maturity range shocked him, but he understood that not every student in the College would be a grand scholar; he expected at least a bit more maturity from the student body.

Joshua reached the western wall of the library and found a few bookcases, coated in thick sheets of dust, with older, leatherbound books taking up the spaces on the shelves. Undoubtedly this was the Dark Magic section. Looking at the spines, Joshua saw titles that intrigued him. *The Dangers of the Assembly of Mages, History of the Dark Magic School, The Unseen Consequences of the Mages' Wars,* and *Kalathan* all sat on one shelf with no sense of order or placement. He grabbed the Kalathan book and opened it. The spine creaked and instantly he knew no one had looked at this book in quite some time. The smell of dust coming from the book intensified as he flipped through the stiff pages, aged and yellow, which rasped as he leafed through them. Skimming the book, he remained skeptical about the information held within such an aged book. *Is this information still relevant?* A valid question but one he would have to evaluate after reading. He turned another page and his breath stopped as he found a detailed depiction of what the author speculated Kalathan looked like.

A terrible image of an amalgamation of animal and person showed on the page. The depiction portrayed a human torso, goat legs, wings from a corvid, though proportionally larger than that of an ordinary bird, a face similar to a lion, and human arms that on the upper arms sported the same dark feathers as the wings on the biceps, though they thinned toward the elbows. Brandings and scars littered the torso, markings from battles, ceremonies, or various sources. The image enthralled him. He couldn't pry his eyes away, despite a pit forming in his stomach at the sight. Beads of sweat formed on Joshua's forehead and threatened to run down his nose before dripping onto the pages. He wiped the sweat away with his sleeve, confused about why the library suddenly felt stifling when it normally was brisk. He knew that Master Averon used spells to control the temperature in the library, something he claimed preserved the books. More believable than that, however, would be that Master Averon, being a stouter person than others, simply was always warm and wanted not to be constantly sweaty.

The abundance of dust within the book tickled his nose, threatening to bring a series of uncontrolled sneezes, though he was able to resist by scrunching his face, wriggling his nose, and opening his mouth repeatedly, his eyes closing as he did so. Going through this process, he almost failed to notice Maja approached from one of the other sections in the library. While he didn't know her at a familiar level, a downside of still learning the other members of the Dark Magic school, she would have been perusing the illusion section.

"Councilor, you look bothered," she said, the lilt in her voice carrying a symphony of concern.

Joshua turned the image in the book toward the Elf. "This picture. I don't know why it both captivates me and terrifies me."

"Yes, the image of the Chaotic One often has that effect on people."

"You seem unconcerned about the image."

"I have seen it many times in my tenure with the Dark Magic school. After some time, it grows less…awful, if that makes sense."

"I see…" he said, pausing and briefly returning his attention to the book. "I have a task for you. Can you see if there are any signs of Dark Magic usage on the continent? This image concerns me and makes me curious."

"Certainly. I will return when I have some news for you."

Maja bowed her head and walked off, disappearing behind a bookshelf. Joshua returned to examining the depiction of Kalathan once again. The image almost felt like it could jump off the page at any moment. Simply by looking at it, he felt like he was keeping the picture from moving, though he knew that idea was impossible. An image, made entirely of ink, could not move. He knew no spells that would allow something like that. Yet, as he looked at the next page, he *swore* he saw movement in the corner of his eye in the direction of the terrible picture. The image still disturbed him, even after examining it for as long as he had.

After a few minutes of staring at the image, thinking it was about to move any moment, Joshua closed the book and brought it with him to the central desk where he once again found Master Averon examining yet another book someone else brought back to the library. The Elf looked up immediately and lowered his glasses, held to him by a thin golden chain, and smiled warmly at Joshua.

"How can I be of service, Councilor?"

"Has anyone else seen this image and thought it was moving?"

"I'm not aware of anyone having that particular sensation. I can investigate why that would be, but I can promise you it will take time, if I ever find the answer for you. Anything else you need from me, Councilor?"

Before Joshua could answer, Maja returned through a portal. "Councilor, I'm afraid I have some bad news."

"Forgive me, Master Averon, but I must leave. Thank you for your time and answers. Today has been wildly insightful."

"Perfectly fine, Councilor. Come back any time. You make me exercise my brain, and that's something I cherish."

"What have you found, Maja?" Joshua asked, stepping away from the library's central desk where Averon was already nose-deep in the stack of books again.

"We have the activity pinpointed on our map if you would like to see it, Councilor."

"Excellent. Let's see this activity," Joshua replied, stepping into the portal behind Maja.

Chapter Twelve

ach of the schools at the Sorcerer's College maintained their own outlying building where they conducted their business. The Dark Magic school was the only one of these buildings that had no windows or doors, leaving it only accessible via portal. Like the other buildings it contained two above ground levels, but also contained three basements, something else that separated it from the other schools' buildings. To conserve space within the central tower, most of the staff maintained their bedrooms in the outlying buildings, except the Councilors. The ground floor contained classrooms where the learning took place. The Dark Magic school, being the only school that didn't have students, unless a new Mage was brought into the fold, rarely used their classrooms, and instead used these rooms for storage and offices. The majority of the Dark Magic school's business was conducted in one of the three underground floors.

The first floor was the independent library the Dark Magic school maintained separate from Master Averon's massive collection of books. Knowing that Master Averon would not be pleased hearing that they maintained their own library, with books that pertained only to their school, they did their best to keep that a secret. Joshua disliked lying to the librarian but knew that Averon's biggest concerns were based on controlling the content that students could consume. Given that the Dark Magic school had no students, and their building could only be accessed by portals, Joshua felt he could easily justify their independent library if word ever reached Averon about its existence. Still, he hated lying to the aged librarian.

The next basement level, a single, open room, was used for spell practice. Temporary walls partitioned off different practice areas to allow for privacy for those learning new spells or manipulating spells. This area provided the members of the school a safe place to practice their spells, be they dangerous, unusual, or anything else. This also prevented other members from pestering each other to learn particular spells while practicing specific ones. On occasion, the Dark Magic members would visit the other schools to learn new spells and then come back here to manipulate or modify them. Some accidents, at times unavoidable, *had* happened. Most of them happened under the previous Councilor's tenure as the superintendent for the school. Joshua did his best to ensure the practice areas were safe places to work on spells. He didn't want any of his team members to feel pressured into trying any spells they didn't want to.

The lowest level of the Dark Magic school, also a single, open room, contained only a large table surrounded by chairs. At the center of the table stood a small stand with a clear glass orb, an exact copy of the one Headmaster Sanev carried with him at all times. The correct combination of spells would cause the orb to project an image of the continent in the air above it. With a few adjustments to the spell originally used for this, their map would show red blips to indicate areas where someone used Dark Magic across the continent. In theory, it would work for the other continents as well, but Joshua feared the amount of power needed to perform such a spell. He feared the power of the spell to monitor Drendil alone, but again he could justify that easily enough if anything adverse happened.

Joshua and Maja walked down the stairs from the practice area to the map room. Reaching the bottom level of the school's building, Joshua approached the table and greeted the other two members of his school. Both were Elves but came from different areas of the kingdom. Girzi hailed from Erith and Myrdin was born in Anselin. The latter still hadn't fully accepted the news of what happened there yet and still seemed a bit frazzled. Joshua had talked with both of them enough to know they were starkly different though they acted almost like sisters. Of the members of the school, both had the longest tenure and were wary of fully trusting Joshua as the new superintendent right away. Especially after the discovery made about Kerron, Joshua fully understood their trepidations.

While every member of the Dark Magic school performed similar roles, Girzi and Myrdin were his hunters. They spent most of their time, either by direction or otherwise, in the map room or the library studying and looking for signs of Dark Magic. They worked tirelessly together and often stood shifts in both rooms, swapping out as they needed to. When they discovered something that needed their attention, they went without hesitation. Joshua appreciated their dedication to the team.

Joshua leaned against the table with closed fists as he looked at the map floating over the table. "What have you found?"

"Dark Magic. Apologies if you were expecting something different." Myrdin stated with more than a drop of sarcasm in her voice. She flashed a smile to show she was joking.

"Do we have any idea what it is?"

"Not that we can tell from here," Girzi said. "We do know it's in the tundra, though. This activity started about ten minutes ago and stopped as you started walking down the steps. We captured a general location for you on the map."

Joshua stared intently at the effervescent cloud that hovered above the table, his eyes only focusing on the bright red dot showing a location in the tundra that started about thirty kilometers north of where Anselin used to stand. *Have we seen any kind of activity in that area before?* he wondered. A recurrence could potentially mean something significant. Regardless, this activity should be investigated, at the very least to see what caused the detection spell to trigger.

"You said the activity lasted about ten minutes?" Joshua asked, looking to Girzi and Myrdin for confirmation.

"That's what we saw," Myrdin said.

Girzi pulled on the thick, singular braid she had draped over her left shoulder. "We saw nothing beyond when it started and ended. It could be something simple given how long it lasted. Want one of us to check it out?"

"It should certainly be looked into," Joshua said, standing up from the table. "Maja, come with me. Let's see what we can find there."

"Yes, Councilor."

"Let us make you a portal to the tundra," Myrdin offered. "You'll have to walk a bit since I haven't been in that exact area, but I can get you close enough."

"Close is better than nothing. Are you ready, Maja?"

"Always."

Myrdin opened the portal between the table and the stairway. Joshua rubbed his temples, feeling the headache still. His head throbbed dully like he had been clenching his teeth too long. He motioned for Maja to go through the portal first. She nodded then stepped through, her robed whispering as they sloshed through the portal's shimmering surface. Joshua rubbed his temples a moment longer and stepped through the portal, inhaling sharply as he anticipated a bone-chilling wind on the other side of the portal. His skin prickled as he walked through the portal the same as it always did.

Just as anticipated, a fierce, bitter wind immediately whipped at Joshua's crimson and gold robes. He preferred wearing his knightly robes over his white Councilor robes for myriad of reasons, chief amongst them being white robes are nearly impossible to keep clean.

These robes were significantly easier to keep clean and didn't make him stand out as much. As the wind thrashed his robes about, Joshua stopped for a moment and took in his surroundings. A spinney rose from the ground about a kilometer to his left. In his mind that direction was west. The group of trees, thinning and withered, looked sad from this distance. Even from this distance he could see their branches thrashing about as the wind raced across the tundra. Ahead of him, Joshua saw a herd of elk grazing on the patches of grass. The herd seemed unbothered by the chill of the wind, but their fur protected them better than Joshua's robes did for him. Overhead, a carrion bird of some kind circled as it scanned the terrain for its next meal. It lazily flapped its wings as it soared, pockets of rising air helping to keep it aloft. It tilted, lifting its right wing and rose sharply. Joshua broke his focus away from the things around him, noting there would be time for watching birds later if he so chose.

He looked to Maja who was simply standing a little away from the portal. "We should split up and see what we can find."

"Sounds good," Maja said, nodding. "Dazzle spell if we find something?"

"I can think of nothing better to do."

With their plan established, Maja turned around and started off toward the copse of trees while Joshua went the opposite direction, toward some hilly terrain. Not wanting to waste any time, he cast the viewer spell and started walking around looking for traces of Dark Magic. As he crested the first hillock, he saw nothing and continued toward the next. He walked down the second hill toward a third and, still seeing no traces, closed the spell to trust his instincts more than his spells. There was a time and place for spells, but this didn't feel like one of them. He stopped on the top of the small hill and looked around, trying to get a good sense of where the Dark Magic user may have been. To the south, beyond the hilly area he was currently in, a large clearing opened up and became progressively greener. Joshua found himself wondering why the herd of elk weren't grazing there but dismissed the thought. To the west, beyond the copse of trees Maja was now investigating, rose a chain of mountains, their peaks topped in snow that was visible even from this distance. *If anything, Maja will probably find something over in the trees,* Joshua thought just as he heard the zip and crackle of Maja's dazzle spell. Facing the woods, he saw the streak of smoke streaming into the sky and started walking in that direction.

The dazzle spell, a simple and effective way for signaling locations, created a ball of light accompanied by a loud scream. Once the ball of light reached its apex, it burst into a greater display of light. This one became a blast of sparkling green and blue, clearly visible against the steel-grey clouds in the sky far overhead. Joshua thought it felt too convenient that she found something so quickly, but he trusted her experience more than he trusted his own gut instinct. She had, after all, been in the school longer than he had. For yet another time, he felt he was right to not trust his gut instinct.

Joshua took a few steps and created a portal, stepping through into the cluster of trees. This was a trick he had learned with Michael while they hunted Vor'Kath along the significantly warmer, southern coast of the continent. He used to need long moments of concentration to craft a portal that would take him anywhere with any level of accuracy or dependability. Now, he could make one in an instant and jump to nearly anywhere within sight in a moment. It was a skill especially handy in combat, although Joshua avoided fighting of all kinds whenever possible. Joshua stepped through the shimmering doorway in the air that all his portals were and stepped directly into the tree line. He continued walking through the woods in a roughly west-northwest direction. He prepared some spells in case what Maja found was dangerous and not a curiosity.

As Joshua weaved between the trees, he noticed moss growing on the northern base of the trees, proving that adage true. Still walking through the trees, he found himself wondering why that was in fact true. He figured the simplest explanation would have to be that moss avoided direct sunlight and growing on the north side of the tree allowed it to do just that. If he really wanted an explanation, he could always go to the alchemist and ask them. Not all alchemists were horticulturists, but enough of them were that he could actually depend on them to know the answer to that question. They would likely welcome the company and the question before divulging some long-winded explanation that no soul should ever *want* to hear. Thinking of this, Joshua wondered why the alchemists were the only school not represented by either a Councilor or a color among the flames leading into the tower. He figured he could always ask Sanev when he rounded a tree and heard a twig snap.

Joshua's hands shot up in an instant as he turned around, his spells at the ready. He stopped an instant before launching a spray of fire at Maja. She tilted her head at the spells in his hands and he released them, the fire fading with a faint *fizz* sound. Maja, holding a finger up to her lips, pointed over Joshua's shoulder. He turned and saw a hill with a cave entrance on the side. The stony edges of the cave were carved with foreign runes which glowed with the faintest purple light. Approaching the mouth of the cave, Joshua readied the same spells he had previously and noticed that no footprints went into or came out of the cave. He knew that meant nothing. The runes alone were proof enough that this place was likely the site for the Dark Magic they detected. Joshua released his spells and opened another viewer, looking for any traces. He found dozens but couldn't tell their age. He could, however, see some of the traces matched those he found in Anselin.

"The Children of Chaos have been here," he whispered.

Maja's head snapped to him faster than he could blink. "What? You're sure of that?"

"I'm positive. These traces are the same I saw in Anselin. They've been here."

"Should we go in?" Maja asked. "I think we may need backup if the Children are here."

Joshua released the viewer spell and looked at Maja. "Do you think we need help with this? You're a strong Mage, Maja."

"We don't know how many they could be. If you think we can handle them on our own, we should go in."

"Well," Joshua said, taking a deep breath and crossing into the mouth of the cave. "Follow me."

*   *   *

They were finally alone together in the lakeside cottage. Esram stood before his nearly finished alchemical project, carefully pouring the last few drops of the potion from his retort into a small glass vial. With the final drops falling into the vial, he returned the retort to the table and retrieved a piece of cork to stop the bottle. He squeezed the material into the narrow neck of the glass bottle and gently turned the vial over a few times. The final step of the process complete, he held the finished potion up in front of a lamp to verify its opacity. He watched the air bubbles exploding inside the vial, a result of the gentle shaking. His potion was finally ready. Daethis, watching Esram while she lounged in a chair, sat up and cast a spell. She gazed into the orb her spell created then smiled contently.

"The Councilor and Maja have reached the cave. The witches will ambush them shortly. You're sure this is what Kalathan wants?" Daethis asked.

"Daethis, my love, are you doubting the plan?" Esram said.

She stood and sauntered over to him and wrapped her wispy arms around his waist. "Why do you think I would ever do such a thing?"

"These are trying times, Daethis. We have to be sure that those who are bonded with us are going to follow through," Esram explained, putting her hands in his.

"I am going to follow through. This world needs cleansed the way our master envisions it. I'm just worried about Maja is all. We need her."

Esram turned around to face Daethis, turning within her arms. "We need them both. The witches are weak and will be defeated easily by them. They have done their part."

"You have the dagger?"

"Yes. It's in a secure place where only I can get it when the time is right."

"Excellent. Everything feels like it's falling into place."

"Indeed, my love. Soon we will rule this world alongside Kalathan."

"I cannot wait," Daethis said before pressing her lips against Esram's.

Chapter Thirteen

ichael sat at his favorite spot in the Cave. Frank had just finished refilling his mug, he had a fresh pipeful of tobacco, and a plate of great food on the way. What more could he possibly want? As he took a long gulp from his tankard, he felt a pang of guilt strike him. He told Joshua he wanted to cut down on his drinking, yet here he was. Drinking. He forgot to mention to Frank that he wanted to cut back and the man continued to serve him the same as he always did. If anything was different, Frank was making his rounds across the bar faster tonight.

The ale today was colder than normal. Michael took another quick drink and as it traveled down his throat, he felt something tickle in his ear and his body shivered without his control. He let the wave of cold wash over him and fade. The shivering stopped momentarily, and Michael proceeded to strike a match and light his filled pipe. He planned to sit at the Cave until Frank told him to go home or until someone came to interrupt his drinking like Joshua did the other day. He hadn't seen Joshua since they went to Anselin but figured there could be something the Mage needed from him. If that were the case, Joshua would know where to come.

Michael took another sip of his beer while his pipe smoldered, tiny tendrils of smoke rising from the bowl and creeping from the mouthpiece. Frank stopped by as Michael set down his tankard, adding fresh ale to the mug. A hefty layer of creamy foam floated atop the amber colored beer. Within a moment of the refill, one of the tavern maids brought a plate heavily laden with food and set it in front of Michael. The knight smiled as steam rose from the chunk of meat and roasted potatoes knowing this was the best part of his day. He wasn't working as a guard captain, the king gave him no assignments, and his beer would be uninterrupted for as long as he could see. *This is perfection.*

*   *   *

Joshua crept through the system of caves hidden under the hill in the woods. He could see very little around him but could hear perfectly fine. Faint voices. Water dripping. Some kind of whistling. Thankfully, the fire spell he held at the ready provided enough light that he could see but only enough to walk through the narrow, rock-strewn pathway. Stalactites reached for the floor and Joshua weaved between them as he walked, also keeping an eye out for their floor-bound cousins. Water flowed down the rocky formations in the cave. As he stepped around a crystalline column, an icy drop of water splashed against the top of his head, the droplet racing for the back of his neck soon thereafter. Footsteps. Maja walked behind him but not as quietly. The soles of her slippers whispered against the moist stone beneath them.

Joshua followed the path and went around a corner and started descending again. This path had dropped significantly since they entered the cave. Joshua saw the flickering of some light at the end of the path; he slowed down and watched the flicker as it danced on the moist wall of the cave. He saw no shadows from people or anything else and resumed walking at his previous speed toward the end of the path. He needed to reach the end of the path and see from where that light came. Surely, it would be the same place he was hearing the whispered voices. As he approached the end of the path, he saw a large, cavernous area opened on the other side. He stopped before the opening to the cavern and Maja tapped him twice on the shoulder as she lined up behind him, her own spells at the ready. Joshua listened to the jumbled whispering and counted to five before he launched himself into the cavern.

He stopped the instant he entered the cavern. Maja bumped into his back not anticipating his hastened halt. Joshua released his spells, took two steps, and gaped at the whole cavern. Like most caverns, this was a rocky, dark place; however, this one's walls were scrawled with foreign runes the same as he saw at the opening. Just like those earlier runes, these also emitted a faint purple light that pulsed brighter and then dimmer in a cycle. The light almost seemed to match his breathing. Joshua inhaled and the runes seemed to get brighter and when he exhaled they grew dimmer. *That's odd.* In the center of the room, on a flattened rock that served as a dais, stood a stone altar. This was a different rock than the rest of the surrounding area, a clear sign that it was brought here for some unknown purpose. In the ceiling above the altar Joshua saw six lanterns arranged in the shape of Deja the Phoenix, the constellation by which travelers found their bearings when lost. This was the sources of the light in the cavern.

Joshua, feeling something forcefully pulling him toward the altar, walked up to the stone slab and looked at what sat on its surface. Once he could see the top of the slab he saw yet more of the purple runes and seven midnight black pieces of some unknown material laid out in the shape of a sword blade. His heart started thundering in his ears as he looked at the shards. They were clearly from a sword blade, but he wasn't sure who would have wielded such a weapon. He continued looking at the sword fragments until Maja said something and startled him back to the matter at hand.

"These are Vor runes," she said.

Joshua suddenly realized whose sword the fragments were from. "Vor'Kath's sword!"

"What's that?" Maja asked, turning away from the runes carved into the walls.

"These are fragments of a Vor sword! *This* is Vor'Kath's sword, or what remains of it. The Children of Chaos are gathering the fragments from his sword!"

Maja walked over to the altar. "How can you be sure?"

"Right here," Joshua said pointing at the biggest collection of fragments in the middle of the blade. "This is where Michael's own Vor sword broke through Vor'Kath's during our fight near the southern ocean."

"What do you think they were doing with it?" Maja asked.

"I honestly have no idea, but it looks like the whole sword wasn't recovered."

"I'll see if there is anything we can glean from these runes in the walls," Maja said.

The other Mage stepped away from the Altar and Joshua continued staring at the pieces of the broken Vor sword that did not belong here in this cavern. There was no way anyone should have been able to recover such a weapon after the way it shattered. Yet here the shards sat in a cave in the tundra on an altar of stone with engraved runes on the surface of the altar. The light from the runes still seemed to match Joshua's breathing, something he was sure was simply in his head. He placed a hand on the altar and for an instant the lights showing in the runes changed color. The change only showed for the briefest flash and was back to the soft purple color before Joshua had time to register if it truly shifted.

Something pulled at him, beckoned him toward the shards. He looked around and saw Maja was intently inspecting a set of the runes on the wall. Joshua, his hand still on the altar, lifted his hand ever so slightly from the smooth, nearly polished surface of the altar. The thing that called to him, persuasive, formidable, and intense, continued to pull at him, urging him to touch one of the shards. A voice in his mind screamed for him not to touch the shards, but this call was stronger than his willpower. He could do nothing to stop his hand from creeping toward the broken sword pieces. Something about the shards promised power. Unlimited, ever-increasing power. He could rule with such power. His fingers grew closer to the largest of the shards. He fought so hard against the power that yanked at him so intensely. His fingers, not even a centimeter from the fragment, lowered and just barely touched the sword piece.

Fizz. A portal opened somewhere in the cavern. Joshua turned around as fast as he could as a bolt of lightning zapped through the air over his shoulder. He felt the heat from the spell and heard it crash into the ceiling, spraying chips of stone everywhere. Time slowed as another bolt of lightning zagged through the air, again missing him. The jagged, blue-white fingers of Magic snapped past him and slammed into the wall not far behind him. Joshua looked for the person casting the spells.

Hags. Two stepped out from the path he walked moments before and into the cavern. They wore simple robes and had matted hair with pieces of teeth, feathers, bones, and other items mixed into their tangled strands. Necklaces of fingers and ears on pieces of string hung around their necks. Their faces, hideous and gaunt, sported clusters of warts around their beaklike noses and their cleft chins. Violet eyes glared at Joshua, the same color as the runes carved into the walls. Their skin, pale as the snow, had clearly not seen direct sunlight in years, if ever. They snarled at Maja and Joshua, showing their yellowed, pointed teeth and forked tongues. They hardly resembled the Elves they once were hundreds of years ago. Joshua nearly pitied these monstrous creatures but knew they were feral and incapable of processing emotions. *Witches!* Joshua thought. Rumors said a group of them lived in the tundra, but he forgot until just this moment. Now he had to deal with them.

The hags split up as they entered the cavern; one went to the left while the other went right toward Maja. Joshua wasted no time and started throwing spells as soon as he could. The hag furthest from Maja was his target. A stream of liquid fire leapt from Joshua's hand, singing feathers and hair from the witch before she moved behind a rocky pillar. Yet another bolt of lightning flashed through the air and Joshua reciprocated with his own, catching the hag in her shoulder. Her arm flopped to the ground and squirmed. A howling screech came from behind the rock and the hag rushed out spells at the ready. Joshua threw another stream of fire which caught the witch squarely in the chest. She was engulfed in a moment, stopped running, fell to the ground, and writhed in agony for a few moments before finally going still. The fire continued to smolder long after the hag stopped moving.

Joshua turned around and prepared another spell, this one a blast of lightning, and saw Maja taking down the hag that approached her with grace and fluidity. As Joshua turned, another spell shot forth from the path that led to the cavern. He threw his prepared lightning spell in that direction and heard a chittering as his spell landed only among the rocks and crystalline formations of the cave system. Joshua prepared another spell, moved toward the opening as silently as he could and waited. A head and arm peeked out from behind the edge of the opening and Joshua threw a spell at the hag without any hesitation. The lightning bolt contacted with her forehead and the body dropped limp within an instant. Maja looked to Joshua and motioned her approval. Joshua sighed in relief as the sounds in the cave died with the last hag.

"*Vile* beasts," Joshua spat as Maja knelt to look at the now-deceased hag with the hole through her skull.

"You should find some pity in your heart for them, Councilor. They didn't choose to become what they are. The Dark Mages manipulated them into what they are today. Also, we invaded their home, and they were protecting what they think is theirs," Maja argued.

"You've learned well to tug at my heartstrings, but right now isn't the time, Maja. Especially not for something so grand as pity. They are the product of choices others have made but also those they themselves made."

Maja looked up from investigating the last hag to fall. "Aren't we all?"

"You're right about that," Joshua said, looking intently at Maja. "I won't pity those creatures for their station in life."

"Choose how you wish. I pity this one who died so needlessly," she said, standing.

Joshua looked at the still smoldering hag not far from him and sighed. *I didn't need to be so aggressive,* he acknowledged. He dreaded that thought as soon as it started floating around in his head. While he disliked needless killing, this was necessary. They attacked first, and he merely defended himself. Perhaps the level of aggression he showed in response to theirs was needless. He could have used a less aggressive spell to defuse the situation differently. He took inventory of their situation and told himself to remember this in the future. Some situations could be dealt with in less violent ways.

With the witches dead, and their deaths considered, Joshua looked once more at the altar in the center of the room. The moment his eyes fell on the polished, carved stone he felt an unrelenting force calling to him the same as before. Something about the shards bothered him. *What did the witches want with them?* Other questions bounced through his head. What was the connection between the Children of Chaos and these witches? Were the Children seeking help with something beyond their power? What could possibly be beyond the power of the Children of Chaos? So many unanswered questions glided through the ether of his mind, all with no discernable answers. Joshua took another step toward the altar and felt the force that pulled on him growing stronger. Another step. Another.

He once again stood at the altar, the shards of what he knew to be Vor'Kath's sword laid out before him, as if an offering. To whom, he didn't know. Again, he noticed the fainted changes in the glowing runes carved into the stone slab. *Reach,* a slithering voice called within him. *Touch.* He fought against the urge, pushed at the shimmering darkness that sat in his mind. That gnashed at him. He turned his attention to the light within his mind. The Allfather. He closed his eyes and inhaled deeply. The Allfather guided him through life. Yet… Power could be his right now. He needed to only reach and touch one of these shards and cast the appropriate spell. He could absorb the power contained within these pieces of pure Magic. His fingers felt the throb of that promised power earlier as they ever so briefly grazed the surface of the shard before the witches attacked.

"I think I've seen these symbols before," Maja's voice echoed from behind him.

"You recognize them?" he asked.

If Maja answered, he couldn't hear her. Every bit of his attention focused on the shards. All he could see were the shards. They seemed to hum, as if they called to him. He couldn't ignore their crooning any longer. Joshua reached his hand toward the shards, his hand creeping toward the dark sword fragments. His vision blurred around the edges as he reached, the shards the only thing he could see any longer. They seemed to grow larger as his hand drew closer. He had to touch them, to feel the power he had no doubt surged through them still. He knew the Vor were beings of pure Magic. He cast a spell of theirs before and since then craved to feel that power again. He wanted the power. No, he *needed* it. He would simply touch…

Cold. Anguish. Despair. Heat. Each of them shot up his arm the moment his skin contacted the largest shard. Despite the faintest touch being the only thing connecting him to the shards, his hand lurched forward, and his fingers closed around the entirety of the shard. He couldn't release his hand and the sensations grew stronger, swirled, magnified until soon everything was just the sensation of heat and cold pulsing up his arm. Darkness enveloped him. Time stopped. Power washed over him. The shard's power. The power of…something familiar yet unknown. In the darkness Joshua saw two pinpoints of light, the faintest contrast against the darkness that made night seem like dawn. These pricks of light shot forward until they turned into eyes. Terrible and dark, they stared into him, into his soul. He tried to run, to hide, to release the shard in his hand but, despite the screaming in his mind, he remained trapped by this strange, dark abomination.

The power of the shard continued to pulse up his arm. He tried to fight, to resist. He felt his willpower begin to flicker like the flame of a candle that caught a gust of wind through a drafty window. He wavered ever so slightly; the sensation magnified. The power of the shard overwhelmed him, washed over him like a wave crashing against the sands of a beach. He felt swept away, yet the eyes continued to stare at him no matter where he looked. He couldn't escape them. Everything became the eyes. A voice, terrible and great, boomed within his mind and when it spoke the eyes changed. They matched the caliber of the voice, the wrath palpable within their domineering gaze. *Welcome, child,* the voice called to him. Joshua shuddered at the presence of the voice within his mind.

"Who are you?" Joshua called to the darkness.

The voice, still disembodied, echoed within his mind. "You have known me a long time, Joshua. Why do you resist?"

"What do you want?"

Everything changed. Joshua saw the mortal realm, trapped within a bubble. Not far from it floated another bubble, another realm. He couldn't see which realm. Another bubble. Another. Hundreds of them floating around him. Each one unique and independent of the others. Darkness. The space between the realms. It…moved. Joshua knew, now, who he spoke to. Who drew him to the shards. Who tempted him with power beyond his control and his thoughts since the day he joined the Order of Ravens. Kalathan. The Light Eater lurked as the space between these realms. A tendril of the darkness, somehow visible among the rest of the darkness, reached for Drendil, the first bubble Joshua saw. This finger of the abyss touched the mortal realm, *his* mortal realm, and the edges of the bubble cracked like a mirror before shattering completely. Flames. Chaos. Disorder. *Madness*. It spread across the image of Drendil the bubble still partially contained. The darkness around Joshua chuckled as the Madness spread. Another tendril of darkness touched the next realm. And the next. More of these fingers of darkness appeared until every bubble shattered and Joshua floated amid thousands of shattering mortal realms.

"Witness me," the voice boomed in his mind again.

Hundreds of voices called out at the same time "He brings Chaos with him."

"Stop him while you can," another voice called from amid the hundreds.

Yet another voice, this one familiar, called. "Release the shard, Joshua!"

"You're killing us!"

A familiar voice called from the sea of darkness. A voice he went years without hearing. One he hadn't heard since that day he thrust from his memory a long time ago. The Celebration of Honey. Prikea. The voice called to him. Soothed him. His mother. Her voice, also disembodied, spoke to him. The darkness around him shuddered. Shifted. Flickered.

"You must stop this, son. You're the only one who can."

Everything around him faded. The darkness, somehow combatted by his mother's voice, receded, shrieking as it rushed back into the shard. Joshua's hand, free of his own control, released the shard. The pulsing heat and cold stopped once his fingers released the sword fragment. Joshua inhaled deeply, gasped for the air his lungs so desperately needed. He fell to his knees and wavered before tipping backwards onto the ground. The cavern around him spun.

"Councilor!" Maja gasped and rushed toward him, breaking her focus from a cluster of runes carved deep into the wall.

"Kalathan is coming. He wishes to destroy not only our realm but every mortal realm."

"How do you know this?"

"I touched a shard," Joshua said, pointing at the altar.

Maja shot him a glance as she helped him regain his footing. "By the Allfather's best codpiece, why would you do such a reckless thing?"

"It was beyond my control. I lost myself for a moment."

"Will you be fine?" Maja asked, releasing Joshua once he felt steady on his feet again.

"I think so. We must destroy this place and these," he said waving his hand at the fragments on the altar. "I'll cast a spell of pure light. That should solve this issue."

Joshua used the spell he received as a gift from Vor'Leanne and flooded the altar with liquid light. The darkness fought against the light, starting first as spots that quickly grew into large streaks of black in the midst of the golden light. The pool of light and dark sizzled and splattered until the sword fragments started to dissolve. Within a few minutes, nothing remained on the altar other than a puddle of the liquid light. The ground trembled and Joshua knew the caves were unsafe to remain in any longer. He grabbed Maja's hand, opened a portal, and rushed through it as he dragged her with him. They stepped through the portal back onto the tundra amid the trees that surrounded the hill. Joshua closed the portal and turned to look at the hill. The runes carved into the entrance now glowed red, the light already intense and only growing stronger with every second that passed.

The ground shook, violent and terrible tremors making it difficult to remain standing. Joshua looked beyond the entrance of the cave, saw stalactites falling from the ceiling, and heard them shattering against the hard, rock floor of the caves. A large split appeared in the edges of the cave entrance, splitting the runes in two. An instant later, the entire hill collapsed in on itself, as if the caverns below were the maw of some great beast swallowing everything in its way. Joshua blinked, unsure of what he had just witnessed. Without their cave, the witches, if any survived the skirmish today, would have to move elsewhere. Joshua made a mental note to send someone up here later to investigate. *Vile creatures,* he thought. Still, seeing the collapsed cave, a thought stuck with him. He had wondered about this just after the witches attacked.

"Someone knew we were here," Joshua said, releasing Maja's hand.

Maja blinked before responding. "That's crazy, Councilor."

"Is it? Someone knew when I was looking at the shards on the altar. I was distracted and wouldn't hear the hags' approach. This whole thing was a trap!"

"Who would have set something like this up though?"

"Esram," Joshua said, looking at the hole in the ground where the hill once stood.

"Who is Esram?" Maja asked.

Chapter Fourteen

There was a long pause as Joshua continued to stare at the hole in the ground where the hill and the cave system used to be. He heard Maja's question but needed time to process everything. Before explaining, he needed to prove his theory correct. Joshua knew Esram was *involved* in the attack on Anselin but had no real way of knowing if he was the mastermind or simply a pawn. After Joshua watched Gordack's memories, seeing Esram kill King Erkan made it seem that Esram was the one behind the entire plot. However, after watching the evidence left behind by the traces, Joshua wasn't sure where Esram fit into the plot against the kingdom. *Is Esram smart enough to handle all this planning?*

"Who is Esram, Councilor?" Maja asked again, finally breaking Joshua's gaze from the collapsed hill.

Joshua quickly explained everything he learned while delving Gordack's memories with Farryn, Bryne, and the headmaster. "I need to speak with the headmaster about what we found here. He needs to know about this."

"Don't mention that you touched one of the shards," Maja suggested.

Joshua stopped, looked at Maja with a great deal of curiosity, then touched a finger to his nose and nodded. He opened a portal and stepped through, finding himself standing directly outside the headmaster's office. Joshua felt spells on the inside and knew that Sanev already had someone in his office but decided, given the nature of his mission, that an intrusion would be welcomed. Delays in sharing knowledge of this nature could mean the end of life as they knew it and not just for Drendil. Joshua kicked himself for touching one of the shards but knew that the vision that came with that action is what he needed to see. Now, others needed to hear about what he found in the cave. Joshua reached for the doorknob and went into the headmaster's office without knocking.

"Councilor, what is the meaning of this intrusion?" Sanev said, standing behind his desk. "I am in the middle of a meeting with your counterpart for the war school trying to figure out what we can do about the Children of Chaos."

"Two things. First, I have more information about the attack on Anselin that you will want to hear. Second, that's a conversation that *I* should be included on, correct?"

Syndra, the War Councilor, looked to Joshua with eyes narrowed. "I suggested that we include you, but *you* were not at the College and this matter is vitally important."

"Please, no fighting. Councilor Joshua, I understand your instincts of barging in, but can this *not* wait a few additional minutes?"

"It cannot. You need to hear this as immediately as possible."

"Fine," Sanev growled. "Would you please excuse us for a moment, Councilor Syndra?"

Syndra stood, bowed at the headmaster, glared at Joshua, and left the headmaster's office. The door closed before Sanev started speaking again, this time his voice quieter than it had been. Joshua knew *that* was a sign of true perturbation when dealing with the headmaster. Joshua prepared for the quiet berating session that he deserved after all that happened today.

"What was that display, Councilor? You have no idea what we were discussing or how close we were to reaching an answer on the matter of the Children. How *dare* you barge in here and demand my time when I'm in the middle of a meeting with—"

"The Children of Chaos found the broken pieces of Vor'Kath's sword," Joshua interrupted. "They've done something with them, but I don't know what. A piece of the sword seems to be missing. While investigating some caverns in the tundra, some hags attacked Maja and me. They've been taken care of, and the shards and cavern have been destroyed. Given this information, added to what we learned about Anselin, I believe there are definite problems on the horizon, Headmaster. Please continue to grit your teeth at me, if you wish, but that will only delay every action that we should be taking to prevent whatever the Children have prepared."

Sanev inhaled sharply and visibly released the tension in his jaw and shoulders before replying. "What piece of the sword was missing? Also, how do you know the finders were the Children of Chaos?"

"I saw some spell traces outside the caves. They were from the same casters I saw in Anselin. I have no doubt that these are the Children of Chaos," Joshua replied quickly. "As for the missing piece, it looked like the hilt and a quarter of the blade was missing."

"What use would the Children have for a quarter of a Vor sword? That's completely illogical for them. I would think they should prefer the whole sword given the amount of power those blades contain."

"I believe the entire situation in the caverns was a trap. The hags knew the moment I…touched a shard…and chose that moment to attack," Joshua admitted.

"You *touched* the shards! Councilor, I must say this is quite beyond alarming to hear. You are supposed to be containing and eradicating Dark Magic, not allowing yourself to be tempted into trifling with it. What was your reasoning here?"

"Again, I believe this whole thing was set up so that I *would* touch the shards. There was something irresistible about them. I couldn't control myself as I touched them. Also, I saw a vision. It was like I was looking at the abyss and all the mortal realms. Once the darkness between the realms, which I assumed was Kalathan, reached into one, all of them started collapsing. I also heard some voices calling out as the realms started collapsing."

"This vision you saw makes sense. If the Children are, in fact, planning some kind of ritual to bring Kalathan into this realm then…" Sanev started then paused for the briefest of moments. "Allfather save us all that's why they need the hilt of the sword."

"I'm not following, Headmaster. What do you think they are planning?"

"I don't know all the details but there may be some kind of ritual. I would, as soon as you leave my office, speak with Averon, and see if he has any books on the subject. We must figure out what they are planning and stop it at once. Have you anything else for me?" Sanev asked.

"Do you have any information about Esram that you aren't telling me?"

"I'm afraid there's more to his story than I let on before, mostly for fear of retribution for my inaction," Sanev said, staring at the wall behind Joshua for a few moments before continuing on. "Well, about six months after I expelled him from the College, I received a flood of reminders that he should have been put down instead. Everything started as perceivable accidents at first. A barn burned down in a remote village, some cattle died, so on and so forth. Nothing that could really be attributed to Dark Magic use on its own.

"Well, then things got serious as Esram got more…daring with his experimentation. Long ago, a village of tribal hunters lived in the tundra not far from where you said you found the caverns. These hunters never posed a threat to the kingdom as they were a small community isolated in an area where no one lived. We kept tabs on them for trading purposes but that was it. Well, one day their chief came to visit the College and requested some aid in dealing with wolf-like monsters. I thought nothing of this because they were hunters, and such things should have been within their bailiwick to deal with. We are Mages, after all. We don't really deal with these types of problems. I digress. About a month after the village chieftain left, rather upset I should say, a merchant arrived from their village to the north with a note addressed to me. The merchant was distraught and terribly shaken. When we pressed what he saw he proffered the note and left as promptly as he could. I should add, for clarification, that this note was written and signed in blood. Would you like to guess at what the note said?"

Joshua didn't even need to think about what the contents of the note might have been as deep within himself he already knew. "Kalathan."

"Precisely. Might you also know whose signature happened to be at the bottom of the page?" Sanev asked.

"Esram," Joshua said, again needing no time to think about the answer to the question.

"You are a shrewd one, Councilor. Now, getting back to this story. This note terrified me to my very core. After it made its way through the Councilors, including your predecessor Kerron, I took the Council and a handful of battlemages to the village to investigate what the merchant simply refused to talk about. Well, the sights were more devastating than I imagined. I dare not think about what we found, lest the memories keep me from sleeping. I asked Farryn after that day if she could cast a spell that would block the memories and she refused. Her rationale was that if I didn't live with the sight of those dead villagers every day then I would forget what led to that and another Esram would escape. At the time, I didn't agree with her and was, in fact, quite cross with her, but now I understand. My lapse in judgement resulted in the loss of so many lives and now threatens to bring so many more to their unfortunate and untimely end," Sanev said, pausing for so long that Joshua wasn't sure he would continue. "I still see their bodies at night when my eyes close, Councilor. They weren't simply killed. They were posed in crude, ritualistic poses with a myriad of props. The bodies had been placed in a circle around a small stone that I know now was a makeshift altar. The village chief's face was removed, and a large elk skull was placed over his head. I have yet to see anything as nightmarish as that scene."

"Why would he go through all that effort? What was the purpose of the mock ritual unless…" Joshua stated, letting his voice trail off as he thought. He stood. "I have to go, Headmaster. I just remembered seeing something about this in the library."

Joshua opened a portal and stepped through, bringing him to the College library's western wall. He grabbed the book he read before Maja took him to the tundra. This was the book with the image of Kalathan that seemed to move. He shuddered thinking about that image and how it appeared to move but knew there was something within the book that he needed. He stopped, looked at the shelf, and grabbed a couple other books, holding them all under his left arm. He took a step toward the portal but heard Master Averon calling for him to stop. Joshua didn't even turn to acknowledge the librarian before stepping through and closing the portal. Once back in the headmaster's office, he carefully dropped the tomes onto Sanev's desk, keeping the book with the moving image of Kalathan in his left hand.

"What is all of this?" Sanev asked, beyond confused by what was happening.

"First, I need to find the ritual details. Second, I need your help with this. I believe this book holds what we are looking for, but it may also be in these others. Lastly, I will need to apologize to Master Averon for stealing his books after all this is finished," Joshua answered, cracking open the book in his hand.

"Please tell me you didn't just grab these and come back through the portal."

"If that's what you don't want to hear, I'm fine not admitting anything."

"By the Allfather."

"He can help us when we've found what we're looking for, Headmaster," Joshua said.

Joshua flipped through pages within the book, skipping the image of Kalathan that he dreaded to even think about. When he didn't find what he sought, he grabbed the next book in the pile, then the next, until he had exhausted every book that he had stolen from the library. He sat down in the leather chair across the desk from Sanev, slumping as far as he could while still sitting in the chair. After a few minutes of staring at a blank spot in the wall, he sat up and grabbed the first book again, carefully examining every page he could until…

"Allfather save us, I hope that's not what they're planning!" Joshua exclaimed.

*   *   *

Esram once again found himself waiting on the other Children to arrive. He leaned against the thick, rough trunk of the tree in the middle of the field. Waiting like this made him grow weary and impatient, especially since the sun was still above the horizon. Discretion could hardly be guaranteed during the day. *Why can't they simply show up on time?* He pondered to himself as a corvid of some kind or another flew up and perched itself in the tree branches above him. He closed his eyes and listened to the bird chitter as Daethis approached. He couldn't hear her footsteps as she walked quietly enough that he wouldn't hear her even without the bird overhead. She knelt next to him and put her hand on his knee, squeezing gently.

"Sorry to be late, my dearest. I had to take a few extra portals to get here," she said.

Esram breathed in the lavender and vanilla of her perfume, his eyes still closed. "You're forgiven. The others are who I worry about."

"Tomorrow is the night. Are you excited?"

"Immensely," Esram said, opening his eyes and looking into hers.

"Where will we begin?" Daethis asked.

"Not until the others are here, dearest."

"Right. I forgot that you don't like divulging *any*thing until we are together as a group."

"I like not to repeat myself."

As Esram finished saying that, two portals opened. Oleg stepped out of one and Maja from the other. Both approached the tree where Daethis and Esram knelt. Sadly, Daethis removed her hand before the others could see. Esram doubted their relationship was a secret to the others, but Daethis preferred the subtlety of their lies and deception. Esram broke his eyes away from her gently-shaped face and made eye contact with both Oleg and Maja as they approached. They appeared not to realize they both arrived at the same time. Esram doubted Oleg knew much of what was going on around him at any given time but would never voice that opinion aloud when the larger Elf was nearby.

"Welcome," Daethis said, her lilting voice cool and collected.

"How are the witches?" Esram asked, though he already knew the answer.

"Dead," Maja replied without hesitation.

"What! How could you let that hap—" Daethis started.

Esram held up a hand, calming her down. "Remember, it was all part of the plan. The witches have served their purpose. We, our master included, have no further need for them."

"Still, that seems like a shame," Daethis argued.

"You will understand in due time," Esram said, standing. "Let's speak in full about all of this on the Holm. Oleg, could you make the portal?"

"Yes," the brutish Elf said before casting the spell.

Esram stepped through followed by Daethis, Maja, and finally Oleg. The smell of grass and saltwater assaulted Esram's nose while the sounds of waves crashing against the beaches filled his ears. Around him he saw the natural bowl-like shape of the island with the altar in the center of the basin. The stone slab in the center of the basin, surrounded by shorter pieces of stone formed an altar with seats surrounding it. Esram longed for their ritual but calmed himself, knowing they had to get all the pieces in places first. *Everything will happen in time.*

"About the witches in the tundra?" Daethis asked, her voice trailing off as she reached the end of her question rather than finishing it strong.

"Yes, Maja, what happened with the witches? Did everything go according to plan?" Esram asked, looking from Daethis to Maja as Oleg closed the portal.

"Everything went according to plan," Maja answered. "The Councilor touched a shard not once, but twice. The trap worked exactly the way we needed it to."

"Excellent. That should mean he is conflicted about power and corruption and everything else he once held dear. What does he know about us?" Esram asked.

"I still don't understand why we couldn't let the witches escape and live. They could come in handy later," Daethis complained, folding her arms across her chest.

"The witches serve no more purpose now that we have this," Esram said, summoning the freshly reforged Vor dagger that had once been the hilt of a longer, slightly curved sword.

The dagger, simply a reforged portion of the Vor sword, looked like a smaller version of a blade used to fight Sir Michael the Valiant and Sir Joshua the Ravenous in the southern portion of the continent less than a year ago. The handle remained the same length as it had before, roughly the length of Esram's forearm, but the blade was significantly shorter because of where the original had shattered. The single-edged point was reformed in what had once been a wickedly jagged scar where Magic had seeped from the shards of the blade. The witches, as Esram knew, performed many unsanctioned rituals with the Vor and communed with the foreign realm to gain access to their purer Magic. With this power at hand, they were able to reforge the blade and imbue it with the same strength it once held. That power now surged through Esram's arm as the others looked on, ogling the glistening, midnight black blade. Oleg reached for the hilt of the dagger, but Esram unsummoned it and the blade vanished from sight, tucked safely away where the others couldn't reach it no matter how hard they may try.

"Such a beautiful weapon exists for only one purpose, Oleg. We must be careful with it until its time comes forth," Esram warned.

"Are we set with everything we need for the ritual?" Maja asked, changing the subject.

"The only thing we have left is to kidnap our sacrifice. Have we figured out his patterns yet?" Esram asked.

"We know he spends a lot of time in the castle and a tavern near his house. We can grab him as he stumbles home from a night drinking. Doing that should give us the lowest number of witnesses possible. Thoughts?" Daethis asked.

Esram thought for a few seconds about this. "I like it. Oleg, you grab the drunk and Maja take care of the squire as we discussed before."

"It will be my pleasure," Maja said, grinning and rubbing her hands together mischievously. "The Councilor is such a short-sighted fool that he won't even realize what's going on until it's too late."

"What does he know about us?" Daethis asked.

"He delved the child that *you*," Maja said pointedly at Esram, "let get away so now he knows Esram's face, name, and background. He's a nosy one. Also, after he investigated Anselin, apparently he's picked up our traces. He saw them outside the caverns, which was a terrible idea for getting him to come to the cave."

"I didn't think he would run straight to the College and tell them what happened. Nor did I expect anyone to delve him. Had I known either of those would have happened, I would have put him down as he ran away," Esram replied.

Maja snorted. "Have you become so soft that you are willing to show mercy now?"

"Eh, it's more fun this way. For the rest of his life, he will carry a memory of what I did to that excuse of a king."

"You're a sick bastard, Esram," Daethis said, stepping away from the group.

"This is why I was chosen to lead our group. We must be harsh to bring forth our desires. The world would just as easily put us down for practicing what we do," Esram proclaimed. "Soon, we will rule those who would rather we die than succeed. I'm willing to go the distance to see this through, but I'm not getting the sense that all of you are equally motivated."

"We all want the same things, Esram. I was just not expecting you to say anything close to that is all," Daethis said, flashing a cruel glance his way.

"We're lovers, and you thought that means I'm soft-hearted?"

"Esram!" Daethis cried. "I told you not to tell anyone else."

"In his defense, we both knew," Maja said quietly.

"The child worries me," Oleg said.

"There's no worries to be had with him—"

"Even if he grows up wanting to seek revenge for the trauma we have undoubtedly caused him?" Daethis asked, turning around to face the group fully. She stood with her nose nearly in the air, full of the lesser nobility that came with her bloodline.

"That thought has crossed my mind, but by the time he grows up to even understand the truest meaning of revenge, this world will have been smoldering for a decade. We *will* bring the Light Eater into this world. Mark my words!"

"As long as you have considered the possibility," Daethis scoffed.

"We are ready to enact this plan tomorrow evening?" Esram asked receiving nods from the other Children. "Good. Let's bring about the end of this mortal realm."

Satisfied now that their formal business was concluded, Maja and Oleg created portals and left the Iron Holm. Daethis turned her back on Esram, who knew she was pouting simply by the way her face wrinkled the sides of her neck. Not wanting to hear anything further on the subject, Esram turned and walked up the hill to his south. As he reached the top, the salt-filled breeze began playing with his hair. His eyes watered as the wind swept across his face. Finally at the top, he breathed in the smells of the ocean, the salty spray of the ocean's waves as they crashed against the stones beneath him and the acrid stench of decaying sea life. Overhead, he heard gulls squawking as they circled the island. As he stood there, admiring the chaos that surrounded him, a pair of willowy arms wrapped themselves around his waist and squeezed gently. Daethis. He placed his hands on hers and returned the gentle squeeze. He closed his eyes as she whispered in his ear.

*   *   *

Once again Joshua found himself envious of Freenel Manor's luscious grounds. Whoever George used to maintain the lawn and gardens was a master of all things green. Joshua stopped to examine a gorgeous, blooming bush. The flowers started as a lilac color that faded to white at the end of the petals. Looking closer, he saw many bees clumsily bumping into the flowers, digging into the pollen, and then buzzing away. He often forgot to appreciate the smaller things in life, like the flowers and busyness of life that surrounded him. Everything seemed random to him, but, as a former priest, he knew the Allfather had planned everything with specific purposes. Life was balance, a lesson he still felt he needed to learn even after all his time studying the things around him. The bees pollinated the flowers, which then brought more bees who gathered the pollen and made honey, which people and animals consumed. Without honey, life would surely continue, but without the bee, even sustaining life would grow difficult. Something so small as humble bees were essential to the continuation of life for every species.

As Joshua contemplated the essential status of the bees, the door to Freenel Manor opened and Michael strode out, unaware of Joshua, who stood in the grass just off the main path. Michael should have noticed Joshua, though. He didn't think himself *that* invisible, watching the bees. Still, Michael strolled to the end of the path and turned to the right, heading up the lane. Even without speaking to him, Joshua knew Michael was heading to the Cave, despite his desire to stop drinking. Finally, curiosity overwhelmed Joshua and he called out to Michael, who started and turned around, his arms tense and a surprised look on his face.

"Joshua! I was just on my way to find you. I was hoping you would be at your estate."

It was such an obvious lie. Michael would know Joshua rarely spent time at his estate. He spent a vast majority of his time in any of the libraries he had access to, either at the College or with the Battlemages where he served during his time in the army. *Oh, Michael.* He expected more from his friend than this.

"Are you heading to the Cave again? I thought you said you wanted to stop going there?"

"That's not where I'm heading, Joshua."

"Like I said before, *you* alone can be the one to make that change in your life if that's what you want. No one else can make that choice for you."

"I understand that. I just…I can't get over what we saw in Anselin. Death surrounds us, Joshua. I can't take it."

"I know what you're going through. There are other ways to get through this besides going to the Cave. Let's talk about this—"

"Just because I'm coping differently than you or am having a hard time with things I have seen and done, doesn't mean I'm wrong! Stop trying to change me into whatever image of me you have developed in your head. Now, if you'll excuse me, I really need a drink."

Joshua stood, still amid Freenel's grounds. A torrent of frustration, anger, and disappointment swirled within him, fighting for dominance in the sudden deluge of emotions that formed. How dare Michael assume anyone was trying to force him to change? Did he really think so little of Joshua that he would jump to that conclusion? They knew each other for the better part of a decade. Surely in that time, Michael would have learned that Joshua only wanted the best for Michael. That was the foundation of their friendship. From the moment they met in Feldring all those years ago, that's all Joshua wanted. It started with getting the nightmares to stop and evolved into this fight over assumptions.

A few moments passed, stretching like a pile of warm taffy candy on a mid-summer day. Joshua continued to allow his emotions to stew, the frustration and anger shoving the disappointment aside. He gritted his teeth and took a step forward, wanting to follow and confront Michael, but stopped. Doing just that would help nothing in this situation. Confrontation would only lead them both further down a rabbit hole that Joshua didn't need to explore. Quickly, he performed the same meditation exercise he completed thousands of times before, casting his emotions and sensations out of his mind until he floated, serene, within himself. Breath rushed in through his nose and meandered out through his pursed lips. He continued this breathing until his face relaxed and he felt detached from himself. He was merely a soul floating within his body, like a leaf on a still pond.

Opening his eyes, he created a portal, no longer caring about the Magic restrictions in the city, stepped through and found himself in the College library, one of his sanctuaries where problems escaped him within the leaves of the myriad of tomes that he could explore. Thanks to the Children of Chaos, Joshua still had much research to complete as he looked for the specifics of the ritual he believed they planned. His rationale was, that by knowing the ritual, he could stop it. The idea seemed sound as he thought it over. Now, standing in the middle of the library, he wondered if he needed to do more.

Chapter Fifteen

ichael trotted down the stairs as he left the castle after a long day of managing the day's guard shifts. The sun, now descending beyond the walls of the city, threw a multitude of color swatches into the sky far overhead. Streaks of pastel oranges, yellows, purples, and reds flooded the once white, fluffy clouds that littered the sky. Michael stopped at the bottom of the steps and admired the clouds as they floated by, bathed in the myriad of rich colors of sunset. He couldn't remember the last time he simply stopped to admire the clouds. *Caw. Caw.* A crow, perched on a nearby wall, took to flight, calling its perturbances as it flew low across the courtyard. Michael hardly thought anything of the presence of the crow. They were a common bird in Drendil and in Shemont. Something tickled the back of his mind that lately he'd seen or heard a lot more of them, but he ignored the thought and started walking through the courtyard in roughly the same direction the crow flew.

Michael crossed the courtyard and exited through the portcullis in the wall that surrounded the castle. He stopped and spoke with the guards, ensuring everything was orderly as they started their shift and examined the controls for the metal latticed gate before moving on. Satisfied with what he found, Michael made his way south through the market where merchants continued packing up their unsold wares after a long day on their feet hawking goods. Some took their goods into shops, while others packed wagons that would make their way to other cities across the kingdom in time. He saw a blacksmith grabbing an empty weapons rack and armor stand and stopped to speak with the smith.

"Good evening, sir," Michael called.

"How can I help you, my lord?" the blacksmith asked, bowing slightly.

"I'm no lord. Are you still taking business today?"

"For a knight of the kingdom, I will take business until I cannot remain on my feet," the smith said as he placed the racks on the stairs of his shop and walked over. "What can I do for you tonight?"

Michael removed his sheathed dagger from his belt and handed it to the smith. "I just need this sharpened. It's been too long, and I accidentally broke my whetstone. Do you also have any of those handy?"

The smith drew the dagger and inspected the blade with his calloused thumb. His face scrunched as he felt the edges of the blade, but he said nothing. After a few moments, he sheathed the dagger, held up a finger, and went into his shop. The door remained open after the smith entered and Michael heard the faintest whisper of some grinding while he waited. Michael hadn't expected the smith to stop what he was doing for him, but he smiled regardless. *Perhaps I'll ask him to sharpen my sword while he's at it,* Michael thought. He stepped around the small table and into the smithy where he saw the smith seated with a pedal-powered grindstone. The smith worked the dagger's blade from hilt to tip first on one side then the other. He lifted the oiled dagger from the wheel only to inspect it and change sides. The smith worked meticulously, and, in a few minutes, he stopped pumping his foot on the pedal. Even without the power of his foot the wheel kept spinning for a few seconds before it slowly came to a stop. The smith grabbed a rag from a table nearby and wiped the excess oil from the blade, removing any dirt and debris that came from the grindstone. He returned the dagger to the sheath and handed everything back to Michael. The smith kept his hand stretched toward Michael and looked at the sword, tilting his head toward it briefly. Michael drew his sword and handed it, hilt first, to the smith who sat back at the grindstone and started sharpening the blade.

Michael walked around the smithy, admiring the weapons and armor the smith displayed. Cuirasses, pauldrons, greaves, swords, axes, and maces all hung on the walls in various places. They ranged from simple pieces with no decoration to ornate pieces the king would proudly use. Michael found himself admiring a sword with a pair of engraved rubies in the pommel. The rubies, large and flattened, shone beautifully with a gold-flecked griffon etched into the surface. Michael looked to the blacksmith who was busily working the edges of Michael's sword. Seeing that the man was distracted, Michael grabbed the sword and examined it closer. He ran his fingers gingerly up the fuller in the blade and checked the balance of the blade. Everything pointed to the sword being exquisitely crafted. The castle blacksmith would be hard-pressed to craft something this pristine.

"Sir, I'm sorry to ask but could you put that piece back on the wall?" the smith asked, the grindstone still creaking.

"Of course. I'm sorry, I wanted to get a closer look at this one. How long did it take you to make that sword?"

"It took me a year. The king himself is coming in the morning to retrieve it. That's my most treasured creation."

"As it should be. I've never held a sword so wonderful before."

"Thank you, sir. Your sword here is nice. I'm guessing it came from Tabish?"

"It certainly did. His weapons are good, but after holding that one," Michael said, pointing at the king's sword, "I think I've ruined myself to his work."

"Don't feel that way. A rushed weapon will never feel the same as one where the smith took his time. Tabish is a wonderful smith. He just can't take his time as often because he works for the army. I, however, can take all the time I want," the smith said, standing and returning Michael's now-sharpened sword.

Michael carefully slid the sword into his sheath and grabbed his coin purse. "What do I owe you for this?"

"It's free of charge, sir. I only ask that you bring them back when they need sharpened. I can take care of your weapons from now on if you would like."

"I can't walk away without paying you. What would you charge a regular army soldier for sharpening two blades?"

The smith deflated slightly. "Ten pence, sir."

"Here you are," Michael said handing over the money plus some extra. "Thanks for staying open for me."

"You're too kind, sir," the smith said with a slight bow.

Michael left the smithy and continued walking south through the market. He walked past a cluster of food vendors who sold salt-cured meats, fruits, vegetables, and everything in between. They packed their wares into wagons attached to teams of horses to prepare for their journey to the next city. With Anselin now destroyed, Michael wondered how that would affect trade throughout the halves of the kingdom. The relationship between Elves and humans was always touchy for reasons Michael never fully understood. Part of that, he figured, was from him not being native to Drendil, but on the other hand, he doubted he would understand it even if he were from this continent.

Michael stopped at the edge of the market and waited for a train of merchant wagons to roll down the street on their way out of the city. He listened to the gentle creaking of the wagon wheels and looked down the road toward his favorite tavern. As he looked, he thought about the fight he and Joshua had the day before. Joshua. The Mage frustrated Michael at times. Michael wondered why Joshua felt the need to try changing everyone around him when he himself had his own flaws. Thinking of the fight churned a storm of emotions deep within Michael. He knew his drinking was problematic for maintaining a healthy life, but he wasn't sure he wanted to change himself. His experiences all troubled him. Death haunted him. He felt surrounded by death itself. What he said to Joshua the day before felt true enough. He was simply coping differently than Joshua who, instead of drinking to drown the memories, was burying himself in an endless string of books and studying. They each had their preferred vice.

The last of the merchant wagons rolled by Michael and he stood in the same place, looking longingly at the carved wooden sign hanging above his favorite tavern. The thought of Rosie's food made his mouth water, and he could nearly taste the beer already. He contemplated, instead, simply heading home to his humble knightly estate, and eating whatever food George had undoubtedly prepared. He would have some fresh ale there as well if he so much as implied a desire for ale. George would even offer to run to the Cave and get some ale from Frank who did send some home with the squire from time to time. Michael considered his options for a few moments before finally landing on stopping at the tavern for at least a few drinks and maybe some food before heading home. He hadn't mentioned to Frank that he was considering the cut back on his drinking as he wasn't sure how the man would take that news. Still, Michael was proud of himself for considering not stopping by the tavern at all. That had to be a step in the right direction.

Michael walked slowly toward the Cave, still contemplating his choice as he stood in front of the door. *You alone cane be the one to make that change,* Michael thought. Joshua's words bounced around his head as he reached for the door. The round metal knob felt good in his hand as he turned it. The latch moved with the same oiled fluidity it always did before finally giving way and allowing Michael to open the door. A small brass bell above the door *ding*ed to announce his presence to all inside. Michael took a step and crossed the threshold and suddenly felt at ease, his brain and stomach calming as he approached his typical stool and was handed his usual tankard filled with his favorite beer. Michael raised the tankard to his lips and sipped at the foam floating atop the amber-colored ale. He tipped the metal mug further and tasted the ale itself as it washed over his tongue. He held the beer in his mouth a few seconds and savored the slightly flowery taste. While he couldn't recall the name of the flower, he could picture its drooping purple petals that faded to white at the bottom.

Frank walked back over with a curious look on his face. "Eating here tonight or waiting until you get home?"

"That answer depends entirely on what Rosie has in the kitchen tonight."

"Roast beef with stewed potatoes and carrots or a venison stew."

Michael took another long drink from his mug while he thought about the choices. "Have a plate of the roast beef sent out when you get a chance, please and thank you."

"Want a refill of your beer while I'm here, Michael?"

"That sounds wonderful, Frank," Michael said, extending out his half-full tankard.

Marcy, this evening's tavern maid, brought the plate of steaming food out by the time Michael could take another drink from the tankard. She set the platter down and walked away while Michael quickly eyed the food. A hearty hunk of beef seated in a puddle of its own juices, red skin potatoes and carrots covered every part of the plate. Michael sometimes wondered how the Cave made money with such large portions, but he didn't care enough to ask Frank such a personal question as that. Scattered around the plate were also slivers of onions, cooked to a translucent perfection. He waited for the food to cool down enough to eat before digging into the potatoes first. He used a knife to cut the soft, whole potatoes into more manageable chunks. The smell of the roasted garlic, rosemary, and a touch of citrus tantalized him, begging for him to start eating already. He took another sip of the floral beer and started eating right away.

The thick chunk of meat fell apart as the fork moved through the strings of cooked beef. The potatoes smushed under the slightest pressure, and the carrots did nothing because they were carrots. Everything was tender, juicy, and exceptionally well-made. He took a silver coin from his pouch and flipped it to Frank, who looked confused until Michael pointed at his food with the fork and patted his stomach. Rosie would certainly appreciate the gift. He worried that Frank would see it as Michael saying something about Rosie not making enough money, but he had known Frank for long enough that if it were an issue, Frank would say something.

After finishing his meal, Michael loosened his belt to the next notch and leaned back, content, and happy. George cooked well, but when compared to Rosie, he was still learning how to mix flour and water without getting clumps. Michael finished his beer and decided against another. One beer was enough for him. He waved Frank over and asked his total for the evening.

"Given the thousand marks you gave me before, I still think you're in the black. If you want to throw more money at me, I won't stop you," Frank answered. "Are you sure you don't want another beer before you leave?"

Michael thought for a brief moment before answering. "Actually, let me get another refill while you're already here, Frank."

"Very well."

With his tankard filled again, Michael watched the bubbles slowly pop and removed his pipe and the small bag of tobacco from the pouch on his belt. He took a pinch of tobacco leaves from the back and pushed them into the bottom of the bowl, evenly coating the bottom. He then formed a ball with more of the tobacco which he placed atop the even layer on the bottom. Lastly, he sprinkled another pinch of loose leaves on top of the ball before striking a match. The flames took to the loose leaves, and he puffed at the mouthpiece pinched between his teeth. His mouth warmed as the smoke came through the polished wooden stem. He blew the smoke out the sides of his mouth as he continued to pull air through the pipe. Once he was satisfied with the amount of fire within his pipe, he vigorously waved the match to put out the flame and set the smoking splinter of wood on his empty metal plate.

With his elbows on the bar, feet on the crossbar near the bottom of the stool, and his pipe clenched between his teeth, Michael contentedly watched Frank work the tavern. The stout man rarely stopped walking. Back and forth from one end of the counter to the next, he constantly moved to fill drinks, take orders for the kitchen, or remove dirty mugs after customers left. Frank only stopped walking long enough to fill pitchers with more beer, then went back to serving his customers.

When Michael eventually finished his pipe, he finished his beer, and stood from his favorite stool, denying yet another refill. It was time to head home for the evening. While George learned not to fret so much about when Michael came home, Michael still didn't like making his squire concerned. George's stomach always wound into a knot worrying about where Michael was, even though Michael's schedule hadn't changed in a long time.

Michael removed a gold coin from his purse and left it on the counter for Frank before making his way to the door. The street was empty, as he expected this late in the evening. His eyes snapped to the center of the road, thinking he could still see where the hellhounds killed that unfortunate woman right outside the Cave about three years prior. Despite how long ago that was, he still looked to where her body fell. Though he couldn't see the blood anymore, that had washed away after countless rainstorms came through Shemont, he thought he could still see the imprints the hellhound's paws burned into the cobblestones. The heel of his boot scraped against one of the loosened stones that made up the street, and he started to fall, but caught his balance before it was too late. He quickly looked around to see if anyone saw that happen, embarrassed to still be so clumsy even as a Knight-Commander of the Royal Order of Drendil. Thankfully, the street was empty when he looked behind him. He turned back around to keep walking and…

Bumped into a gargantuan person who had not been there even a moment before. The Elf towered over Michael and was so wide at the shoulders that he consumed Michael's vision. His dark robes, hanging ominously still, reminded him eerily of Vor'Kath. These robes at least moved in the gentle breeze that danced down the street. Michael stepped back to avoid a confrontation, but, as the Elf raised his right hand, Michael's snapped to the hilt of his dagger, and everything went dark before he could even move the blade within its scabbard.

Chapter Sixteen

s Joshua walked toward the castle, he reflected on how he no longer dreaded these meetings with the king and headmaster. They happened so frequently that now even the Master General no longer felt the need to act as a gatekeeper for the Mages' arrivals. They were simply allowed to walk up to the king's office and await his permission to enter. Joshua was thankful that Jacob understood the gravity of the situation and these meetings to not interfere with them. Joshua hardly thought of Jacob doing his job as being an intrusion or anything along those lines. It simply felt like a hassle having to wait outside the castle for the man to come down and retrieve the visiting Mages. Joshua felt bad interrupting the king's busy days with what felt like less than an update on their progress, but the king himself insisted on having a daily meeting to discuss just that, so Joshua and Sanev complied.

Joshua had spent the last couple of days entirely in the library at the College, either the official one or the one the Dark Magic school maintained on their own. He scoured books for any details on the myriad of suspected rituals the Children of Chaos performed. The more he studied this group and their antics and rituals, the less he found himself understanding why Mages left the College to join them. There appeared to be too many rules and regulations within the Children of Chaos and even within their predecessor group, the Assembly of Mages. The number of rituals both maintained was mind-boggling as well.

Joshua reached the top of the shallow staircase that led to the castle and walked in through the open gate without any of the guards stopping him. They, at this point, should already recognize him as a regular visitor. Whether or not they knew his business, Joshua didn't care. He simply needed to be allowed into the castle without issue, something he thankfully was granted. He walked into the main hall of the castle and noted the servants cleaning and wondered why they didn't do that at night when the castle was closed to visitors. It would make more sense for them to clean at night, but Joshua figured this may be a reason he wasn't the person who ultimately made these decisions. Joshua guessed that was the king or queen. From the main hall, Joshua went through a doorway into a spiral staircase and went up two levels and left the staircase which led to a hallway with some patrolling guards. At the end of the hall, he found another staircase and climbed another two flights of stairs to yet another series of hallways. He walked down one, which had more guards stationed at various doors and patrolling. He passed the door marked with Deja, the phoenix constellation. This door, with the stars painted silver, marked the Master General's office. One guard, posted outside the office door, nodded ever so briefly as Joshua walked by. The next office, this door on the inside of the hallway, had a double door and a guard posted on each side of the door. This was the king's office. Joshua knocked and waited for the king's permission to enter.

As he waited, Joshua reflected that King Orson II had certainly calmed since taking on the responsibilities of being the sole ruler of the Kingdom of Drendil after the incident at Anselin. Those first few weeks were unpleasant for anyone around the king. Normally a level-headed person, Orson was on edge as he scoured through the laws and traditions, trying to decipher his obligations as the king. For so long, two kings oversaw the kingdom and Orson still seemed a little unsure how to handle the Elven half of the kingdom. During those couple weeks Orson's language showed itself as much gruffer than normal. On an ordinary day, Orson wasn't known for his pristine language when flustered, and anything would cause him to explode into a rage many would consider unfit for a king. Joshua heard whispered stories of the king's sharp tongue and fiery temper from the castle staff who thought they were talking quietly enough. Joshua found himself thanking the Allfather that nothing from the Anselin investigation caused him to personally see the king's ire. *May it forever stay that way,* he thought as the king called from the other side of the doors. As

Joshua opened the door, Headmaster Sanev walked up, rushing toward Joshua so they could both walk in together.

"Good morning, gentlemen," the king said, rising from behind his desk.

King Orson II, a regal and composed man, stood nearly two meters tall with midnight black hair with silver peppered throughout. Most of the lighter hairs gathered at his temples except for a small patch right at the top of his hairline. His steel grey eyes, which seemed as welcoming today as they did any other day, sat under thick, black eyebrows. His powerful jawline could cut gems if needed. Joshua had a hard time placing the king's age between his rigid posture and the still-youthfulness in his face. Joshua noted extra stubble growing under the king's flat nose. He knew Orson had ruled the kingdom for at least two decades, but by the smoothness of his face, except the hint of wrinkles around the edges of his eyes, it would be impossible to tell. The Duke of Griffin's Perch looked much more grizzled than the king, somehow. Joshua assumed some of that could be the result of the spell that befell the duke a few years prior.

As Joshua and Sanev entered the office, King Orson took his seat again. "What updates do you have for me today, Councilor?"

"Since the incident with the witches, I have scoured every text the College has concerning the rituals the Children of Chaos have performed or documented in the past. Thankfully, being an organization built of pride and acquired power, they document many of their processes," Joshua said.

"Not to rush you, Joshua, but I am a busy man what with the kingdom to rule. What have you found?"

Joshua quickly explained what he found in the caves in the tundra for the king. "All of this leads me to think they are planning a deeply upsetting ritual that involves the hilt of the Vor sword. While I have ideas about the nature of the ritual, I don't have any concrete evidence as to what they are preparing."

"Stop beating around the bush. Just say what you think they're planning, Councilor."

"Sorry, Highness," Joshua said. "I believe the Children of Chaos are planning to summon Kalathan into our realm. It may just be Esram planning this too."

"Allfather save us," Sanev breathed.

"By the Allfather!" King Orson slammed his fist on the top of his desk, startling Joshua. "What the *fuck* is bringing them to do *that*?"

"To be honest, they are a twisted little group, Highness," Joshua answered once his nerves settled.

"What gave you that inclination, Councilor? Was it the attack on Anselin, the assassination of my counterpart, or something else?" the king sniped.

"Sire, that's a bit unnecessary," Sanev said calmly.

"What I meant by that, Highness, was they seem to put their own needs in front of society's. They are simply doing what they think is for their greater good. It is no different than us doing what we can to put the Children down when we see fit."

The king merely grunted at this. "I still can't get over the fact they want to bring Kalathan *into* our realm. That baffles me."

"Is there nothing else this ritual could be doing?" Sanev asked.

"After the vision I got from touching one of the shards on that altar, I doubt they are doing anything less than summoning him," Joshua said.

King Orson's eyes snapped from Sanev to Joshua in an instant. "Hold on. You're saying you *touched* one of the shards?"

"Yes," Joshua answered without hesitation.

"I don't think I'll ever understand why you would do that, but let's move on," Orson said. "You were saying something about you think the Children are going to *summon* Kalathan into our world."

Joshua took a deep breath and quickly explained the vision he had when he held the shard of the Vor sword in his hand. He left out a few minor details, such as the voice at the end belonging to his own mother, but he told as much as he could. Joshua realized, telling Sanev and Orson about the vision, that he hadn't talked through what he saw during that vision before. It felt liberating to talk about it finally, though he knew the others in the room would have preferred him not touching the shard. That amount of pure darkness could be dangerous to anyone, especially someone who swore an oath to eradicate Dark Magic throughout Drendil. Joshua knew that what he did was dangerous, but sometimes a risk needed to be taken in order to take the next step toward saving the world. *Sometimes risks are with the cost,* Joshua thought to himself. The logic seemed sound in his mind. Perhaps the others just didn't see that. Maybe they simply didn't think touching the shard was worth the knowledge he gained from it. Without that vision he would be fumbling around in the dark trying to figure out the Children's next move. Unless…

"They *wanted* me to touch the shards," Joshua said, cutting himself off. "That was part of their plan all along. Headmaster, I believe there is something dreadfully worse going on than I had initially anticipated."

Sanev's ears twitched vigorously, and his face contorted slightly before he regained his composure. "What do you mean, Councilor?"

"I am starting to believe that Kerron wasn't the only Dark Mage in my school."

"Preposterous! We had them all tested. Every Mage who was in the school after we discovered Kerron's betrayal has been removed and dealt with. What makes you think this?"

"It's just an inkling of a suspicion right now, Headmaster. I have no proof to go on, but Maja found the cave where the shards were staged on the altar. She admonished me for killing the witches so aggressively, and she stayed behind to further the investigation in the tundra while I went to speak with you," Joshua said, his thoughts racing faster than he experienced before. "When did Maja join the Dark Magic school?"

"She was selected by Kerron before the end of his tenure, but we vetted her. I had considered throwing out the recommendation altogether. She's a strong Mage though so I erred on the side of caution and allowed her into the school under a six-month probation period."

"You're saying there may be a Child of Chaos in your school which serves to eradicate Dark Mages?" Orson asked, stroking the thick stubble at his chin, leaning back from his desk.

Joshua rubbed his temples, applying a bit more pressure than he needed. "That's the only thing that makes sense. Headmaster, when did her probationary period end?"

"I believe it was after your fight with Vor'Kath. You would have been unconscious in the medical ward. Syndra would know better. I had her covering for the Dark Magic school while you were incapacitated. Should we ask her for details?"

"That's not necessary, Headmaster. I think I know what's been going on. I need to look through some books in my school's library to confirm though," Joshua said.

Once again, Sanev lost his composure for a brief moment, his ears twitching more than before. "I'm sorry but your what?"

"Well, since I've let the cat out of the bag, I suppose it's time you know that the Dark Magic school maintains their own private library that's outside the control of Master Averon. This is something that, I was told, started with Councilor Seldanna when the school was formed. Until now its existence was a secret. I'm not saying that Master Averon does a poor job maintaining the books—it's actually quite the opposite—but these books are better kept out of the hands of the general populace at the College. This is a precaution I've had no issue continuing," Joshua explained quickly. "We should refrain from letting Master Averon know, simply so he doesn't throw a conniption over books not under his direct control."

"I have no qualms with any of what you just said. I only ask that you, please, never mention your private, unmanaged library outside of the present company or your school members again. I would *despise* bearing witness to Averon's reaction to hearing about it."

"Can we, once again, *please* get back to the conversation at hand? I really could care less about where you Mages keep your books or who maintains them. I believe, given what the Councilor has mentioned, that there are significantly larger problems at hand than that," King Orson said, cradling his face in his hands, his fingers interlocked together.

"Sorry, Highness," the Mages said in unison.

"I believe we were discussing the possibility that Maja is a Dark Mage?" Orson said, looking up finally.

"We were. I'm not starting to doubt that, but there would be one reason for the Children to have infiltrated the College. Would either of you like to wager a guess to the why?" Joshua asked, looking back and forth between Sanev and the king.

"Purely for chaos," Sanev stated calmly.

"Precisely. They want to sew chaos where and when they can. Infiltrating the College, destroying Anselin, killing King Erkan, putting King Orson and the rest of the kingdom on edge, the shards, the hags, and finally the ritual to summon Kalathan…all of that causes chaos in its purest forms," Joshua explained. "We have to figure out where they would be performing the ritual, for starters."

"Don't dally on this, Councilor. I doubt the Children are going to be waiting a long time for this kind of thing to take place," the king said.

"As you wish, Highness. I will simply pop by our library to find a couple tomes on the subject and do a little research," Joshua said, pausing to think briefly. "Should I grab Michael to help me with this?"

"I would recommend grabbing Michael this evening. He's currently working a shift as a guard commander, and I hate having to backfill positions like that. Do your research first, then retrieve him for the interesting bits," Orson suggested, tapping his fingers on the arm of his chair anxiously as he spoke; Joshua noticed but said nothing about that. "Anything further for me?"

"No, sire," Joshua said.

"I'm finished here, Highness," Sanev said, standing from his chair.

After leaving the king's office, Joshua made his way through the castle much as he had on his way to the king's office. He passed many offices where officials of varying levels of bureaucratic power worked on a myriad of projects that would keep the kingdom running or improve its efficiency. Before hitting the last staircase which would take him to the main halls, Joshua stopped by a guard and asked where he could find the guard commander's office. The guard, quite helpful after Joshua identified himself, provided directions and Joshua followed them toward another wing in the castle he rarely visited.

As he walked, Joshua thought about the last conversation between Michael and him. He hated the things they said to each other, and Joshua felt it best to apologize. However, once he came within eyesight of the office, a plain wooden door which bore the king's rampant griffin under a cluster of three stars Joshua felt his stomach growing uneasy. He had never popped in on Michael during his workday before and didn't know how Michael would handle it. Joshua may have been ready to apologize, but now he wondered if his friend was ready to even hear the apology. Joshua stopped in the middle of the hallway as the door opened and a guard who wasn't Michael walked out. By the plumes on the guard's helmet, Joshua knew him to be a captain, likely stopping by with a status report for Michael. *Garrison work seems so droll,* Joshua thought. As the door inched closed, Joshua tried to get a glimpse inside the office to see if Michael was busy before he stopped in, but it shut before he saw anything in the room. Unable to see through the solid wooden door, Joshua decided against talking with Michael just yet. Instead, the Mage decided he would simply stop by Freenel Manor after his research. *I can apologize then,* Joshua thought, satisfied with the decision. Everything would work out better that way.

Joshua left the castle, tracing his steps back to the central part of the structure where he could find his way back to the main hall and finally outside. Walking down the stairs to the courtyard, Joshua heard a crow *caw*-ing, which intrigued him as corvids seemed to be following him lately. He thought about it for only a second before shaking off any further thoughts and left the courtyard, crossed through the market, passed Freenel Manor, and made his way out of the city where he could safely cast spells again. As he walked, he wondered when the king would lift his ban on spells being cast within the city. While not a major inconvenience, and the exercise was certainly appreciated, Joshua found it wasted a significant amount of his time having to walk out of the city before he could cast a portal to the College. Finally, where he could do so, Joshua created a portal that would take him to the Dark Magic school's library. He hesitated for the briefest of moments, thinking of his new suspicions toward Maja, but ultimately stepped through the portal into the library.

Chapter Seventeen

oshua studied a smattering of books within the Dark Magic library for a couple hours, looking for anything that may be helpful to finding where the Children of Chaos would hold a ritual to summon Kalathan. Rather than looking alone, he recruited Girzi and Myrdin for help. With nothing better to do, they both seemed beyond excited to help with something. Joshua appreciated their enthusiasm and for the moment avoided asking about Maja while he mulled internally about his inkling suspicions of her. Before broaching the subject, he needed to ensure his fears were well-founded. He could think of fewer ways to do so much harm as to confront a person about being a Dark Mage, only for them to be clean.

Joshua knew he must stop and consider all options. Afterall, it could be a coincidence that Maja happened to find the caves *and* the activity that alerted the school to the tundra. Thinking about it, Joshua couldn't shake that the situation seemed just a touch *too* coincidental. There was just too much he couldn't ignore. Finally, Joshua couldn't take it any longer and broached the subject of Maja with the others.

"Where's Maja? I would really appreciate having a fourth set of eyes on this project," Joshua said, hoping he was covering his tracks well enough.

Girzi didn't look up from the books she poured over. "The last I knew she was still in the tundra taking care of the witches as you ordered."

"I haven't seen her since she went through the portal with you," Myrdin said. "It's weird that she hasn't come back yet."

Joshua inhaled sharply. "Do you think there's anything off-putting about her?"

"Not really," Myrdin said, looking up from her book.

Girzi also looked up from her books. "Why do you ask, Councilor?"

"It's nothing, really. Just think there's a coincidence that keeps catching me."

"My grandfather used to say that coincidences meant you were looking in the right place," Myrdin said, returning her attention to the books. "Maybe you just need a fresh set of eyes to evaluate whatever is concerning you?"

"Precisely, Myrdin," Girzi said. "We often get too wrapped up in the small details and can't see the bigger picture. What's bothering you, Councilor?"

Joshua, ready to tell the others what he was thinking, flipped a page in the book he was reading and found a list of varied ritual sites used by the Assembly of Mages. "I can't say for sure, but this may be helpful. Take a look at this."

"Oh, I've seen this list before, actually. I think we have some of these set up for the map to automatically detect any Magic activity so we can investigate," Myrdin explained.

"Do you think the Children would use the same locations as their predecessors?" Girzi asked as she tugged gently on the end of the thick braid that hung over her left shoulder.

"There's enough of a chance for it," Joshua said, placing a smaller piece of paper between the pages. "This is certainly nothing to turn our noses up at. I think I'll go find Michael and let him know we have some things to look into. I'm sure he'll appreciate the work."

"Do you want us to come with you?" Girzi offered.

"No, you stay here and continue looking. If you find anything else, earmark it for when I get back. Thanks for your help with this. I know it's nothing quite as glamorous as hunters are used to, but everything helps."

Girzi and Myrdin nodded and smiled as Joshua stood from the tableful of books and created a portal to Shemont. They wasted no time waiting for him to leave before returning to the stacks of books on the table. Joshua returned his focus to the matter at hand and stepped through the portal. On the other side, he stood in the grass on the north side of the road heading east from Shemont. He stepped onto the packed dirt road and walked as quickly as he could toward the city without breaking a sweat or running. Within a few minutes he was walking across the bridge toward the portcullis that led into the city. He stopped momentarily to allow a merchant wagon to work its way through the gate and was once again walking toward Freenel Manor. Joshua walked down the main boulevard that cut through the city and stopped in front of Michael's estate contemplating whether he was right to just stop by unannounced. The two of them hadn't spoken since their fight the other day, something Joshua deeply regretted. They both said words neither meant and Joshua at the very least wanted to apologize for what he said.

Still, there was a good chance that fight drove Michael to drink more, which Joshua also regretted. He looked down the boulevard toward the Dwarven Cave then back at Freenel Manor and decided to try his luck finding Michael at the tavern before he just stopped at the manor without warning. Joshua made his way down the street toward the tavern with the wooden sign hanging above the door. He admired the craftsmanship of the sign for the briefest of moments before he pushed the door open, the small ding of an equally sized bell chiming his arrival. Frank, the owner of the Cave, waddled toward the end of the bar where Michael normally sat and greeted Joshua heartily.

"Greetings, good sir! Have a seat where you please and we will be with you shortly."

Joshua waved his hand dismissively. "I'm actually here looking for Michael. Has he been here tonight?"

"Aye, he was. He left about an hour ago, so I would check his estate. George will know where he is if he's not there."

"Thank you kindly, Frank," Joshua said, turning toward the door.

"Any time. He's not in trouble, is he?"

Joshua stopped, hand on the door, ready to open it and turned to the tavern owner. "Why would he be in trouble?"

"No particular reason. It's just the last time you came here looking for him he wasn't happy about it."

"We had a job to do. I didn't mean to be so harsh with him," Joshua said.

"I hope you find him, whatever you need him for."

"Thank you, again, Frank."

Joshua left the Cave and returned to Freenel Manor, walking down the boulevard where he could still see the marks in the cobblestones left by the hellhounds' fiery paws. He walked slower than earlier, thinking about what he wanted to say to Michael. Clearly, Joshua's words had driven his friend to drink more than before. This was something Joshua couldn't live with. As a former priest he was supposed to lift others up around him, encourage them to see the light of the Allfather in life around them, and ease their burdens. Instead, he simply made Michael's harder to carry. *Francis would be ashamed of me*, Joshua thought. Joshua stopped in the middle of the empty street and thought about that for a moment. Francis, the head of the Order of Ravens at the time of Joshua and Michael left for Drendil, would not have been ashamed of Joshua for the fight between him and Michael. Francis would, however, have reminded Joshua of one thing: mortals are imperfect and have their shortcomings no matter how good their intentions may be. Joshua simply had to remind himself of that.

Joshua reached the side street in front of Freenel Manor and stopped to admire the grounds once again, which even in the dimness of twilight looked impressive. He was happy with the choice to have George and Harold talk about the groundskeeper that Michael employed. *I should stop by Valenton Hall sometime tomorrow,* Joshua thought. He hadn't stopped by his knightly estate in a while and figured it would be good to see the grounds and Harold while he could. He saw plenty of time away from Shemont in his future with the investigation into the Children of Chaos. As Joshua stood outside Freenel Manor he noticed lights flickering inside and a shadow cast against the front room window. Based on the size of the shadow, he assumed it to be George and figured the squire was simply looking to see who was standing outside. Joshua thought he walked quietly enough but apparently his presence was known inside the house already. Joshua started walking up the walkway lined with trees but stopped the moment he reached the stairs leading to the front door. Blood.

In the years that passed since attaining knighthood, Joshua had stopped by Freenel Manor many times to visit Michael. In all that time, he knew George to keep a meticulously clean home, despite Joshua's habit of stopping by unannounced. The sight of dried blood put Joshua on edge. The door, left slightly ajar, gave Joshua the slightest glimpse into the front room, but he couldn't see anything clearly enough to know what was going on inside. He prepared two spells and burst through the door to find Maja standing over a pale, mutilated body. Joshua took a moment to assess the situation. George sat propped up in a leather, high-back chair with a book discarded on the floor beside him. Stab wounds littered his bare chest, leaving streaks of dried blood which stained his simple cotton pants. George's head tilted back as far as the chair would allow it, revealing a deep, ghastly wound that stretched across his throat from ear to ear. Blood had poured from the wound down his chest and arms, dripping from his fingertips onto the book. Joshua felt a white-hot fury building within him as he looked at George's stiff body propped up in the chair, staged the way it was. Maja turned toward Joshua slowly, a menacing grimace spread across her face, contorting her lips but not touching her eyes.

"Councilor, I'm so happy that you've chosen to join us tonight," Maja chuckled.

"What have you done, Maja," Joshua whispered, his voice beyond hoarse.

"Is it not obvious?"

"Where's Michael?"

"He's safe…for now. You should release those spells before someone else gets hurt."

"Where's Michael?" Joshua repeated. "Take me to him."

"All in good time, Councilor. I need you to release those spells before you get hurt."

Joshua mustered all the strength and power within himself and threw his readied spells at Maja. A fury of light and darkness caught each other in the air in front of George's mutilated body. Memories of a fight similar to this flooded Joshua's mind but he fought them back, pushing them aside as he drew yet more strength from the Magic within him. Every scrap of power he could wield now raced through his hands. The pure light, his gift from Vor'Leanne, pushed back the flood of darkness Maja cast until her spell broke and she stumbled backward, crashing into the wall behind her. Joshua released his spells and heard himself shouting into the room. He readied the spells again in case Maja wasn't finished yet, and the shouting fell silent. Joshua started panting, regaining his composure. He took a step closer to Maja and another rush of darkness flew toward him. Joshua cast the light spell in his left hand and subdued the darkness again, taking another step. More darkness. Light. Another step. Finally, standing a meter away from Maja, everything stopped. Joshua continued panting and Maja melted into a sweat-covered, defeated husk of a person. Even her grimace faded.

Joshua released the light spells and began to lower his defenses. As he did Maja's hands lit up with yet another spell. Pure darkness sloshed from her fingertips, flowing wickedly through the air toward Joshua. He brought up a reflective barrier spell, the one he learned from the book he received from the Order of Herons priest in Erith. The darkness reflected back onto Maja and Joshua watched in horror as she aged decades in the blink of an eye. Her hair thinned, turned white, and fell out, her skin grew wrinkled and translucent, and her eyes became more deep-set as her face contorted from the instant aging that took place. A moment later the flood of darkness stopped and all that remained before Joshua was a pathetic, wrinkled mass of skin clinging to frail bones all covered in robes that no longer fit properly. Now, Maja panted and gasped as she leaned against the wall, a remnant of what Joshua once thought to be a promising Mage.

Joshua continued panting, his deflective spell still holding steady. "Where's Michael?"

"I…can't tell you."

Joshua, anger coursing through his veins, threw a bolt of lightning into the wall above Maja's decrepit head. "Tell me!"

Maja somehow withered further and tried to shrink further away from him. "They took him for the ritual."

"Where did they take him?"

"I'm telling you nothing further," Maja rasped.

Another bolt of lightning snapped toward Maja, this time striking within a hand's length of her. "You will tell me *everything*, Maja."

Tears raced down her face. "There is an island. It's off the western coast of Drendil. That's where they're waiting."

"What are they waiting for?"

Maja continued sobbing. "I-I-I can't tell you!"

Joshua readied another lightning spell but didn't throw this one. His fist clenched until knuckles popped. The lightning grew stronger in his closed fist. His teeth clenched. Muscles in his temple and neck tightened beyond what he thought possible as he poured more of his strength into the lightning spell. His hand started aching as his fingernails buried themselves in the palm of his hand. His hand shook under the tension in his arm.

"Tell me what the Children are waiting for," Joshua whispered.

"They're waiting," Maja started before swallowing dramatically, "for you."

Joshua released the lightning spell into the floor. "What do you mean they're waiting for me? Tell me everything you know!"

"There's a trap. The Children are waiting on the island for you to arrive. They're going to bind you, use a potion to paralyze you but keep you awake, and start the ritual to bring Kalathan into the realm. There's nothing you can do to stop them," Maja explained.

"How many of you are on this island?"

"Three."

"Are there Children beyond this group?"

Maja hesitated momentarily before answering. "Not that I'm aware."

"Is Michael safe?"

"For now, he is. That may change as the ritual starts. I don't know all the details."

"Why did you lead me to the shards?" Joshua asked.

"There's a lot of moving pieces with that. It's too hard to explain right here, but—"

"Make me a portal to this island."

"I will do *no* such thing!"

Joshua ground his teeth together. "Make me a portal there, now!"

"No!"

Joshua unclenched his teeth and looked at Maja. As he looked at her aged, decrepit form, he felt a surge of pity flood within him. Disgust followed immediately after. *How can I feel pity for someone who betrayed me?* The muscles in Joshua's jaw tightened as he fought with himself. *Why am I so conflicted?* Clearly, he was getting no further information from Maja. He knew he couldn't keep her alive.

The oath he swore wouldn't allow any other outcome. Joshua wavered for a moment, releasing his reflective spell and Maja snapped at the opportunity, forming another spell of pure darkness. Before she could finish, Joshua cast a spell of lightning which shot through the air and punched right through Maja's wrinkled forehead like a hammer through a plaster wall. Her body went limp and the spell forming in her hand collapsed on itself with a boom that echoed through the room. Books, rattled by the concussion, fell from their places on the shelves.

"Destroying one evil in your world may not save it," a familiar voice echoed inside Joshua's mind.

"I wish I listened to her," Joshua sighed, looking at the chaos in the room around him.

"One is the mastermind while the other is the puppet. The master can always find a new puppet," Vor'Leanne continued to caution within Joshua's mind. Her voice came through so clear that Joshua would have thought she were standing beside him. He found himself wondering how she could have been so right and so quickly. Had he even listened to her? He admonished himself for forgetting her warning so hastily. As he thought about Vor'Leanne's warnings, another thought floated through his mind, a faint whisper within the maelstrom of emotions battling within him. *Could Kalathan have planned all of this the whole time?* This thought, fleeting and effervescent as it was, cemented Joshua where he stood. He took stock in everything that happened since he arrived in Drendil for a brief moment. Vor'Kath, aligned with Kalathan from the beginning, failed repeatedly. It felt more than likely that Kalathan would want his bungling puppet replaced by another.

"If you remove this threat, it is likely that another may simply take his place. And that new threat may be stronger, more determined," another caution came through from Vor'Leanne.

"Allfather save us," Joshua breathed.

Joshua looked around the room once more and noticed George's eyes were still open, staring emptily at the ceiling. Joshua walked over and closed them gently while saying a prayer to the Allfather to guide his soul to the afterlife he deserved. He hated the thought of what George must have seen in that final moment and wondered if he could delve the man to see it. He wished not to waste time, but this amount of carnage seemed like too much for Maja to achieve on her own. Joshua shook his head, trying to break those dark thoughts free. This wasn't a fate anyone deserved, no matter what kind of life they chose to live. He chided himself, again at missing the signs that Maja might betray him. Then, mid-admonishment, Joshua wondered if there *were* any signs that pointed to her being a Dark Mage. While only devoting a few moments to that, he came up empty-handed and set his attention back on the room.

As he looked around the room for anything that might point to what happened and where the Children of Chaos prepared for their ritual, a thought struck Joshua. He couldn't make a portal to the western coast of Drendil without first being there, and riding his horse, even at the fastest speed it could handle without dying beneath him would take days at the least. He didn't have time for that. However, someone in this room likely visited that very island. He could delve

Maja's still-fading memories and see enough of the island to make a portal there and stop the Children before they could further the ritual. *She warned you about a trap,* he reminded himself. He would simply have to go through the portal with spells at the ready. Nothing short of that would work. He could go to the College and bring a platoon of battlemages with him, but he felt confident facing three Dark Mages at once. *How strong can they be?*

Joshua prepared the delving spell and stopped, thinking about what he was about to do. Surely, something like this would break the oath he swore as he took his position on the Council. This seemed like the kind of thing the College would detest greatly. The question of whether his plan was possible flashed through his mind, but he focused on the gravity of delving a dead Mage to access the fragments of their memory that remained so he could portal somewhere. *I'm attempting to save not only this realm but* all *mortal realms. I think I can justify my actions here,* Joshua thought confidently. Sanev would understand. Joshua inhaled deeply and lowered the delving spell into Maja's bloodied, wrinkled head.

Chapter Eighteen

The Children of Chaos, gathered on the Iron Holm, gathered around the stone altar to which they bound the drunkard. A viewing orb, a small translucent ball that floated in the air, showed the front room of the drunk's estate where Maja waited for the Councilor. They watched everything as it unfolded. They watched as Maja betrayed the Children, as they planned. Esram smiled knowing that everything was falling into place. Soon, the Councilor would come to the Iron Holm where they would be waiting for him.

A fierce wind cut across the island from west to east, rippling at the Children's dark robes and the ropes that tied Michael to the altar. A hint of salt and decay from the sea formed a nearly overwhelming conglomerate smell as it mixed with the slightly sweet aroma from the grass and threatened rain. High overhead, thick, unnatural-looking clouds covered the sky. The clouds, so thick and dark that nothing could be seen beyond them, threatened to drop sheets of rain on the ritual site. Esram loved the chaos that indeed thrived within nature.

Esram and Daethis watched the viewing orb while Oleg tended to their captive knight. Oleg maintained a series of spells that monitored the knight's breathing, heart beats, and his brain patterns. Esram, being an alchemist, didn't understand how Oleg knew all of these medicinal spells, but he didn't question it either. He looked briefly at the spells and shivered thinking of all the work that went into keeping someone in this particular state of unconsciousness. As he watched Oleg, Daethis squeezed his arm, signaling that she wanted him to look at the viewing orb again. Esram broke his attention away from the large Elf and the complex web of spells he manipulated. A flash of light showed within the viewing orb and Maja's body went limp in an instant. Unfortunately, they didn't have sound coming through the viewing orb, but they didn't need sound to understand what happened.

"He's already killed Maja. I fear the Councilor may be stronger than we anticipated. You know this could be a problem, right?" Daethis asked.

"She was a liability to the group. Her resolve was weaker than we needed," Esram stated.

"Darling, you'll love what he's doing now. It's so…devilish of him."

Esram looked into the viewing orb and gasped. "He's *delving* her? I didn't think that worked against corpses."

"Maybe if the person has recently died it can work. I thought his morals would prevent him from defiling a corpse, but here we are. You know what he is looking for, right?"

"Us," Esram smirked. "He's falling right into our trap like a fly in a spider's web."

"He would make a good addition to the group, Esram."

"I don't think he would break his moral code the way he is if he were still in the dark about what we are doing here. Those morals are rigid and, I thought, unflinching. We likely will never convince him to join us."

"Never say never. We may yet convince him that the College is only tying his hands rather than letting him be free," Daethis said.

"Everything is ready," Oleg said, turning his attention away from the altar.

"Esram, we need to prepare the illusion," Daethis reminded.

"That is simple enough. Oleg, cast the spell."

"Yes, master," Oleg replied, his voice more tart than usual.

Esram and Daethis started walking up the hill while Oleg readied the illusion spell. Within a few moments everything would be ready for their special visitor to arrive. The illusion would create four prostrated bodies set up before the altar, as if the Children waited for a specific time for the ritual to start. The illusion also hid the saltire where they would bind Joshua for the duration of the sacrament. The cross itself was a simple contraption of wood and iron nails. There was nothing significant or special about it. Esram smiled and reached into his pouch where the small vial rested, wrapped in several layers of cloth to protect it. The potion he worked so hard to create would come in handy for this part of their plan. The concoction would paralyze Joshua long enough that the Children could bring him into their spell without him trying to interfere or intervene. Without being able to touch his own Magic, Joshua would be powerless to stop everything he would witness tonight.

As they crested the hill, Esram turned and took a final look at the Iron Holm. Oleg finished the illusion spell and things…changed before Esram's eyes. Suddenly four prostrating bodies appeared in the space between the altar and the stone benches that filled the space in the island's bowl. The people in the illusion all matched the Children of Chaos. There were two males, one significantly larger than the other, and two females. Their arms stretched toward the stone altar where Michael, not part of the illusion, still laid bound by simple ropes to the legs which supported the thick, stone slab. The wooden saltire a few feet from the altar disappeared as the illusion spell took shape over everything. Esram's smile broadened as the spell took shape and began to look more convincing. The spell didn't have to be strong to be effective. It only had to convince the Councilor that the Children were caught unprepared while they simply snuck up behind him and forced the potion concoction down his throat. Esram watched as Oleg anchored the spell to one of the stone benches and made his way up the hill to join the others. Their guest would arrive shortly and Esram wanted all the Children ready to receive their guest. He hated the idea of being ill-prepared for someone so integral to their ritual.

*   *   *

Within the front room of Freenel Manor, Michael's knightly estate, Joshua prepared a delving spell that he planned to drop into Maja's fading mind. He hesitated as he put the spell together, knowing that if the College discovered this, they would likely remove him from his position as the Superintendent of the Dark Magic school. Delving of itself wasn't frowned upon, but defiling corpses certainly was an activity the College disliked. Without doing this, Joshua would never stop the ritual from happening. The Children also had Michael and Joshua felt compared to save his friend from something that caused the pit in his stomach to sink like a cluster of bricks.

Joshua cast aside his inhibitions about the delving he already prepared and quickly lowered the spell onto Maja's head. Once settled in the right position, he sank the dangling tendrils into her skull where they pierced her brain. A cloud formed over Maja's limp, lifeless body and Joshua began searching for memories, checking the most recent ones first as they would be the most volatile. He saw her standing outside the collapsed cave meeting with Esram and two Elves Joshua didn't know. He recognized the largest of them from when he and Michael investigated Anselin, but the other he had never seen before. Each of the Children of Chaos wore dark, hooded robes except Maja who wore her College robes, white with a black stripe around the cuffs and piping along the hems and collar. This memory was getting him no closer to saving Michael, so Joshua cast it aside and moved to the next one.

He saw the front door of Freenel Manor and stopped, not wanting to see George's final moments. Joshua closed his eyes and felt a lone tear drip onto his cheek thinking about what the squire went through once he opened the door. The wickedness that Maja clearly exhibited, as witnessed by the disarray and chaos in the room, was enough for Joshua to have some idea of what happened. *Some things are better kept unknown,* he reminded himself. Again, this memory, unwatched, got him nowhere closer to finding the Children, stopping them, and saving Michael, so Joshua again cast this one aside in search of the island.

He tweaked the delving spell slightly, looking for more lasting memories that may still exist in the fading consciousness of his former associate. From the experience Joshua had delving others, he found that short-term memories were generally more accurate to specific, smaller details while long-term memories were more stable for watching. Perhaps there was a lasting memory of the island that Joshua could use to find his way there. He scoured through memory after memory, seeing glimpses of Maja's hidden past. He saw a memory of her father as he put on his armor, marked by the black chimera on a grey background that belonged to Anselin. Grief and sadness shot through Joshua as he watched the memory. Maja's father picked her up, embraced her, kissed her forehead, and set her back down, then left their home for what Joshua knew to be the last time. Guessing from her size, he placed her around eight years old. *Such a tragic loss at an early age,* he thought before memories he buried within himself started bubbling to the surface. He, too, lost his parents at an early age. Joshua wasn't a Dark Mage, though. Joshua marveled at the difference in life experiences that led two people with similar backgrounds down two vastly different paths throughout their lives.

Joshua continued manipulating the delving spell, once again looking through recent memories that may let him see the island where Maja said the Children waited for him. He stopped what he was doing and wondered if he should be jumping at the chance to stop the Children without any backup. These were, after all, three powerful Dark Mages and, other than fighting Vor'Kath and the hags in the tundra, Joshua had little experience fighting another Mage. He considered his fight with Maja and how that could have gone much more poorly if he slipped for even one moment. *Could I handle* three *mages on my own?* Even if he were to try getting help now, would he arrive at the island on time? He was already wasting time looking through decades of memories locked inside a dead woman's decaying mind. Frustration welled inside Joshua as he debated what to do with himself.

Joshua went through a few more recent memories until he found what he was looking for. He stopped on the memory he wanted and saw a group of five Mages wearing dark robes standing around a stone altar. The image was fuzzy as the state of Maja's mind worsened. He could see shapes but couldn't really make out faces or any real descriptive details about who was standing around the altar. He could see water nearby and knew this was the island he looked for. One of the figures he knew to be Esram, only because he took charge of some kind of ceremony where an orb was created. It floated above the stone altar and everything around the group descended into darkness. Joshua reversed the memory briefly and looked at the altar for a moment before he realized it was just like the one the witches had in the caverns. This one didn't have any runes carved into the smooth, polished surface but it seemed like it matched the other.

Feeling like he saw enough of the island to make a portal there, Joshua discarded the delving spell and took a step away from Maja's body. He looked around the room one final time but saw nothing else that needed his attention. Joshua slowly walked back to the front door, trying to disturb as little as he could. As he moved toward the front door, he noticed the trail of blood that went from the front door to the chair where George's body remained propped as if he had been reading. Joshua examined the blood and figured that George was likely dead before Maja even stepped into the house. *Such a shame,* he thought, looking at the disastrous scene again. He knew Michael would be devastated if he had to see or hear about this. Joshua shook his head to clear away the thoughts of Michael seeing this and breaking down and left the house to find a guard. The least he could do was report this scene to someone who could get the entire situation cleared up. He also needed to explain the sound of spellcasting that anyone within earshot had likely heard, despite the king's ban on Magic use within the city. Joshua saw a guard not far away from the manor and ran as far as he could toward the other man.

The guard started seeing someone running up to him. "What is wrong, sir?"

"There's been a situation in Freenel Manor that requires some attention," Joshua replied.

"Take me there," the guard said, his hand going to the hilt of his sword.

As they jogged back to Michael's estate, the stiff soles of the guard's books clicking on the cobblestone, Joshua quickly explained why he was in the city and what he saw when he walked up to the front door. The guard cringed hearing about the blood but, upon seeing the scene, all color drained from his face.

"What exactly happened here?" the guard asked, looking to Joshua for reassurance.

"I'm not sure what happened before I got here but this," Joshua said, waving his hand toward Maja's body on the floor, "happened after I got here."

"I won't report your Magic use to the Guard Captain. It sounds like you were provoked into this. I'm sure anyone else looking at this would understand. Go save Sir Michael. The kingdom needs him very much," the guard said.

"Thank you. I will do what I can to save him," Joshua said.

The guard turned his back on Joshua as he continued looking over the scene in the front room of Freenel Manor. Joshua stepped away and imagined the island he saw within Maja's withering memories. He pictured the grass dancing in the coastal wind and the spray of the water as it crashed into the rocks that formed the base of the island. He saw the hills that formed a bowl in the center of the island and the lone tree at the top of the hill, its branches waving in the same wind that pushed the grass. Joshua imagined the salty smell that clung to the air from the sea on the western side of the ocean. He felt the bitter sting of the wind on his bare skin even in this time of the year. He felt his skin prickle as the imagined wind blew across his skin. Joshua opened a portal as he continued thinking about the island and stepped through.

Chapter Nineteen

oshua stepped through the portal and saw the Iron Holm exactly as he saw it in Maja's memories. The island stretched out beneath him as the hill fell toward the bowl where the altar stood. He looked to his left and saw the lone tree, its branches waving in the wind that indeed made his skin prickle. Joshua returned his attention to the altar beneath him. He saw the stone altar with several stone benches arranged before it. He saw four figures prostrated before the stone slab, two near each corner between the altar and the benches before it. Joshua looked closer at the altar and saw Michael lying atop the stone slab, his ankles and wrists bound to the legs of the altar with what looked like simple pieces of rope. Joshua had no doubt that's who he saw there in the center of the bowl. The leather pauldrons, boots, and greaves with the crimson tabard gave that away. Most other officers in the army wore metal armor, but Michael always preferred leather armor for ease of movement. There was something else that Joshua could just barely sense. It was another spell but not near the altar. It was…behind him?

"Greetings, Councilor. We are so happy you could join us for this wonderful ritual today," a smooth, calming voice called from the direction of the spell.

Joshua spun on the balls of his feet as quickly as he could, readying spells in each hand as he made his way around. Before he finished preparing the spells, something struck him, severing his connection from Magic altogether. The shock of that happening, something he had never experienced before, brought him to his knees. He looked up and saw three Elves, one of average size, a tall and willowy one, and one gargantuan. The largest of the three stood just over two meters tall and weighed at least eighteen stone. Between the scars that littered his face and the slight right-hand hook in his nose, Joshua assumed the giant also happened to get into many fistfights throughout his life. The willowy Elf, by contrast, could have hidden behind either of the other two if she were just a smidge shorter. Joshua could only describe her face as gaunt and haunting. The last Elf Joshua knew to be Esram, if only by the jagged scars that smothered the left side of his face from jawline to just above the sideburns and mouth to ear. In person, versus seeing them through someone else's memories, the scars looked much more menacing. The left side of Esram's mouth was pulled back toward his ear, giving him a permanent grimace on that side. *Bryne really did a number on this man's face,* Joshua thought briefly before the large Elf grabbed him and lifted him off the ground.

"I do apologize for cutting you from your Magic so severely, Councilor. We just don't need you touching that just yet. For now, drink deeply," Esram said as he dumped a foul smelling, dark liquid into Joshua's mouth from a green, glass vial.

Joshua started to cough, but the large Elf placed his hand over Joshua's mouth to keep him from spitting out any of the concoction. Joshua reluctantly swallowed and wished he hadn't as the aftertaste was nearly worse than the initial bitter taste of the liquid. He pulled his face away from the Elf's calloused hand and grimaced and tried to bring the vile substance back up. He felt another spell hit him and the muscles in his throat numbed within an instant. As his throat went numb, he knew he had no way of removing that foul potion from his body now. He started evaluating the situation. The Children of Chaos simply waited for him to arrive, cut him off from his Magic, and forced him to consume…something. He now felt empty, cold, and mundane. Even without his connection to Magic, he had never before felt this way. He reached for the Magic within his mind but bumped into something unseen, yet still just as much there. He could see the precious power he now craved but was prevented from getting close to it. *How unfair this is,* Joshua lamented to himself.

"What," Joshua said, mustering all his strength to speak, "have you done to me?"

"Oh, that's quite simple, Councilor. I spent the last few days perfecting a potion which will leave you paralyzed and block you from reaching the Magic you so desperately need to defeat us. Isn't it magnificent how something so simple can make someone so utterly useless?"

"I can still—"

"You will regret it," the brutish Elf said.

Joshua felt the muscles in his neck give and his head lolled backwards. He started thinking of any alternatives that he had, but everything required some amount of movement in his muscles which, at this point, he had none of. He could have kicked the gargantuan Elf in the groin, but the only thing Joshua could feel below his shoulders was a cold and tingly sensation. He cried inside his mind for his muscles to respond, but his body wouldn't listen. Joshua prayed to the Allfather to regain his strength, but again nothing happened as the large Elf effortlessly hauled Joshua onto his shoulders. The Children of Chaos walked toward the ritual site. As they did the entire scene *flickered* like the flame that consumed a candle and the four people kneeling before the altar vanished. Michael remained where he was as Joshua realized everything had been part of an illusion. A wooden cross appeared as everything faded. He swallowed the lump in his throat as realization came about who that was reserved for. *Please, Allfather. I'm begging you. Give me my strength for just one moment.* He knew that's all he would need. He pushed against the invisible barrier in his mind for what felt like eons as they walked down the hill and tied him to the saltire. As the last binding attached his wrist to the crossbeam, darkness enveloped Joshua. He floated in the emptiness for what felt like an eternity, his body and all senses cut off from his mind. He was simply a… void.

Chapter Twenty

The Children gathered around the altar. Esram kept his eyes on the blinded and deafened Councilor while they readied themselves for the ritual. Daethis and Oleg spoke together quietly enough that Esram could hardly hear them. He had so rarely heard Oleg speak so much, it was surprising. *Why was it so easy to capture the Councilor?* Esram wracked his brain, wondering why one so powerful could be severed from his Magic so readily. There should have been more resistance. He expected a whole fight between Joshua and the Children. Yet, there had been nothing. They threw the spell once and it worked. *Perhaps he was distracted?* It was possible, but not likely. Esram considered this a few moments longer while his companions finished their preparations. Daethis tapped him on the shoulder when they were ready to commence the ritual. Esram nodded but held up a finger as he walked over to their captive. There were some final remarks that must be made before they started the world's end.

Esram removed the spells that covered the Councilor's eyes and ears. "You know, I must thank you for everything you've done for me, Joshua."

"What have I done for you?" Joshua's voice was flat and emotionless.

"You killed Maja for me. I spent many hours trying to figure out how to do that myself. She was good within our group, but inadequate in many ways. She asked too many questions that a child wouldn't need to ask. She became a liability to me. To us, even. Thank you, Councilor. You have served our group valiantly," Esram said, only half mockingly.

"You're so welcome," Joshua responded, his voice still emotionless. His neck muscles were still paralyzed but Esram could see Joshua moving his eyes between himself and the altar.

"Oh, there's no need to worry about your dearest friend here, Councilor. I assure you nothing averse will happen to him. He will feel little to no pain in what is coming."

Joshua's head twitched as he attempted to raise it as he spat fierce venom. "Touch him and you will die a most gruesome death."

Esram smiled with both sides of his mouth seeing such emotion finally. "You interrogated Maja thoroughly, so I know that you're already aware of what we are planning. You, Councilor, were the only thing we needed before the ritual could start. How does it feel knowing that you will not only witness the end of this realm but participate in helping bring about that destruction?"

"I'm not helping you, Esram. I can't even touch Magic right now."

"You're unable to, but we can connect to it for you freely. Isn't it wonderful, Councilor? Everything that we needed is here now."

"Why are you doing all of this?" Joshua asked, once again failing to raise his head.

"Years ago, a fight happened between me and one of your colleagues. He instigated everything, yet *I* was expelled from the College despite not harming another student. These scars I carry with me everywhere I go," Esram said, pointing at his mutilated face, "are the work of Bryne. Yet, your headmaster expelled me from the College. Have you heard the full story of what happened to me? I'm *sure* that Sanev has been wholly honest about the *difficult* choice that he made. Let me clear your mind of that miserable mockery of the truth that the College is no doubt continuing to spread about me.

"After our fight, Bryne ran to Sanev with bullshit evidence that I was studying Dark Magic. In complete fairness to Bryne, I was doing just that, but his evidence didn't show an inkling of that. Do you know the *evidence* that Bryne had against me? He said I was casting a spell that he didn't know. Bryne was an oaf, and any student could have accidentally crafted the spell I was going to cast at him. Sanev expelled me from the College when the rules clearly state there is no tolerance for violence or aggression between students. Daethis can attest that Bryne instigated the fight between us. Yet, he was never expelled from the College. Do you know why that is, Councilor?"

"I don't know, Esram."

"He was never expelled from the College because he uncovered a Dark Mage. Actions of such caliber often can cause the College to overlook the sins one has made, so long as they aren't as unforgivable as going outside the College's teachings and guidelines. Regardless, since the day that Bryne attacked me, I have been outcast by any societal group beyond the Children. Everyone sees me as a monster and a menace because of these scars I carry on my face. Since that day I have plotted my revenge against not only the College but the *world*. Today, I will fulfill not only my own vendetta but a prophecy! Do you feel special yet, Councilor? You are helping to fulfil a *prophecy!*"

"Your expulsion was fair and according to the rules, Esram. If anything happened the way you say it did—"

"My *face* bears scars that will never fade. What part of the truth are you denying, Councilor? Bryne couldn't fully control the spell he cast, and now I bear the sigil of that mistake for the rest of time. What, within your precious rules, allowed him to throw lightning that was beyond his control into my face?"

"He was defending himself, Esram!" Joshua shouted, regaining an ounce of his former strength, something that shouldn't have been allowed with the potion.

"Bryne started the whole affair. He bullied me relentlessly because he was larger than me and I couldn't stop him physically."

"That gives you the right to attack him?" Joshua demanded.

"I was defending *my*self, Councilor. You weren't there. How are you going to sit there, bound to that cross, and claim to know how things happened? You are only reciting one side of the story and that side has covered up that Bryne should have been expelled as equally as I was."

Joshua sighed and released any scrap of strength he had left in him. "You're right. He should have been expelled too."

"I know you are only saying that to agree with me, Councilor, but I appreciate the fake sentiment the same. Now, if you have nothing further to say, we really should be getting started with this ritual," Esram said, walking back toward the altar.

Joshua waited a few moments before speaking again. "You can't usurp Kalathan once he's in this world, Esram. You're a fool if you even think you can."

Esram stopped dead in his tracks and turned, furious, to look at the Councilor who stared directly at him. "You know *nothing* of which you speak. I aim not to usurp my master but to fulfill his Will and bring this world, and every other mortal realm, crumbling at his very touch."

"Esram, we should get started soon," Daethis said, touching him gently on the arm.

"Now, Councilor, you shall behold the awesome might that you at the College have fought for so long. This is the very power you witnessed when you touched the shards. Prepare yourself," Esram said, quickly turning toward the altar where Daethis and Oleg already waited.

Chapter Twenty-One

oshua cried inside his mind for his arms and legs to struggle against the bindings that held him to this strange cross. Whatever ingredients had been in that potion still kept him from so much as wiggling his fingers, let alone actually fighting against the ropes that bound him. He was entirely captivated with no chance for escape on the proverbial horizon. His mind continued yelling at his arms and legs to do something, anything, that would get him off the cross and stop the ritual before it could start. No amount of internal yelling did anything as his limbs remained wholly unresponsive. Joshua struggled to understand everything going on as he attempted to struggle on the cross. Still, he continued pleading to the Allfather to give him a momentary respite from this paralysis to no avail.

While all of that happened, he also kept an eye on the Children of Chaos as they prepared spells to begin their ritual. The large, brutish Elf revealed a series of spells connected to Michael where they monitored him as thoroughly as a battlefield medic would watch their wounded. With a wave, the spells dissipated, and the large Elf woke Michael up. Joshua watched as his friend's eyes opened to the sight of thick, roiling clouds far overhead which seemed to threaten rain but never bring it. Michael immediately started struggling against his own bindings before Esram leaned in and whispered something to him, calming him instantly. Together, the two of them looked toward Joshua and Michael whimpered ever so quietly seeing the Mage. Joshua thought he saw a tear leave Michael's right eye as the two of them maintained eye contact.

"Councilor, I do believe there is a detail I failed to clarify for you that you may only now understand. For this ritual to work, we need a sacrifice. We also need an item of great hatred, something which I'm sure both you and Sir Michael here are familiar with," Esram said, holding his left hand out where a short, dark blade with too long of a hilt materialized in his hand. "I'm sure you were wondering what happened to the other piece of the Vor sword. Well, here it is, reforged into something which will bring about what should have happened at that tower southeast of here. Neither of you should have walked away from that fight. As I understand it, Councilor, you nearly didn't, correct?"

"You will do nothing to Michael, Esram. Everything you do to him I will do to you tenfold," Joshua promised through gritted teeth. A single tear dropped from both of his eyes.

"You don't understand, Councilor. You are powerless in this situation. What can you do but watch everything unfold?" Esram asked as he released the blade. "Now, if you will allow it, Councilor, we have a ritual to start."

Lightning streaked through the sky and within a few moments thunder pealed strong enough to shake the cross and rattle Joshua's teeth. Esram whispered something else to Michael who continued struggling against the spells that bound him to the altar. While Esram leaned in toward Michael, the other two Children rearranged the lamps that surrounded the altar. They brought them to the area between the stone slab and the benches and formed them into what Joshua initially thought to be a lopsided circle. As he continued to watch them arrange the torches, he realized they formed the torches into the shape of the six-pointed constellation of Deja the phoenix. *Why would they be using Deja as their guide?* His thoughts raced as he tried to find a connection between the phoenix and Kalathan. As the Elves started lighting the torches, Joshua realized they saw themselves as travelers lost on a journey, looking for guidance to their "home" with Kalathan.

With each of the lamps lit, Esram turned and started a simple ball of light spell. This floated in the air just above the torches and outshone all six torches. Joshua watched, still yelling internally for his limbs to respond. As he did, he felt something painfully hot grab the Magic within him and pull as much of it as possible though him. Joshua felt every strained, tortured tug as Esram commandeered his

Magic and used it to create a massively complicated spell Joshua had never experienced before. Threads of darkness entangled the other elements and built what he could only describe as a bird's nest of a spell, empty but somehow organized. With the bulk of the spell together, the other Children joined in and immediately began adding to the chaotic nature of the spell. Joshua saw an opportunity to delay the inevitable.

"Esram! You're mad if you think Tusur will do your bidding," Joshua called, yelling to be heard above the whipping of the wind that picked up after the clap of thunder.

Another bolt of lightning streaked through the thick, black clouds overhead as it raced toward the mainland before Esram answered. "Tusur will not walk this land tonight."

"You can't possibly think that Kalathan will destroy only the College then leave."

"I fully anticipate that he will destroy first this realm then the other mortal realms. I have prepared for that, and you have foolishly walked into the trap we laid out for you, Councilor. The legends were wrong. They never said that Tusur would eat this realm. They said a great dragon would do just that. I like to think that prophecy leaves room for interpretation."

"But Kalathan isn't even a dragon!"

Something quickly and painfully jabbed Joshua in the stomach. He lurched as far forward as he could with the bindings as bile and blood spewed from his mouth and dribbled down his chin onto his robes. Another jab struck from the other side and more blood sprayed.

"Never speak his name again unless it is to beg mercy from my cruelest master," Esram warned, turning his attention from the concoction of a spell being formed above the torches.

Joshua groaned as blood and spit dripped from his chin onto his chest. "You ignored my point, Esram. Your *master* isn't a dragon."

"You are testing my patience, Councilor."

A spike of searing pain shot through Joshua's head as even more of Joshua's Magic strength rushed through him into Esram's control like water through a sluice. Joshua tried to fight the power drain he was experiencing, but nothing he could do was working. He also tried fighting against the bindings holding him to the cross again, but still nothing changed on that front. He could feel nothing of his extremities. Everything below his neck and shoulders simply felt severed. Joshua watched in horror as the mass of spell energy that floated above the lamps grew in size as Esram funneled out more of Joshua's power. The other Children added to the spell but much less than Joshua himself was contributing against his will.

As the Magic flowed from Joshua into the Children's spell, the pain swelled, and darkness started closing in around the edges of Joshua's vision. He struggled as his eyesight tunneled aggressively. He shook his head as forcefully as he could with his weakened neck muscles and blinked repeatedly, hoping to force away the encroaching shadows. Despite his efforts, and his screaming, which was drowned out by the now howling wind, the blackness continued to enclose around his eyes. Streams of sweat now poured down his face, drenching the already blood-soaked robes he wore. He no longer cared about the beads of sweat that fell into his eyes. Nothing compared to the searing agony in his head as Esram continued to funnel more Magic from his captive Mage. Joshua nearly gave up resisting the darkness when something moved within the small tunnel of light that he could still see through.

Michael's feet shook against his rope bindings. He was working his legs, attempting to loosen the cords. Joshua raised his head and brought Michael into the now receding tunnel that enveloped his eyes. A fragment of hope smaller than a grain of sand began blossoming within Joshua's chest. He no longer felt cold as the fierce wind whipped at his robes. *Perhaps Michael can get us out of this after all!* Joshua's thoughts raced as he watched the horror of the ritual unfold before him. The sight of the growing mess of a spell made his mind hurt nearly as much as his Magic being used involuntarily by someone else.

Still, Sir Michael the Valiant, Knight-Commander of the Royal Order of Drendil continued working the cords against the sharply pointed edges of the altar to which he was bound. Joshua felt he could hear the fibers in the robes fraying with the friction that Michael was causing but he knew that was his imagination, because of the howling wind ripping across the island. Right as the bud of hope starting to bloom within Joshua at the idea that Michael would free himself from the altar and save them both, Esram anchored his portion of the spell to the orb floating amid the torches and turned to face Michael.

Chapter Twenty-Two

sram anchored his portion of the spell and passed control of Joshua's Magic to Daethis who would continue working on her portion while still torturing their guest from the College. As he spun, he started chuckling at the sight of Joshua, dripping sweat, blood, and spittle. Despite his Magic strength and his ability to overpower Maja within a matter of a minute, Esram had reduced the poor Councilor to a driveling shell of his former self. *If only I hired a scribe to record this moment for posterity,* Esram thought to himself, still chuckling. He took his attention off Joshua and as his eyes landed on the drunkard lying on the altar, rage welled inside Esram. *The bastard is trying to escape!* He watched as Michael slowly moved his ankles and wrists to drag the ropes against the edges of the altar. Wasting no time, Esram cast a spell of air that struck Michael in the side of the head just hard enough to make his body go limp. He could now consider the escape attempt ended and Esram felt pleased about the way he handled the situation. He briefly considered if other options existed but dismissed the thought. Mercy had no time or place on this island. Tonight was about only two things: revenge and destiny. Nothing else would stand in his way. Still, Michael looked up at him with such a pained look in his eyes. Esram placed his hand on Michael's forehead as if to assure him that everything would be over soon.

"Daethis, is everything ready for the next step?"

"Whenever you're ready darling. I would suggest you make the sacrifice soon though. This spell will become unstable if we don't do something quick," she replied.

"Councilor, are you ready to witness the terrible fury and fire that my master shall bring with him?" Esram asked, looking to the saltire.

"Esram, you don't have to do this. Stop and think for a moment about what you're about to do. Once you start this, there's no stopping it."

"You speak to me as if I haven't craved this very moment for years, Councilor. I know exactly what I'm about to do. Bear witness, Councilor and remember, we couldn't have brought this about without you. I would commend your participation, but why waste time?"

Esram stuck out his left hand and reached for the Vor dagger in his mind, picturing the place where the witches put it after reforging the blade. The hilt materialized in his hand in the blink of an eye. Such power and rage coursed up his arm and into the rest of his body as his fingers closed around the hilt. Only on a handful of other occasions could he recall such concentrated hatred being in his control. One of those times ended with him receiving a ball of lightning to the face. Thinking of Bryne only added to the rage that burned within his hand. Esram's lip curled in a snarl as he thought about that day yet again.

The blade itself felt out of balance. The hilt was too long for the length of the blade and while Esram understood the why of this, he found himself not caring. He looked at the blade closely, something he had not done yet. Deep within the midnight black surface, which gleamed like a gemstone of terrible beauty, he could see some kind of liquid darkness flowing inside the blade, as if the witches dipped it in a pool of liquid hatred before reforging the blade. The darkness that swirled and cavitated within the blade was viscous but much thicker than water.

Not wanting to delay any longer, Esram adjusted the dagger in his hand, so the blade followed down his forearm, the single edge toward him. He held the blade carefully to not cut himself and become the blood sacrifice the ritual needed. *What a pitiful end that would be,* he thought, chuckling to himself as he moved down the length of the altar toward Michael's head. Once again, Michael started struggling against his bindings, but this time Esram allowed it to continue. He didn't want this to feel like killing a fish. There had to be some resistance and fight in the sacrifice, if only for his own amusement and satisfaction. Esram raised the blade over his head as he breathed a few words as part of the ritual. He had studied the words in the Vor tongue carefully to ensure he would speak them correctly when the time came. Theirs was a harsh language, but it seemed much more suited for this kind of activity than his own tongue. Even the Elvish tongue did this phrase no justice. Besides, the ritual demanded it be spoken in Vor.

"O Dark One, hear my plea. Come to this realm and bring about destruction."

With that said, Esram brought the Vor dagger down and planted it firmly and forcefully into Michael's chest. The blade struck one of his ribs and bounced into the space between it and the next one down before plunging fully into his heart. Michael gasped and his entire body stiffened as the blade melted into his heart. He continued choking as the dark shard of a once-furious sword disappeared. Joshua screamed from the saltire where he now wriggled and shook himself against the wooden frame. *That could be a problem,* Esram thought before turning back to the spell Oleg and Daethis maintained.

A funnel-shaped cloud ran from the spell to the growing black stain in Michael's chest. The instant the tendril touched the sacrifice, a river of blood flowed upward toward the massive spell that writhed, seething as if it were alive. The amount of blood required for the ritual mixed with the massive shapeless spell which turned a sickly crimson then black. Esram repeated the plea again, still in the Vor tongue. He started chanting the phrase, each iteration growing louder and stronger until he shouted and the muscles in his neck strained as they fought to keep up with his fervor. With the last repetition of the phrase, the ground trembled. The stone altar rattled against its legs. The benches nearby toppled to the ground and broke with the furious shaking. The clouds far overhead now swirled vehemently until they formed a perfect circle of melding shades of black and grey. The island itself split, the crack running north from the ritual site toward the grassy, flat area. Where the crack stopped, a wicked portal opened, its edges forming into what looked like stone with Vor runes appearing. The runes, spelling out the name of his master, glowed a deep red with a black center. A voice boomed from the other side and Esram, enrapt by the entire process, fell to his knees and prostrated himself before the might of his terrible master.

*   *   *

Joshua watched in horror as Esram stuck out his left hand and the remains of Vor'Kath's sword appeared. The hilt. The piece that was missing from the cavern in the tundra. Joshua's eyes went wide as he realized the fool he had been this whole time. *Of course, they recovered the whole sword!* Why would they have only recovered the shattered blade? What made everything worse, Joshua realized they had not only recovered the blade but someone, likely the witches, reforged the broken hilt into a dagger. Joshua wished, not for the first time, that his legs would respond to his internal shrieking and weren't bound to this wretched cross. Not so he could escape, but so he could kick himself for such folly. Joshua pushed against the barrier in his mind that kept him from touching the Magic he needed to stop everything that was about to happen.

Esram spun the dagger in his hands, repositioning it so the blade followed his forearm with the edge toward him. Joshua continued pushing, trying to get to his Magic. The Children were no longer siphoning it from him, and the agony of that experience had stopped. Right now, that was the only thing Joshua could be thankful for. *Allfather, please, I need my strength. Help me stop this!* Joshua continued to plead, hoping beyond everything that he would regain his strength for even just the briefest moment he needed to stop this. All he needed was one spell and he could stop everything he knew the Children planned. Everything Esram wanted. He could stop it all with only a single spell, yet his Magic eluded him, staying behind some invisible wall he couldn't push through.

Esram raised the Vor dagger with the hilt that was too long above his head and Joshua froze. No longer did he shriek in his mind for his arms and legs to struggle against his bindings. He withdrew from the Magic he couldn't touch. Everything froze for an instant before Esram plunged the dagger downward toward Michael's chest. Joshua's throat burned and rasped before he realized he was screaming. Time felt like it stopped as the blade fell, moving centimeters with each blink. The jagged point of the dagger touched the woolen fibers of Michael's tabard and ripped through them with ease. Joshua screamed louder as he watched the blade pass right through the leather armor Michael wore under his tabard. Michael's own body did nothing to stop the dagger from plunging through his skin, between his ribs, and into his heart. Everything stopped for a moment as the blade stopped, collar-deep in Michael's body. Within an instant everything continued moving at regular speed and Joshua watched as Michael's body contracted pulling against the cords that bound him to the altar. His shoulders came off the altar screaming as the blade dissolved into a growing black stain over his heart.

Joshua continued yelling, his voice now hoarse as he continued pouring his anguish into the rasp that left his mouth. He closed his eyes and prayed to the Allfather again, longing, hoping for a way to stop this and save Michael. There had to be a way to reverse the knife blade that pierced Michael's heart, to remove the still growing black stain from his chest, to instead plunge the dagger into Esram. There must be something that could be done. Joshua's mind howled for his body to do *something* and, almost imperceptibly, his fingers contracted. Joshua felt it, knew his fingers had moved to his command. Once more a small grain of hope started growing. He didn't know if this was the Allfather answering his pleas or the potion wearing off. Either way, he started moving what he could, trying to find a way to struggle against the ropes that bound him to the wretched cross.

The ground started trembling. The altar under Michael rattled. The benches nearby fell from their legs and the stone slabs shattered on the ground. The clouds overhead swirled into a circling mass of despair. A cleft appeared in the ground and ran north from the ritual site. Once it reached the flat, grassy area, a portal opened and formed into stone. Vor runes appeared, glowing red and black. Joshua's eyes went wide as he saw the runes and he wriggled more furiously against the ropes holding him. He didn't know enough of the Vor language, but eight runes appeared on the portal, and he could only think of one thing they spelled. Kalathan. These were the same runes he saw in the tundra.

The witches had carved the Light Eater's name into the walls and the altar repeatedly. *No wonder something felt off about that place,* Joshua thought briefly, knowing that changed nothing. There was nothing he could do about the past. He had to instead focus on the now as he continued fighting against the ropes and the invisible wall that still stood between him and the Magic he needed to stop this ritual.

"My Children," a voice boomed through the portal, "gaze upon my face and see Chaos, for I am come!"

Esram and the other two Children fell to the ground, prostrating themselves before a voice that Joshua knew belonged to Kalathan, even without seeing anything coming through the portal yet. Tears stung Joshua's eyes as they welled up, the saltiness familiar yet unwelcomed. He blinked the tears away and they fell onto his cheeks, leaving warm trails that turned cold in an instant with the wind that still ripped across the island toward the mainland. His vision blurred again as more tears formed and Joshua continued blinking them away to no avail. Those he blinked away were simply replaced with others in an instant as he looked at Michael. He no longer struggled against his bindings and while he still breathed, it had slowed tremendously. Joshua continued pushing against the barrier that stood between him and the Magic he needed. He could still reverse this. If only he could get to the Magic. A hurricane of fury formed within him, and he pushed against the wall again. This time, it gave way like butter under a warm knife. He reached through the barrier and touched the Magic beyond.

Chapter Twenty-Three

As the Magic surged through Joshua's entire body, everything changed around him. Colors turned more vibrant, sounds became clearer, and smells grew more pungent. The Magic he craved now coursed through every vein of his body, every fiber of his being. After even the short amount of time the Children denied him his Magic, the sensation of being reunited with it was pure bliss. He continued moving as much of his body as he could until he could finally tug on the ropes holding him to the wretched cross. He shook himself violently against his temporary prison but gained not even a scrap of freedom.

Not far away, on the altar, Michael now whimpered in agony. He no longer cried or struggled against the ropes that held him to the stone slab. His chest heaved as he gasped for breath. Joshua looked but could no longer see any remnants of the dagger. *It must have fully dissolved into his chest,* he thought, greatly disliking the idea of such concentrated darkness absorbing into Michael's body. Joshua knew he had to act quickly if he was to stop the ritual, neutralize the Children of Chaos and save Michael. Joshua tried to call out to Michael to get his attention, but no sound came from his throat. Not even a raspy squeal emitted. He needed to speak, to keep Michael's attention off the agony in his chest. He just had to keep Michael's mind off everything. If only he could speak.

The portal's surface shimmered, catching Joshua's attention. As he looked to the portal, he noticed that not only was the portal growing in size but the grass around it was decaying before his eyes. Every bit of life drained from the grass, and it withered before crumbling into a fine dust carried away by the wind that swept across the island. Not only the grass, but everything alive wilted. The wildflowers scattered through the grassy field slowly turned into unrecognizable twigs that only moments before had been daisies, asters, and blazing stars. Joshua set his eyes on the portal once again, his heart thumping like an aggressively played timpani drum. Without thinking he started the breathing exercises he learned as a young priest to get his heart beating normally again. This started to calm him down but soon that changed.

The surface of the portal rippled as Joshua watched its shimmering surface stretched and broke around a gargantuan face covered in scales and spikes. Two horns rose from the back of its skull; the horns, which looked like bare bones, pointed nearly straight back with a small rise near the ends which slightly pointed them toward the sky. Impossibly sharp teeth showed in its mouth as it shrieked coming through the portal. A long, slender neck followed, as did a body with massive wings and a wicked tail covered in barbs. The creature, which looked like a mammoth lizard, was covered in silver and light blue scales, each about a foot wide. Joshua felt his jaw drop as the behemoth finished coming out of the portal, unfurled its fleshy wings and took to the sky with more ease than Joshua imagined. Besides the basilisk in the desert, the largest lizard Joshua had seen was only a meter long. He knew this could only be a dragon of mythological existence based solely on its size alone. A beast of legends, dragons were said to breath fire and other elements. He wondered what form of Magic this monster could let fly from its mouth.

From snout to tail, the dragon stretched forty meters in length and its wings easily spanned beyond that distance. Each of its four paws bore four gargantuan toes with a large talon at the end of every digit. While the talons didn't look overly sharp, Joshua knew they would have no trouble ripping through a man in an instant. Everything about this monster seemed like a weapon, ready to take down anything that got in its way. Joshua's heart skipped beats as the beast reached an altitude where it could bank. It started circling the island as the portal shimmered again. Joshua shook his head vigorously and took a deep breath. The Children of Chaos summoned a *dragon* and something else was coming through the portal. He couldn't imagine where this portal connected or what else stood on the other side ready to walk out in a few moments.

Yet another dragon emerged, this one slightly larger than the first by a few meters. Its scales, a variety of green hues, and its size was the only way Joshua could tell the difference between them as they both flew around the island. The shrieking of both dragons filled Joshua's ears, drowning out everything else around him. *Allfather save us they have* two *dragons in our realm,* Joshua thought to himself. As the second dragon finished its first lap of the Iron Holm, another emerged from the portal. This dragon was again a different size and color from the previous two. The third dragon, deep blue littered with white patches, was thirty meters long. It took to the sky and joined its terrible brethren as a fourth emerged. This dragon, red and orange in color, was the same size as the previous and had no time to flap its wings before a fifth emerged from the portal. That dragon, covered in yellows and oranges, also started flying right before a sixth dragon broke through the shimmering surface of the portal. Yet another dragon poked its head through the portal, looked to the sky and shrieked to match the others. The cacophony of bestial screams overwhelmed Joshua. He thought, hearing the dragons calls, that they were singing to each other. *Do dragons even have a language of their own?* he pondered as he watched them fly. The last dragon to emerge from the portal boasted brown scales that shone in the flickering light of the torches set before the altar.

Joshua watched the sky in horror as the monsters flew together, their mighty wings flapping almost silently. Finally, together, they cried in unison and let out bursts of different elements from their mouths as they flew. Two breathed bursts of fire, one let out an icy cloud that dissipated quickly, and the other three let out green clouds that fell to the ground like a sickly rain tainted by something foul. Within moments of their elemental spewing, the dragons grew silent except the faint sound of their wings flapping. The Children of Chaos, looked to the sky, their eyes wide with wonder except Esram who looked somehow cheated. Joshua thought the expression on his face was like that of a small child whose mother promised a candy but later denied him that very treat. His shoulders slumped as the ground began trembling more violently than before. Overhead the clouds grew somehow darker, blocking out any hint of fading sunlight that came through the thick, dark billows of moisture that amassed over the island. Joshua knew that whatever was ready to come through the portal this time would be significantly worse than the six dragons flying overhead.

The portal rippled. Wavered. Shimmered. The once smooth surface shifted like water after someone threw a handful of stones into a stagnant pond. As the ripples reached the edges of the portal, they bounced back toward the center until the entire portal was wriggling and looked on the verge of breaking. This continued for a few moments until an arm reached through the semi-liquid surface. The hand and forearm looked human, but above the elbow the skin changed, and thick, dark feathers sprouted from the skin. The feathers looked much like those on a raven. Another arm protruded through the portal, this one grasping a black, metal scepter as long as Joshua was tall with a sloshing eye suspended in a clear, glass orb surrounded by four raven wings at the top. The eye looked right at Joshua, peering into his soul as if it knew he was partially responsible for summoning what was now coming through the portal. Joshua thought he heard a voice speaking in his mind as the rest of the body appeared through the still violently shaking surface of the portal.

The Children of Chaos returned their faces to the ground as what Joshua knew to be Kalathan finished coming through the portal. Even had he not seen the image in the book at the library, he would still have known what this *thing* was called. He felt his stomach lurch into his throat as the image of the book was now a living thing in front of him. Just as he saw in the image this was an amalgamation of human, raven, and goat pieces. A human frame covered in feathers was supported by goat legs much like a faun. The biggest differences between Kalathan and a faun was the goats head that sat upon the broad shoulders and the wings that spread from the shoulders. Fur the same color as the feathers covered the legs and chest. The only scrap of clothing that covered any bit of this beast was a tattered and frayed loincloth of the same color as the fur beneath it.

Allfather save us. They summoned him, Joshua thought, feeling his legs go numb and limp as he watched Kalathan finish stepping through the portal. Even his hold on Magic left him as he watched in horror as the biggest mistake in mortal history unfolded before his eyes. Joshua felt entirely responsible for what he witnessed today. Joshua, not anyone else, had heard but not listened to the warnings of the Vor. Joshua, no one else, had cut down the Light Eater's puppet forcing him to find new minions to carry out his will. He alone would answer for what he had done sooner rather than later. He knew his soul faced damnation before the Allfather's throne for not only allowing this to happen but also for being part of the ritual. He doubted the Allfather would care that his participation was forced. It felt like a minor detail compared to the presence of the conglomeration of animal and human pieces standing between the altar and the portal. The Allfather would have no choice but to send Joshua's soul to this very being for an eternity of torment. No other price would carry enough weight for this befallen tragedy.

Epilogue

Esram dared not lift his face from the ground despite the dirt flooding his nose. Blades of grass tickled the insides of his nostrils. The culmination of his life's work stood before him, yet he dared not even sneak one glimpse at his dark master. Kalathan's presence was one they longed to bask in for decades, and for the time being he was content with merely basking. He had an eternity before him to consider the consequences of the temptation to look at Kalathan's sacred face. Esram found himself relaxing every muscle in his body now that all of his work was finished. There was still so much more ahead, but the biggest hurdle was now behind him.

"My Children, I praise you for fulfilling my Will," Kalathan said, his voice ripping through the air. Despite coming from a goat's head, the voice sounded completely human.

His eyes still closed, Esram saw the flickering flashes of light coming from the dragons as they spewed clouds of elemental destruction. He heard their cries, the bestial roars that drowned out even the incessant shrieks of the gulls that perpetually flooded this island. The skin on his arms and the back of his neck prickled as he took in everything at once. The dragons, his master, the major victory he gained in this battle with the College, everything was falling in place. He could finally rest with the fulfillment of prophecy before his eyes. Everything fit together like the pieces of a complex puzzle. A single tear squeezed through Esram's closed eyes and splashed on the dirt beneath his face.

"Witness Chaos," Kalathan's voice tore through the air, a small boom following it.

*   *   *

"Witness Chaos."

Joshua gasped in horror as he watched Kalathan's wretched body morph in front of him. His entire body rippled and shook like the portal had moments before. His arms shifted and grew in size and Kalathan lurched forward, ending up on his hands and knees, his back arching outward as he continued morphing. Everything about him grew starting with his wings which expanded rapidly, followed by his arms and legs. His torso expanded and his neck lengthened. His face, terrible and unsightly, shifted and shook back and forth until it too started growing. Joshua felt his stomach lurch again as Kalathan started to take shape and the shaking intensified. Soon the trembling stopped and Kalathan looked exactly like a dragon, the same as the six that flew through the air far over the Iron Holm. Unlike the other dragons, Kalathan kept the feathers but only on his wings. The rest of his body sported black scales with red streaks. Spikes sprouted from his entire body. Four horns grew from his head, two reaching backwards and two that started going back then turned toward his snout.

Finally in his new form, Kalathan flapped his feathery wings and leapt from the ground. Soon he took to the sky and joined the other dragons as they continued to circle the Iron Holm. Together, the dragons all breathed their elemental clouds. Kalathan let loose a black flame that roiled like boiling water. The Children of Chaos rose from the ground and watched as their master and the dragons broke out of their circular pattern and flew toward the Drendil mainland. Joshua felt his stomach sink as the dragons disappeared from sight within a few moments. There was nothing he could do at this point to stop the summoned dragons, and Kalathan, from destroying the entire world. Joshua had lost. The College had lost. Everything felt…lost.

…To Be Continued…

9 781737 962403